Gabe

Silicon Valley Billionaires, Book 2

By Leigh James

ISBN: 978-1945340130

Published by Jack's House Publishing, LLC

Cover by Kristina Brinton

Sign up for Leigh's mailing list at www.leighjamesbooks.com.

CHAPTER 1

GABE

I woke up and rolled over, stretching, my limbs loose and relaxed as I pulled Lauren's warm body closer. Her soft moan brought back memories of last night, when I'd blindfolded her and tied her up.

Among other things.

I grinned against her bare skin as she slept. Lauren Taylor, reigning queen of the biotech industry and, until quite recently, a *very* uptight virgin, had been letting her wild side out to play lately. I trailed my fingers down her side, wondering if she'd be up for an encore performance this morning.

My phone rang, and I grabbed it, hoping she would sleep awhile longer. On the caller ID, I saw Timmy's number. I'd thought Lauren's security guard was asleep in the guesthouse next door. Because he never called to chat, I said, "What's the matter?"

"Mr. Betts, we've had a breach."

I jumped out of bed. "Is someone here? At the house?"

"No, sir. Not here. I'm afraid it's worse—it's Hannah."

Hannah was Lauren's younger sister. "What?"

"Someone's taken her."

"*What?*"

"Someone kidnapped her from Lauren's house. I just got the call."

Lauren sat up and rubbed her eyes.

I needed to stay calm for her sake. "What about the security guards?"

"They shot the two guards outside. They also shot Wes—he was in the house with Hannah."

Wesley was Hannah's bodyguard and boyfriend.

Fuck. "Did anyone make it?"

Lauren's head whipped around. "What's going on?"

I motioned for her to hang on.

"Wes is the only guard who made it," Timmy said. "He's at the ER right now—I don't know what his condition is, except it's bad. But Hannah's alive, thank God. The security tape shows them leaving with her."

"Have you talked to the police?"

"They're at the scene. Do you want me to go too?"

"Sit tight for right now. Call Paragon and let security know what happened. I'll talk to Lauren and call you back."

"What happened?"

I sat down and took her hand. "That was Timmy. There was a security breach at your house. Someone broke in and took Hannah. They shot the guards and Wesley, but he's alive. He's in the ER."

Her face went blank, as if the information didn't compute. "I'm sorry? What?"

I squeezed her hand. "Hannah's been kidnapped."

She opened her mouth and then closed it.

"Timmy said the police are at the house—they'll open an investigation. We have the security tape. I'll call Agent Marks at the FBI and let him know what's happened."

Lauren still looked dazed.

"Babe, do you understand what I said?"

"Is my sister…*dead*?"

"No," I said firmly, hoping she'd believe me.

She sat for a minute, staring out into space. Then her gaze focused back on me. "Two of our men are dead, though."

"Yes."

"And Wesley…" It seemed as if the news was sinking in.

I reached out to hold her, but she flinched away.

She jumped up, grabbing some clothes. "We killed Li Na's guards. Now she's evened the score."

Li Na Zhao, the Chinese healthcare CEO, had been after Lauren's technology, her company, and Lauren herself, not necessarily in that order. I knew where Lauren was heading with this line of thought. "Babe, this is not your fault."

She laughed bitterly, pulling a sweater over her head. "Tell my sister that when she's crying because Wes got shot—that is, if we ever get to talk to her again."

"We're going to get her back. It's going to be okay."

"It is *not* going to be okay!" She hustled past me to the kitchen, shaking her head as I followed close behind. "Hannah warned me—she told me to walk away from Li Na, to let her have the patch—that it wasn't worth dying for. But I didn't listen to her, because I never listen to her! And now she's suffering for it."

Lauren had recently tricked Li Na by agreeing to partner with her on a version of the patch, Lauren's game-changing biomedical invention. But with my help, Paragon surreptitiously launched the technology, winning the race to rule the global healthcare market.

Apparently, Li Na didn't intend to let Lauren enjoy her victory lap.

I didn't know what else to do, so I fired up the coffeemaker while Lauren paced and cried. "This is my fault. I don't know what I'll do if they hurt her—"

"Don't think like that."

She stopped. "I *have* to think like that. My poor sister…" She shook her head when words seemed to fail her.

I wished there was something I could do to comfort her, but as long as Hannah was missing, there'd be no comforting Lauren. Other than me, Hannah was all she had.

We stayed in the kitchen for the rest of the morning, fielding calls from the police, the FBI, the hospital, our attorneys and our security teams.

Wesley was alive but in critical condition.

No one knew where they'd taken Hannah.

Lauren continued to pace, two hectic spots of color in her cheeks. She wasn't crying anymore, but she also wasn't talking.

I watched her warily. "Babe, we should probably eat something. This is going to be a long day."

"She's probably dead," she said flatly.

"She's not—"

Lauren whirled on me. "I know you're trying to make me feel better, but stop. *Please.* I just want…I just want it to be yesterday. I want to go back. But I can't, so I need to prepare myself for the worst."

Her phone buzzed against the island, and she lunged for it. She tapped at the screen and then stood there—I could see her hands shaking as she read.

"Lauren?"

"It's Li Na. She sent me an email." She shoved the phone at me.

It seems I finally have something that you want. I'll be in touch.

I clutched the phone hard, on the verge of shattering it. "I'm sending this to Dave and Leo—to see if they can trace it—maybe we can give it to the FBI." If anyone could help reverse-trace this, it was the leaders of our Paragon's IT team, Dave and Leo.

Lauren nodded, her face a pale mask.

"I called my brothers. They're already on a flight. They want to help." She hadn't met Levi and Asher, and this wasn't how I'd planned on introducing them, but since they ran a private security company, there was no time like the present.

"Are they…familiar with this sort of thing?"

"Yes—Levi's ex-military. His company handles all sorts of cases, including high-profile kidnappings. He'll know what to do." Levi and Ash couldn't get here fast enough. Waiting to hear back from the police and the FBI was making me crazy. They were telling me nothing, probably because they had nothing to tell.

But Levi would get results. That was why Betts Security was widely recognized as one of the top security firms in the country.

Lauren licked her lips. I poured her a glass of water, and she stared at the clear, level liquid. "I'm going to let her have it," she said after a minute. "Li Na, I mean. The patch. My company. I'm not doing this anymore—I can't. I'll email her back when I can formulate a coherent thought."

"Okay." It would've seemed crazy for her to say that even yesterday, but this was new territory. "I understand. I'll help you do whatever you need."

"I can't lose Hannah. I would never… I could never…"

I put my hand over hers and squeezed. "I know."

"Do you really think she's still alive?"

"Yes—Li Na isn't going to hurt her right now. She wants your technology, Lauren. She knows that your sister is going to give her the bargaining power she's been looking for. Li Na's a lot of things—and completely fucking crazy is at the top of that list—but she's not stupid. She did this for one reason: to get you to crack."

She threw up her hands. "Well, she wins."

"And that's okay. We'll get your sister back, and then we'll go after Li Na."

"I don't even care anymore. I just want Hannah safe. Li Na can have Paragon. I'll just…start over, or not." She looked around the house. "I could hide here for the rest of my life, I guess."

I pulled her against me. "I would say I like the sound of that, but I can't. You're too brilliant to keep from the world." I kissed the top of her head. "We'll figure it out."

She buried her face in my chest, her shoulders shaking.

I held her close. "*Shh.* Don't."

Lauren's phone buzzed again, and we both jumped. She grabbed for it. I could see over her shoulder it was from a blocked number. "It's her—I know it."

Right before she hit the speaker button, she motioned for me to be silent.

"Hello, Lauren," Li Na said, sounding infinitely pleased with herself.

"Where's Hannah?"

"Safe. For now." Li Na paused to let the implied warning sink in. "And she'll stay that way if you're more cooperative than you've been in the past."

Lauren clenched her fists together but held herself in check. "Tell me what you want."

"The same thing I've wanted all along—I want you to sell your existing technology to me. And the rest of your company. I want the patents, the contracts, the equipment—everything. And I want you to consult for me."

Lauren's brow furrowed. "Don't you think the FBI's coming after you at this point, now that Clive Warren's dead and you've kidnapped my sister? Not to mention shot three security guards? And what about the Chinese authorities?"

Li Na snorted. "I'm not worried about it. I'm helping to reinvigorate Shenzhen—my people won't touch me."

The city of Shenzhen, which housed Jiàn Innovations' headquarters, was considered the Silicon Valley of China. Li Na was practically royalty there.

"As for the FBI," she continued, "they don't seem that concerned. Clive Warren was an admitted criminal. They haven't been in touch about the circumstances of his death. With respect to your sister, I'm sure the authorities are curious. But are they launching a full-scale investigation against me? I doubt it. I'm on Chinese soil, and I covered my tracks. If you have this call traced, it will lead to a cell tower in the Southern District of Russia. I would describe myself as largely unconcerned."

I wanted to reach through the phone and throttle her, but I kept my cool for Hannah's sake.

Lauren's body stiffened with tension. "So you think you're just going to get away with this?"

"I don't see why not," Li Na said casually, as if discussing the weather.

"I need my sister back *now*," Lauren said. "Selling Paragon and preparing everything could take months. I can't let you keep her that long."

She was right—we needed to get Hannah out as soon as possible. If Li Na kept her in less than pristine conditions, she would never last. I didn't want to consider what else might happen to Hannah—things worse than a dirty mattress or unappetizing food.

"I anticipated that response," Li Na said, "and I would allow you to trade yourself for her, if you prove you're taking meaningful steps toward the sale. Once you show me a P&S and other supporting documents, your sister will be released and I'll take you in her place. You can work remotely to finalize the transfer, someplace secure. I won't hurt you, Lauren. But you'll be alone—no security detail and no FBI—I learned my lesson the hard way last time. No one will save you if you try to cross me again."

Lauren's throat worked as she swallowed hard. "I understand." She didn't dare look at me.

"And I won't stop with you," Li Na said, her voice calm and decisive. "I'll come back for Hannah and for your Mr. Betts too. I hear you're back in his good graces—"

"I'll do it," Lauren said. "Just tell me where you want to make the trade."

Oh HELL to the NO.

"I have to go. I'll be in touch." Li Na hung up.

I clenched my fists in rage. "No."

Lauren started pacing again, seemingly lost in her own thoughts. "No, what?"

"*No, you are not turning yourself over to Li Na.* She's not ever touching you again!"

"She's never touched me! Even when she held me prisoner in Menlo Park, she only ever fucking *Skyped* me. I can't let her keep Hannah. It's me she wants!"

I stood in front of her so she couldn't pace and plan. "She can't have you."

"Of course she can—I have to get my sister out!"

"You're not in the right frame of mind to make decisions."

She looked at me as if I had three very annoying heads. "So what? There's only one decision to make—to save my sister! I'll do whatever Li Na wants—anything to get my sister back."

She tried to maneuver around me, but I grabbed her shoulders. "You're not thinking this through. If Li Na wanted you, she could have taken you in the first place. But she didn't do that. She went after Hannah because it would *hurt* you. Because it would *bind* you to her."

I watched her warily, trying to ascertain whether she could understand, given her highly agitated state. "She has you exactly where she wants you—finally. I don't care what she promises you. She's not going to let Hannah go. She'll take you, and then she'll make sure that some guard's holding a knife to Hannah's neck the entire time you do her bidding."

Lauren shook her head. "I won't go to Li Na until they give Hannah to you. Once that's done, leave and take her with you."

"They aren't going to give Hannah to me." I fought the urge to shout. "They'll keep you both, and then Li Na will kill your sister when it suits her. And when she finally gets her hands on the international cash cow that is Paragon and has it up and running—once she's used you up—she'll kill you too. And I won't let that happen."

"This isn't about you. This is about my sister, who's the only family I have left, who's in trouble because of *me*!"

"You made me a promise to never put yourself in harm's way again."

"This isn't about me either. It's about what she's going to do to my poor sister—"

"This isn't your fault. And I'm not going to lose you, babe. Not now. Not ever. We'll find a way to get Hannah back, I promise. But it's not going to be trading your life for hers. You're staying here with me."

Her eyes went wild with fury. "*No, I'm not.* This isn't your choice. It's not some power game we're playing in the bedroom!"

"You're right. It's not." My voice had a sharp edge. "This is life or death."

I grabbed my phone. My eyes never left Lauren's face as I made the call. "Timmy, I need you watching the perimeter. My brothers are landing at SFO this afternoon, and our attorneys are on their way. We need to go on lockdown. Assemble the team. No one else gets in or out of here. Got it?"

I hung up and nodded at Lauren. "Did you hear that? *Lockdown.* You're going nowhere unless I give you express permission."

Lauren looked stricken. And as if she might punch me. "You can't do this."

I crossed my arms. "Watch me."

CHAPTER 2

GABE

She'd stormed off then, a litany of curses flying after her along with her long blonde hair. Lauren had to understand that I was doing this for *her.* I wanted Hannah back too—of course I did. I loved her like the little sister I'd never had. But there had to be another solution. One that didn't involve my girlfriend being held captive, or worse.

Lauren slammed the door to the bedroom. *Fuck.* She would never see my side of this without a fight.

I stalked around the kitchen, feeling trapped. I wanted a bourbon. I wanted to punch someone. Smashing crystal glasses against the stone fireplace would do the trick too, but instead, I did the adult thing—the northern Californian version. I grabbed a protein shake and my swim trunks and headed outside to the pool, slamming the stupid drink down on the pool deck. I changed and eased myself into the water. I would vastly prefer to crush something or, preferably, someone. But here I was, swimming laps.

Sometimes being a responsible adult sucked big, hairy balls.

The cool water didn't ease my anger, but I swam until my muscles burned, not letting myself think about what she'd said. If Lauren tried to trade herself for Hannah, I would lose it. I'd learned the hard way with her. She'd gone behind my back before, trying to get evidence from Clive Warren, her former board member who turned out to be a traitor. But I would never let her be that vulnerable again.

I pushed the thought from my mind as I did another lap, oblivious at first to the warm sunshine and the ache in my muscles. I swam until all thought ceased, until I could feel only the burn in my lungs, arms, and legs. Finally, I pulled up to the edge of the pool…and next to a pair of Italian loafers.

My older brother, Levi, pulled down his sunglasses and inspected me. "You training for something?"

I wiped the water from my face. "I'm trying to keep from throwing shit."

Levi laughed, and I noticed there were more lines on his face since the last time I'd seen him. "Things are going well with Lauren, I take it?"

"She spoke to Li Na Zhao earlier. Li Na wants Paragon free and clear—and she wants Lauren to trade herself for Hannah."

His smile vanished. "I'm guessing that's why there're guards all over the place—to keep your girlfriend from doing just that?"

I climbed out of the pool, careful not to soak Levi's suede loafers—I needed him on my good side. Despite being a big, bad security agent, my older brother was very particular about his clothes.

I grabbed my protein shake and a towel and sat, looking at my house. Lauren was in there, somewhere. Probably cursing my name and packing a bag, for all the good it was going to do. "Hannah's the only family she has left. Lauren's out of her mind right now."

"I don't blame her. Blatant kidnapping and murder are sort of a big deal." Levi took off his shoes, rolled up his pants, and sat on the pool deck, sticking his feet in the water. "Fucking California," he sighed, looking around at the mountains and the sunshine. "It always makes me feel bad for Boston. Like my hometown is an ugly stepsister or something."

"You could always relocate. We need increased security."

Levi nodded. "Clearly—Silicon Valley's tough, huh? Security business is booming out here. How's the guard doing? The one who made it?"

I grimaced. "He's in surgery. The hospital won't release any information to us, but we have one of our guys there, waiting."

"If he comes to, I'll need to talk to him. See if he remembers anything that can help us."

"Okay. So...what's next? And where's Asher?" Asher was our youngest brother and one of Betts Security's top analysts.

"He's meeting with your team. They're doing a perimeter scan and catching Ash up on your systems. We haven't been out here in a long time. He needs a refresher course. He's also going to check out your copter and the helipad in case we need it—have you *ever* flown that thing, or landed it here?"

"It hasn't come up."

"Ah, the discretionary income of a billionaire CEO." He laughed, then scrubbed a hand across his face. "Back to what we're doing—we're going to get Hannah back as soon as possible, obviously. My team's flying in tonight. What were Zhao's instructions?"

I shook my head. "She didn't give any specifics. Yet. She just said that she wants to buy Paragon and she wants Lauren. She said she'd be in touch."

"Then we'll be ready for her."

"But I'm worried about Lauren—she'll do anything for Hannah. She would die for her—she wouldn't even think twice about it. I love Hannah too, but I can't let that happen. Do you understand?"

"Of course I do." He shot me a look. "Does Lauren know who she's dealing with?"

I nodded. "Li Na's crazy, but she's brilliant. She's obsessed with Lauren's technology, and she's ruthless. Lauren knows who she is."

The smile reappeared. "I meant you, little brother."

I looked back out at the water, which was calm, level, and clear—a sharp contrast to how I felt. "Oh, she knows, all right. And she's not happy about it."

***

LAUREN

After a while, I heard voices out in the kitchen, but I didn't care. I stayed in the bedroom, pacing a hole in the oriental rug, trying to figure out a way to escape.

I needed to save my sister—that was nonnegotiable. I would do whatever Li Na wanted. I'd analyzed the situation from every angle, and I knew this wasn't an equation with more than one answer.

I paced, cursing Gabe. He'd gone from my boyfriend to my jailor, and an angry fire coursed through me every time I thought about what he'd said. *"Did you hear that? Lockdown. You're going nowhere unless I give you express permission."*

Someone knocked on the door. Assuming it was Gabe, I said, "Go away."

My attorney, Bethany O'Donnell, stuck her pretty face into the room. "Can *I* come in?"

"Do you have news?"

"No," she admitted, "but can I come in anyway?"

I shrugged and went back to pacing.

Wearing a crisp, dark suit, Bethany came in and sat on the bed. "How're you doing?"

I just shook my head.

"I'm sorry about Hannah. It's horrible. Gabe said you heard from Zhao?"

"She called me. She wants Paragon, and she wants to trade Hannah for me. But Gabe won't let me go."

Bethany nodded. "Come on out, and let's talk about it. Gabe's brothers are here. The one who runs the security company was just telling us he has some insight with how to deal with this. Let's listen to him."

"I'm not going near Gabe."

"Jesus, Lauren." She narrowed her eyes, annoyed. "He's just trying to keep you alive. You're no good to Hannah dead. Let's *go.*"

Bethany never minced words, and my sister *did* need me, so I slunk into the living room behind her clicking heels. I nodded mutely at Gabe and two athletic, good-looking men who must be his brothers, and Kami Robards, Gabe's attorney.

"Can I get you anything?" Gabe asked me, his voice tight.

"I don't want anything except my sister back."

His brothers shot each other a wary look.

"So sorry to hear about Hannah," the older one said, his tone soothing as he approached me. He was a little shorter than Gabe, powerfully built, with the same dark hair and slightly darker brown eyes. He took my hand. "I'm Levi, Gabe's older brother. I run Betts Security." He released me and dropped down next to Gabe on the couch.

The younger one came forward. He was taller than Gabe, with lighter hair, a slightly slimmer build, and hazel eyes. "I'm Asher. The youngest. It's nice to meet you, Lauren—I just wish it was under better circumstances." He patted my shoulder and then sank down beside them, forcing me to confront the rugged male beauty of the Betts brothers.

Gabe's gaze met mine, but he quickly looked away.

"We're here to help." Levi leaned forward, his crisp white button-down shirt straining against his chest. "I've been involved with multiple hostage situations over the years, in private practice and when I was in the military. We'll get Hannah home safe." He turned to Gabe, who appeared to be examining a spot on the floor. "Gabe told me you spoke with Zhao this morning. You're certain she's the one who took Hannah?"

"Yes. It was her guards—she basically admitted it." I swallowed hard. "She wants my company, and she wants to trade Hannah for me."

Levi nodded. "Gabe mentioned that too."

"Li Na said that she would only release Hannah if I sell her my company. She wants the technology, the contracts, the equipment, everything," I explained. "She said she won't accept anything less."

"And you're willing to do that?" Levi asked.

"Absolutely—I don't think I have a choice. But it's going to take some time, and that's a problem," I said quickly. "I don't think my sister can handle being a prisoner for long. Li Na agreed to accept me in exchange for Hannah while the sale's being prepared. But she said I have to show her I'm taking 'meaningful steps' in the process before she'll make the trade—so I have to start getting the documents together."

"Is that where you left things?" Levi continued to look at me while Gabe studied the floor.

I jutted my chin defiantly. "Yes. I said I would do it."

"We need to think that through, Lauren, and consider all the options. Li Na isn't going to let your sister go easily. She's been chasing you for a while, and she finally has something you want."

Gabe shot me a heated look. "That's what I said."

"What about the FBI?" Kami interjected. "Aren't they doing anything to get Hannah back?"

Bethany cleared her throat and sat forward a little. "I spoke to Agent Marks on my way here. He said local police are investigating, and the FBI has also opened an investigation. But he said they have no verifiable leads yet."

"That's not much of an update," Gabe said. "He told me the same thing this morning."

"Li Na was confident they wouldn't be knocking down her door any time soon," I said. "She also said that the Chinese authorities wouldn't touch her. The FBI ran into a dead end connecting her to the guards who held me captive in Menlo Park, and they've never linked her to Clive Warren's death. Our tech guys traced her communication from earlier—it leads to a Russian proxy server. She's covered her tracks. She's safe, sitting pretty in her luxury condo on the other side of the globe."

Bethany turned to Levi. She tucked a strand of platinum hair behind her ear, the enormous diamond-stud earrings she wore reflecting the light, and pursed her perfectly lacquered lips in disapproval. "The FBI will want to talk to you sooner rather than later. Since you're taking over here, can you at least tell me a little more about your company? How exactly do you operate? Are you licensed? Are you legitimate? I don't want my client associated with anything illegal."

"Bethany, let's worry about that later," I said, exasperated.

She shrugged her petite shoulders, not backing down. "Let him answer."

At first glance, Bethany appeared refined and icily gorgeous with her long, stick-straight blonde hair and impeccably tailored suits, but once she dug into something, she was like a pit bull in a china shop. Normally I *loved* her for her rabid protectiveness, but not today.

I patted her hand. "I just want to get my sister back. I don't care if it's illegal. In fact, I hope it is—maybe we'll actually get something done before it's too late."

"Sorry, Lauren, but we're a perfectly legal operation." Levi turned to face my attorney. "We're a legitimate private security company. We're licensed, and all our men are properly trained and licensed. We handle a lot of government contracts. We get called in on cases like this all the time."

Bethany raised an eyebrow at him. "What's the name of your firm?"

"Betts Security."

"Never heard of you," Bethany said. She seemed unimpressed by Levi, no matter how pedigreed, muscled and well-dressed he was.

"And what's *your* name, again?" Levi asked.

She crossed her arms. "Bethany O'Donnell."

"I've never heard of you either," he said under his breath. "But let's get back to the matter at hand. I wouldn't expect a lot of cooperation from the Chinese government. Even with the FBI involved, she'll never be extradited. Corporate espionage is a big game in China these days. The government itself is involved in hacking North American companies."

"So what can we do?" I asked. With every second that passed, I felt as if Hannah was slipping further from my reach.

Levi watched me. "Li Na wants Paragon because the patch is more sophisticated than anything else on the market, right?"

I nodded. "She's stolen from me before. But it didn't do her any good—she couldn't get the technology to work with just her own team."

He looked grim. "So she's failed at that, and she wants more than your sloppy seconds. That's why she keeps coming back. What drives Paragon is the force behind it—you. Your company is built around you, Lauren. She needs you in order to dominate the market the way she wants to."

"What are you saying?"

His gaze held mine. "When she says she'll hold you until the sale goes through, it's a lie. If she gets you, she'll *never* let you go."

Li Na's obsession with my technology was like a nightmare I couldn't wake up from. "I don't care. I just want my sister to be safe. She shouldn't have to suffer because of me."

"It's okay," Levi said. "We'll get your sister back, and we'll keep you safe."

"*How?*" My scientific brain needed details, not assurances.

"We'll tell her that we'll do what she wants and go from there. I'll figure it out with my team, and I'll keep you and Gabe involved in the details."

"And what about her—Li Na?" I asked. My voice sounded flat and faraway to my own ears, as if I were underwater, sinking.

Levi's eyes, so much like Gabe's, brightened at the question. "I'll take care of her, eventually. I think it'll count as a public service."

* * *

"I'll call you if I hear from Agent Marks again. I told him to go through me for now," Bethany said.

"Okay. I appreciate that."

Bethany packed up her things. "He doesn't have any useful information anyway. And listen to what Gabe's brothers are saying. They know what they're doing."

"You didn't seem too impressed by them earlier."

She shrugged, pulling the strap of her briefcase over her shoulder. "I had to do that—I have to vet the people around you. Protecting you is my job. But I researched Betts Security before I came over here, and they're legitimate. They have the experience necessary to help."

"Then why did you say you'd never heard of them?"

She shrugged. "Because I like to make people sweat."

I shook my head—that was classic Bethany.

"I just want you to sit tight, okay? I'll field any calls from the police. Don't speak to anyone without telling me first. I want your involvement with this as limited as possible—we need to keep things on an even keel since the product launch is still so new."

"Fine." Until now, my whole life's focus had been protecting my technology and bringing it to market. But I could no longer pretend to care about the patch. Now that Hannah was gone, I could see my priorities had been hollow. "I need you to help me get the sale prepared. Are you free for the next few weeks?"

"No, but I'll clear my schedule. I'm all yours." Bethany headed to the door. "Do what they say, Lauren. We need to get your sister back. I can't picture Hannah going more than a week without a manicure, let alone wearing the same outfit two days in a row."

"I know." My voice came out thick.

"And make up with Gabe, okay?" Bethany kept her voice low. "He doesn't want you to get killed. Seems pretty reasonable to me." She stopped to wait for Kami Robards.

Gabe was talking to his lawyer in hushed tones. After Kami hugged him and left with Bethany, he shot a wounded look my way.

I melted a little. *Damn him.* I was still angry, but I knew he was trying to protect me. And I knew he was hurting too.

"Gabe." He looked at me, but then my phone rang. "It's her," I announced to the room in general.

"Answer it and get over here," Levi barked.

I answered the phone, making a beeline for Levi. "Yes, Li Na?"

"Are we in agreement about the details?" she asked, as though we'd never hung up. "You start the process of winding up Paragon and send regular updates to my counsel in San Francisco. She'll be in touch. If you're in compliance and things are moving smoothly, we'll arrange a trade."

"I already talked to my attorney. We'll start the process today." I prayed my sister was okay and still close by. "Can we do this soon—the trade?"

"I'll send you further instructions when I'm ready." Her tone was curt.

Levi scribbled something quickly and held up a note. *Proof of life*, it read.

"I need to know that my sister's okay before I agree to anything. I need… proof." I looked at Levi helplessly, not knowing what specifically to ask for.

"She can call you."

I swallowed hard. "I want to *see* her. Now."

Li Na sighed. "She can Skype you. Get your computer set up. But Lauren, if you do anything with this video, like give it to the FBI, you're going to regret it. Your sister will pay the price for your indiscretion. Do you understand?"

My heart hammered in my chest. "Yes."

"Get set up for the video conference. We'll be in touch soon." Li Na hung up without further explanation.

I headed to my laptop and opened it with shaking hands. "Does this mean Li Na's *with* my sister?"

"Not necessarily," Levi said. He came over and maneuvered the keyboard out of my hands, deftly setting up the site. "Gabe, call your tech people. Tell them to get a line on this. I want it traced."

Gabe got on his cell phone immediately, talking to Dave and Leo at Paragon.

"What can I say to Hannah?" I asked.

Levi shook his head, continuing his work on the laptop. "Not a lot. Don't ask her too many questions—where she is, if they've hurt her, if they've said anything specific. That could get her into trouble. Just ask if she's okay. I'll review it afterward for anything I can find that's useful."

"But what about—"

"Lauren," Levi interrupted me. "One step at a time. Now put on a brave face for your sister. She needs you. Ash and I will be over here." He jerked his thumb to the back of the kitchen, where they would be out of sight.

"Where do you want me?" Gabe asked his brother.

I reached out and grabbed his hand, holding on for dear life. My anger receded all at once, my need for him winning out in a landslide. "Here. Right next to me, where you belong."

His shoulders relaxed a little. He squeezed my hand and stood by me as the screen came to life, an image of Hannah appearing. My little sister looked like hell. She was pale beneath the traces of her tan, and her eyes were puffy from crying. What was left of her normally meticulous mascara was smudged beneath her eyes.

I clutched Gabe's hand. "Hannah?"

"Lauren!" she shouted, looking at the screen wildly. "I overheard the guards talking about the plan—do *not* turn yourself over to Li Na! It's a trap! They're—"

"Hannah. *Hannah!*" The last thing I wanted was for my sister to get punched in the face, or worse, before I even had a chance to talk to her. "Calm down. Stop yelling. Are you okay?"

She looked at me, her eyes wide. "No, I'm not okay! They shot Wes, Lauren! He's dead! In my kitchen!" Tears spilled down her cheeks. "He's dead, and it's my fault, and I swear to God, if you give in to *one* thing that bitch asks for, I'm gonna rip—"

"Jesus, Hannah! *Stop!*"

She glared at me through the screen, but at least she stopped yelling for a second.

"Please listen to me. Wes is alive. He's hurt, but he's *alive*."

"Are you…are you sure?" Hannah looked too afraid to be hopeful.

I nodded while Hannah collapsed back into tears. "Oh my God. Okay," she said, sobbing. "I saw him. I saw it happen. I thought he was dead."

"It's okay," I said. "Everything's going to be okay."

She wiped her face roughly and looked back up. "It is *not* going to be okay. These fuckers…" She jerked her thumb in the direction of her captors, off-screen.

"They shot him right in front of me! And I swear to *God*, if you negotiate with these *terrorists*—"

"Hannah, stop! You're going to get yourself ki—hurt," I said hoarsely. "Calm down."

She opened her mouth to protest again, but Gabe cut her off. "Listen to your sister, Hannah. Please."

She looked at Gabe desperately. "You!" she cried. "At least someone with some sense! Don't you *dare* let Lauren do it!"

"She's not doing anything—"

"Stop *lying*!" She turned back to me, another tear spilling down her cheek. "I know why they took me, and I know what Li Na's after—*you.* Don't you do it, Lauren. You're the important one. The special one. You have a gift to share with the world."

I clutched at my heart, which she was breaking. "You're special—you're the most important person in the world to me."

She shook her head savagely. "I'm *average.* I'm *nothing.* Don't you dare trade yourself for me. I'd rather die. I'm not kidding, Lauren. I'll never forgive you."

Someone in the background barked an order that I couldn't make out, and the screen went dead.

"No!" I smacked the keyboard and then the screen, hoping I could somehow bring the image of my sister back. "No, no, *no*."

Gabe pulled me into his arms, but his touch offered no relief.

My sister, the unrelenting optimist, seemed to have accepted defeat.

I could feel myself teetering, off-balance, very close to the verge of hysteria.

I turned to Levi. "I want you to get her. To do the public service thing."

He looked at me, clearly not understanding. "What's that?"

"Take care of Li Na, like you said you would," I said, my breathing ragged, my heart pounding. "Nobody makes my sister cry like that and gets away with it."

CHAPTER 3

GABE

A few hours later, Lauren went with me to see Wes. I thought it would be too much, but she insisted.

"Hannah would want me to. And he was working for me when this happened. Of course I'm going."

She didn't say another word on the drive to El Camino Hospital. Her hand was limp and cold beneath mine, but at least she was letting me touch her.

Eddie, Paragon's security manager, was in the waiting room, his large frame sprawled across two of the small, uncomfortable chairs. He stood when he saw us, his normally ruddy complexion gone pale. "He's out of surgery. They moved him to intensive care, though. The bullet nicked his heart, and when he was shot, he went down hard and hit his head on the granite island. They had to put him in a medically induced coma because they're worried about the swelling in his brain."

Lauren clutched my hand. "Oh my God."

Eddie's reddish brows furrowed into a deep V. "It's for the best, Ms. Taylor. They said he'll be able to heal this way, and that he has a better chance of making it."

"Why are they releasing this information to you?" I asked. The hospital staff had refused to disclose anything to us over the phone.

"I'm his emergency contact," Eddie said. "Wes's closest relative is his brother, who's deployed right now."

"Of course—I remember." Wes had shared that his parents were deceased. His mother had died recently of cancer, and his father had passed ten years ago from a heart attack. His older brother was a career marine.

"Do the doctors have any idea if there's permanent damage?" I asked. I knew medically induced comas were used only in the most extreme cases, where the patient had suffered a brain injury.

Eddie shook his head, looking devastated. "They don't know, and they don't know how long he'll need to stay under."

"Thank you for being here. I'll set up a rotation so that one of our team is always on duty, in case there's news. I want a list of the physicians involved—I have some friends who do rounds here. I want to make sure he has the absolute best care."

"Good." Eddie sank back down onto his chair. "But I'm staying for now. This kid…he's a good kid. I gave him the assignment. I feel responsible for him."

"Wes is great at his job, and I know he loved being with Hannah. He's tough—he's going to be okay," I said, trying to lessen his guilt.

Eddie perked up. "Any news about her?"

Lauren nodded. "She's alive. I spoke to her. I actually got to see her on Skype. We're trying to negotiate with the people who have her. I'll catch you up to speed when we're back at the lab and can talk."

"Okay."

"Eddie—do you think we can see Wes?" I asked.

"I can check with the nurse."

A few minutes later, Eddie came back with the nurse, who smiled at us kindly. "You can come with me, but you can only see him for literally a minute. Okay?"

We followed her to a private room. My heart plummeted when I saw him—I wouldn't have recognized the figure on the bed. Wesley's handsome face was bruised and bandaged beyond recognition, and there were myriad tubes connecting him to various machines.

Lauren took a deep breath before straightening herself and going to him.

She took his hand in hers. "Hey, Wes, it's Lauren. I don't know if you can hear me, but I hope you know I'm here. I want to say thank you." She started crying, clinging to his hand. "*Thank you* for protecting Hannah. I'm so sorry this happened to you. I want you to know she's okay, and I'm going to get her back, and she was so happy to hear you're alive."

Her shoulders shook some more, but she calmed herself. "I want you to get better. We're all rooting for you. We're here, and we're rooting for you. Gabe and I are here, and when I get Hannah back, she'll be here too. We're your family. We love you, and we want you to come back to us."

Tears streaked her face as she turned and headed quickly from the room.

I went to Wes's side. Memories of my father's brief hospitalization before his death crept up, but I pushed them back. "Hey, buddy." I placed my hand over his. "I saw the tape—I saw how you protected Hannah. She's fighting to come back to you. So you fight too. You fight this and come back. You have a whole life to look forward to. And we're going back to that island, dammit. All of us. So get better—I need my ally and my drinking buddy." Wes and I had gotten friendly during our recent vacation. I admired him. He was only twenty-seven, but he'd already served our country and was an important piece of Paragon's security team. He was strong too—we'd worked out together, and I'd seen his focus and commitment.

I squeezed his hand. I hoped he could find that focus and commitment now, and use it to come back to us.

Lauren's eyes were red-rimmed on the way home. I didn't bother to ask if she was okay.

***

LAUREN

I poured myself a straight vodka when we got back to the house. I put approximately two-point-five ice cubes in the glass, watching as they floated around hopelessly, inundated by the alcohol. I felt the same way—lost and floating, about to disappear. Seeing Hannah sobbing and then Wes connected to all those tubes had gutted me.

I kept hearing Hannah's words. *"You're the special one. I'm average. I'm nothing."*

Oh, what I wouldn't give to be the average one.

Levi and Ash both had their laptops open in the kitchen. There were papers everywhere, spread all over the island. "Any luck?" I asked, not knowing what constituted luck in this horrible context.

"No, but I don't expect any." Levi rubbed his eyes. "I need you to understand—this is just the beginning. You should get emotionally prepared for the long haul, and for the waiting, because it's tough. Even a week feels like a lifetime in a situation like this."

"Today felt like a lifetime." I took a sip of my drink. It tasted terrible and it burned, but at least I felt something other than panic and despair.

Levi patted my hand. "We have some time to look for your sister. Li Na has asked you to do something and said she'd keep Hannah alive while you did it. I believe that. She hasn't killed her for a reason. And we're looking for her, but it's not going to be easy, and we're *not* going to find her tonight. Li Na could have her hidden anywhere—a condominium, an office, a house she's rented. It's going to take some time for us to track her down, and I *need* you to be patient."

Gabe put his arm around me. "We'll both be patient, but *I* need to know that you're doing everything in your power. Promise me—us."

Levi sighed. "I promise. *Again.* And yes, I'd love a bourbon, since you asked."

I grabbed my own drink and laptop and nodded at the men. "I'm going to bed."

"You want company?" Gabe asked.

"No… I'm going to start working on the sale prep. I have to make a list and figure out my next steps. At least I'll feel like I'm doing something." I nodded at Levi and Asher. "Thank you both. It means the world to me that you're helping—I don't know what I'd do if you weren't here right now." With no updates from the police or the FBI, I was relying on Gabe's brothers to find Hannah and somehow get this nightmare under control.

I headed listlessly to the bedroom, arranging my computer on the bed. And then, once I'd settled in, I started sobbing.

I couldn't believe Hannah was gone. God only knew where she was and what was happening to her right now.

Her words from this morning played over and over in my head: *"Don't you dare trade yourself for me. I'd rather die."* I'd thought my heart couldn't hurt any more, but it broke all over again as I wept. My sister had always been the one constant in my life, and I loved her more than anything. And Wesley...big, strong, young Wesley was inert in a hospital room, connected to more tubes than I cared to count. He was in a *coma*.

What on earth had happened to my world today?

But I knew the answer. It was Li Na, and she wasn't going to rest until she had my company. I wiped my tears away roughly and snapped open my laptop. She could have it. She could also *shove* it—and I'd love to work on getting creative with the logistics of that—but I couldn't dwell on anything so pleasant right now.

I had to get back to work.

I grabbed my phone. Even though it was getting late, I knew my attorney would be up working. "Bethany?"

"Did you hear something about Hannah?" she asked immediately.

"No. I was going to start a to-do list... I thought we should talk, start planning..." Instead, I erupted into a fresh round of tears.

"Oh, Lauren. I'm so sorry." Hannah had been her client first, and Bethany loved her too. "Just go to bed, and please get some rest. I'll see you in the morning—we'll make all the lists and do all the things, just like we always do. It's going to be okay. I promise."

We hung up, and I glared at my laptop, a headache settling between my eyes. I could accomplish nothing tonight in my current state. I closed the computer, grabbed my drink, and took another burning sip.

And then, remembering every single terrible moment of the day, I cried myself to sleep.

Chapter 4

GABE

I wanted to follow Lauren to bed, but I knew she needed some time alone. So instead, I poured myself an extra-large bourbon and one each for my brothers.

"How's the security guard?" asked Ash.

"Terrible. The bullet nicked his heart, and he fell and hit his head *hard*."

"Was there brain damage?" Levi asked.

"They don't know yet. They put him into a medically induced coma because his brain was swelling. He's a young kid—it was awful to see him like that."

"Do they think he's going to make it?"

"I don't know." I gulped my bourbon, anxious to feel it hit. We'd spoken to the attending physician before leaving the hospital, but he didn't have answers. "They're hoping the coma will help him heal and let his brain take care of itself without stressing the rest of his body. But I have no idea what's going to happen. It's too early to tell."

"I'm sorry," Ash said. "He's Hannah's boyfriend, right?"

"Yes. He was assigned as her bodyguard, and they hit it off. They're both in their twenties."

Ash stared into his drink. "Jesus."

"Listen, I need you to understand—we have to get this done. I'll pay you whatever it takes."

I probably could've ordered them to do this—I owned a minority stake in Betts Security. When my brothers started their company, we did a cross-purchase deal with my company, Dynamica, to fund the startup. Levi's company had been very successful, and part of his success originated from our agreement. Levi owed me, but I held off reminding him because he got douchey whenever I did.

And I needed effective Levi. Not douchey Levi.

"I already told you I'm going to put my best men on this case, including myself and Ash," Levi said. "And *of course*, I understand this is personal and it's urgent. I know you like to be in charge, but you're going to have to let me do my job."

I poured myself another drink. "I'm not going to fight with you. You guys are staying here, you're working for us, and I want to help." I turned to Levi. "Just please don't be a dick. Because then I'll have to break your nose again, and Mom wouldn't like that."

Ash laughed, but Levi glowered at both of us. "If I recall correctly, you had some help—it wasn't exactly a fair shot."

I shrugged. "Seemed fair to me." Ash *had* held Levi when I punched him, but as far as I was concerned, that was water under the bridge.

"Let's forget about that for now." I brought the decanter over and poured them each a conciliatory drink. "What are the next steps for getting Hannah back?"

Ash pointed to a picture on his laptop. "The security tape showed part of the license plate on the kidnappers' car. We're beginning there, trying to track the plate down. I'm sure it's stolen, but it's a place to start."

"And then we're going to work with the FBI and the police to see if they have any leads, which I'm sure they don't." Levi finished his drink and helped himself to another—apparently, his successful business hadn't dampened his taste for bourbon.

Not that I had a lot of room to talk. Not tonight.

"Once we get a lead on the plate," Levi continued, "we'll start the search. We'll cast a wide net and try to ascertain their whereabouts. In the interim, I'm going to find out as much as I can. Maybe something will come in handy—I'll research Zhao's real estate holdings, or corporate entities of hers that may own real estate—to see if I can find anything local. And we'll work around the clock. We've got you covered."

That was all I could hope for. "Okay. And Levi?"

"Yes?"

"Thank you for being here. This means everything to me. I won't forget it."

I went to my room and found Lauren curled up on the bed, weeping. My heart broke as I gently took her into my arms and kissed her cheek. She sobbed and held on to me.

"Can I get you anything?"

She shook her head, still crying.

I cradled her in my arms, wishing I could take her pain away. "Shh, I've got you."

I held her until she finally fell asleep. It took a long time for her body to relax. I tucked her in, brushing the hair back from her face. Her features smoothed out as she finally became oblivious in sleep.

I gently kissed her forehead. "I love you, babe. More than anything," I whispered, careful not to wake her. "And I am going to make this right."

***

LAUREN

The next morning, I called an emergency meeting with my board of directors. I shivered as I strode through the doors of Paragon, followed closely by Timmy and two of Levi's guards. Gabe and Levi had both insisted that my personal security be tripled, but I wasn't worried about myself. All I could think about was Hannah.

Several employees stopped to ask about Hannah. She was a favorite with the staff, always irresistibly upbeat. I answered their questions carefully, saying that we were working on getting her back. I updated them about Wesley—that he was in a medically induced coma, his prognosis questionable.

California sunshine streamed through the windows, but gloominess and paranoia pervaded the atmosphere. My staff looked pale and worried. Eddie had extra guards patrolling the building. We were locked up like Fort Knox, and everyone was on edge.

I nodded at Stephanie, my assistant, as I headed into my office.

Her face was pinched with worry. "Are you okay, Ms. Taylor?"

"No…not at all. But I have a team working on getting Hannah back. And I believe in them."

"What about the police?" Stephanie asked.

"They're looking. So is the FBI." Stephanie loved my sister, and I wanted to give her some hope. They were always chatting and comparing notes on shows like *The Bachelorette* and other things I'd considered silly. "I promise to keep you posted."

Her eyes showed a spark. "Thank you. I'll be praying for her."

I headed into my office, closing the door behind me. When I considered those things now—the shows, movies, and celebrity gossip Hannah unselfconsciously enjoyed, things I'd always teased her about—it made my heart hurt. What she'd said still haunted me: *"I'm the average one."* I'd made her feel that way. Me, with my monomaniacal work habits and my scornful disinterest in normal life. I'd never meant to make her feel average in comparison. Hannah was my heart.

I looked out the window. The grounds surrounding Paragon were covered with dew in the early morning sunlight. How many times had I gazed at this same view, making plans for my company? Even though I had a million things to do, I wandered around my office, feeling lost. Paragon had always been my sanctuary. I'd hidden inside for years, happy to be lost in my research. My ignorance had been bliss, but now I was about to sell my company—my life's work—to the corporate Antichrist known as Li Na Zhao.

I checked the patch's sales data from the weekend—we'd surpassed expectations, again. The patient satisfaction surveys were almost unanimously positive: people loved having a quick, efficient, noninvasive medical test. My technology was a runaway success.

Which made this situation that much more maddening.

I wouldn't be able to control what Li Na did with my company. The patch currently sold for a low price, so most consumers could afford it. Access to affordable healthcare was an important piece of improving the overall health of the planet. I didn't want my technology priced out of reach, but I knew Li Na would ruin everything I'd worked for by chasing a larger profit.

My phone buzzed, making me jump. "The board's ready for you," Stephanie said.

I felt anything but ready. "Okay. Thanks."

I took a deep breath as I headed into my meeting. My board members had been with me from the beginning. They'd always believed in me and in the patch—now, they were going to witness Paragon's devastating end.

I sat down and straightened myself, preparing to deliver the blow. "What I'm about to tell you *must* be kept confidential. I can't risk the public or our partners finding out any details. It could compromise Hannah's safety."

The board members murmured worriedly to each other as I gathered my courage.

I took a deep breath. "I'm selling the lab to Jiàn Innovations. If I don't pull this transaction together soon, with your blessing, they're going to kill Hannah."

Allen Trade put his hand over his heart. "Jesus, Lauren."

Mimi White winced. Angela Blakely folded her hands together, looking stricken.

This was it. Everything we'd worked for would be taken from us, and this was how it would end, after so much promise.

"What about the police?" Angela asked after a minute. "The FBI? Isn't anyone doing *anything*?"

"They're involved, but there's a limit to their power." I shook my head. "My security team believes the Chinese government will refuse to extradite Li Na. With respect to what we can do on American soil, our options are limited. Any legal options would take months or years. We don't have that kind of time."

"What about Wesley? And the guards who died?" Mimi asked. "Jiàn Innovations can't just get away with *murder.*"

I swallowed hard. "My team's looking for the people who did this, and so are the FBI and the police. When we find them, they'll be arrested. But connecting them to Li Na will be difficult—we found that out when Clive Warren was murdered. I know in my heart she's responsible for his death, but I can't prove it. I have emails and text messages, but they're routed through third-party proxy servers on foreign soil. What I have might not be enough to indict her, and frankly, we don't have time to wait and see."

"All this, and Li Na's safe in Shenzhen." Allen sounded bleak. "But I understand your position—it breaks my heart to see the company sold like this, but our hands are tied."

I nodded. "Exactly. Of course I don't want to sell—especially not to Li Na—but I don't have a choice. The only thing that matters is getting Hannah back alive. Bethany's started drawing up the paperwork. I'll reach out to our investors next week and make the announcement to the employees after that. This is going to happen very fast—but I promise to keep you posted."

The meeting wrapped up shortly after that. There wasn't a lot more to say, but there *was* a lot of work ahead. Bethany came to my office to start preparation for the sale. We worked silently for hours. Bethany's laser-focus mirrored my own, and I found her presence soothing. At least all the work distracted me from thoughts of Hannah.

I reviewed the draft of the Purchase and Sales Agreement and supporting documents as Bethany prepared them, distancing myself from the ultimate meaning of the words. I forced myself to look at them analytically, as if I didn't have a stake in the outcome of the sale. I didn't want to think about what I'd lose. I had to stay focused on what I'd get back.

When we'd finished first drafts late that night, Bethany emailed them to Li Na's attorney in San Francisco. She closed her laptop, grabbed her briefcase, and headed for the door. "I can't believe we're doing this."

Bethany had been with me from the beginning, so this was hard for her too. But she surprised me by turning and smiling before she left. "It's a good thing I believe in karma," she said, trying to sound upbeat.

"Why's that?"

A glimmer of sympathy lit Bethany's eyes—she knew how much I was hurting. "Because Li Na's going to get what's coming to her, eventually. And I'm going to enjoy the hell out of that."

I smiled wanly. "I hope you're right."

She swished her blonde hair over her shoulder and headed out. "I'm always right," she called. "That's why you pay me the big bucks. Now use that big, beautiful brain of yours and figure out a way to screw that bitch over, once and for all!"

I watched Bethany as she disappeared down the hall. Figure out a way to screw Li Na over, indeed. That was exactly what I wanted.

But what can I do to her? What's her weakness?

My phone buzzed with a text from Gabe, interrupting my train of thought. *Babe. It's late—come home.*

I almost felt guilty that I still had Gabe to go home to. God only knew where Hannah was, and Wesley was in a coma at El Camino...

Still, I clutched my phone and hustled to the door. I needed to be with him. We were the only thing that still made sense.

***

GABE

Lauren finally got home at midnight. I pulled her into my arms. "Are you okay? I mean, I know you're not...but I still have to ask."

She shook her head against my chest. "Just take me to bed."

As soon as the door to our bedroom closed, she started bawling. "They didn't find anything today, right?"

"No." I wrapped my arms around her again. "Levi said it was going to take a while. I'm so sorry..."

She sobbed against me. "It's not your fault. But I just keep thinking about Hannah... If they're *doing* anything to her... I feel so helpless, I feel sick!"

I kissed the top of her head and rocked her back and forth. There was nothing I could do for her except hold her. I got her out of her work clothes and into one of my Harvard T-shirts. Then I held her for a long time, stroking her hair and rubbing her back until her sobs finally subsided and her breathing evened out.

"I wish I could take your pain away," I whispered when I thought she'd fallen asleep. My heart broke for her. "I would give anything."

She pulled me against her, awake after all. "You can... You're the only one who can. Even if it's just for a few minutes. Just make me feel *something*."

She rocked back against me, making me instantly hard. Now that I knew she wanted me, I suddenly had a burning urge to fill her, to take refuge in her.

She turned toward me, our tongues tangling, and an electric jolt went straight to my cock, which throbbed thickly against her thigh. I needed to be inside her.

I rolled her onto her side so I was pressed up against her back. I took the T-shirt off and ran my thumbs over her nipples, which beaded instantly under my touch. She rubbed her ass against me, moaning, as I nipped at her shoulder and neck, showering her with kisses. She leaned back against me, giving herself to me. It made me feel powerful...important. Like I might be able to make everything better, even if just for a few minutes.

I wanted to give that to her. To give myself to her so I could make her forget the pain.

I trailed my cock up and down her slit, getting it slick with her wetness, and she ground herself against me for a few glorious moments. I felt my whole body come alive, responding to hers. Her breath came fast and hot, her movements increasing our friction. I grabbed her hips and positioned her against me, my knee between her legs to open her up.

My cock throbbed against her. I couldn't wait anymore.

I entered her swiftly, all the way. *Holy fuck.*

"Oh!" Lauren cried. Then she reached around, grabbing my ass and pulling me in deeper.

I'd learned to follow Lauren's lead, to listen to her body, and I knew what she wanted. She wanted me deep, and she wanted me hard. I groaned and bucked my hips, already wanting to explode inside her, needing my own release.

I leaned up on my arm, angling myself deeper inside her. I was close to the edge, and I wanted to come, but I held on, because when I came, this would be over, and *it felt so good.*

I could feel Lauren's orgasm building as her tight body gripped me harder, pulsing.

I moved over on top of her, covering her body with mine, fucking her mercilessly while she stayed on her side. I was in even deeper in this position, and I felt Lauren's orgasm begin to rip through her, her body shaking and clenching around me in climax.

She came, calling my name, and I fucked her through her orgasm.

And then *I* came, finally spending myself into her, giving her everything I had, my thoughts going incoherent, eclipsed by pleasure. She clung to me afterward, and I kissed her sweaty forehead, wrapping my arms tightly around her. "Don't you ever leave me. I mean it, babe. I couldn't bear it."

"I won't," she said, breathing hard. "I promise."

I ran my hand down her cheek. "Whatever happens next, we face it together."

"Together," she promised, just before drifting off.

I watched her as she slept, not wanting to take an eye off her, needing to believe she meant it.

CHAPTER 5

GABE

Lauren went back to Paragon the next morning, promising to be home before midnight. She was exhausted, but her eyes had the fiery determination they got when she obsessed over something. She was determined to show Li Na the sale was moving forward and Hannah should be released.

We hadn't talked any further about the proposed exchange. Lauren knew where I stood. I hoped my brothers found Hannah soon, so we didn't need to have the discussion again.

It hadn't exactly gone well the first time.

As an added precaution, I'd asked Timmy to secure the house with updated electronic security devices and private codes. I wasn't above locking Lauren up if necessary, even if that counted as a dick move. I had to keep her alive and safe.

I called my friend Dr. Edward Kim, a neurosurgeon who had privileges at El Camino, who I'd asked to check on Wes.

He picked up on the first ring. "Hey."

"Hey, sorry to bother you. Did you check on my friend?"

"Yeah, I saw him this morning. I just reviewed his most recent CAT scan. It looked good—the swelling in his brain has gone down a bit, and all his vitals look consistent."

Hope made my heart skip a beat. "Do you think he's going to be okay?"

"It's too soon to tell," Dr. Kim said, "but sometimes these medical inducements really do help the patient heal. It looks like your friend's progress is moving in the right direction. I'm cautiously optimistic. By the way, I had him added to my patient roster. I talked to the neurologist—he's a friend of mine—and we'll be working together from here on out. I feel good about it."

"I can't thank you enough, buddy. I owe you."

"Perfect—I've been dying to play at CordeValle again."

We'd played golf at the exclusive club last spring, and he'd been impressed. If Wes pulled through, I'd get Dr. Kim a lifetime membership. "Consider it done. Thanks again."

I called Lauren immediately. "I just talked to my buddy, the neurosurgeon. He checked on Wes. He said the prognosis is good. They ran another CAT scan, and it showed Wes is healing."

"Oh my God." I could hear the relief in her voice. "That's amazing!"

"He's only cautiously optimistic, babe. But I think we can be too."

"Okay. Wow. I just wish I could tell Hannah somehow."

"Ask Li Na's attorney if you can arrange another Skype."

"I will. That's a great idea—maybe if I could think straight, *I* would've thought of it," Lauren said. "Thank you, honey."

"I love you."

"I love you too."

"Are you…doing okay?" The question remained ridiculous in light of the circumstances, but I had to keep asking it, to try to maintain some sense of normalcy.

"Bethany's here. We're working."

"I'll let you get back to it. I'll see you tonight. Love you, babe."

There was a knock on my door as I hung up. Ryan, my assistant, stuck his head in, his electric-blue glasses shining in the early morning light. "Gabe? I have those reports for you."

"Send them to my laptop."

I pulled up the data Ryan sent me and reviewed the most recent reports from my international partners who handled the patch's distribution. The international sales were tracking the domestic numbers—the patch was unequivocally a global mega-hit. I'd made more money on my partnership with Paragon than I'd projected. I'd always known that the technology would be a bestseller, but its success had blown by every marker.

I'd been interested in Paragon long before I met Lauren. I'd watched the company's growth from afar for years, admiring the team she'd built. I'd speculated that with the board of directors she'd assembled, she'd been working on something fantastic, and I was right. For purely business purposes, I'd wanted Dynamica in on the ground floor with Paragon. That was why I arranged a meeting with Lauren in the first place. But since the first time I met her—at lunch at Grove, the day my life changed forever—I only wanted *her*.

Once I got to know Lauren and saw her brilliance firsthand—and understood the game-changing nature of her invention—I wanted to help the product reach as many consumers as possible. I knew the patch would be a winner, and I could help launch it on a global scale right out of the gate. I believed strongly in Lauren's vision and believed in the good the patch could bring the world. I'd also known it would be profitable, and it was—even with its thin initial profit margin, it was making my company millions.

But profit wasn't the point, and it never had been.

I closed my laptop and started pacing. Lauren had worked tirelessly her entire adult life to bring the patch to market. It had the potential to improve global health on a massive scale in the years to come. I didn't want a corporate terrorist to take it away. I knew Li Na would defile Lauren's vision for her invention. I clenched my hands into fists as I continued to pace. I didn't want Paragon to go out like this—bursting into flames under the misdirection of a greedy, corrupt, and criminal CEO.

Lauren's technology deserved more than that. *Lauren* deserved more than that.

Feeling restless, I grabbed my phone and texted Levi. *Any progress?*

My phone remained silent for a minute, so I went back to pacing. My thoughts went in a hundred different directions as I tried to think of a way out. My phone dinged, and I grabbed it.

There is no progress yet. Please stop driving me fucking crazy, Levi wrote back.

Knowing I was about to tick him off, I picked up the phone and called him anyway.

He answered on the first ring. "Jesus, Gabe. I'm trying to work."

"I understand, but that doesn't answer my question. Did you guys figure out the license plate number yet?"

"You left here two hours ago. Do you remember that I have other clients and other cases to manage?"

I raked my hand through my hair. "Yes. But you promised me you'd give this your full attention."

Levi sighed. "I *am* giving it my full attention. But we haven't uncovered the rest of the plate number *in the two hours since you last asked me.* Now please go back to work and let me actually get something done."

"I *hope* you actually get something done. I'll check back with you later."

Frustration ate at me as I put the phone down and started pacing again. I had plenty of my own work to do, but it could wait. What couldn't wait was saving Lauren's sister and her company. The clock was ticking... Why did it seem like Lauren and I were the only ones aware of that?

I grabbed my coat and my laptop, hurtling past a surprised-looking Ryan. "I'm going out for the day. Cancel my meetings."

"Okay?" Ryan wasn't used to me leaving with the day booked like this, but these weren't normal circumstances.

This was the new normal. It would require some getting used to.

Levi looked less than thrilled when I rolled through the doors of my house a little while later. "Don't you have a multibillion-dollar company to run?"

"Yeah, I do. But I figured I could do it from home today. Wonders of the Internet and all."

Levi rolled his eyes and appeared to say something under his breath, but luckily I couldn't hear it. At least Ash looked happy to see me. "You're telecommuting for the rest of the day? Nice. We still haven't tracked down the full license plate, but I'm going through a stolen vehicle database, and I think I'm getting closer."

I looked at Levi. "See? *This* is what I'm looking for. Progress."

Levi grabbed his laptop and cell phone and headed outside toward the pool.

"You really shouldn't go there," Ash said, jerking his thumb at Levi's retreating form. "You know how he gets when people tell him what to do. It's not going to help—and you need all the help you can get right now."

"I know. But it just doesn't feel right for me to be sitting in my office. Every hour that goes by, Lauren's closer to losing her company, and her sister could be moved farther away from us. I don't trust that Li Na will deliver Hannah, so I'm hoping we can accomplish something in this brief interim—like saving the only family Lauren has left. Is that fair?"

"Of course it is." Always the reasonable one, Ash nodded. "I'm just saying that for sanity purposes, you shouldn't get into a pissing contest with Levi right now. You know he wants to prove something. Let him do it."

I set my laptop on the island and fired it up, pulling up some compliance reports I needed to review. "What do you mean he wants to prove something? To who?"

Ash shook his head. "To you, dumb-ass. He's always wanted to prove something to you."

"So let him. There's no better time than the present."

Chapter 6

LAUREN

A few days later, Bethany and I finalized the first draft of the Purchase and Sale Agreement. We'd completed the task in record time, and we were both exhausted. My vision blurred from reading so much, and from lack of sleep.

"Bethany, please get the package together for the attorney. Send her all the documents we've prepared so far, then ask for an update." I stood up, stretching. "And I'm going to ask Li Na if I can talk to Hannah."

Bethany looked skeptical. "You think she'll agree to that?"

"We've accomplished more than I thought was possible over the past few days. We're sending them proof of our progress, which is exactly what she asked me for. It can't hurt to ask, right?" I wanted to see my sister, alive and as okay as the situation would allow. If Li Na's men had done something to her, the deal was off. "I'm showing Li Na my due diligence—the least she can do is reciprocate."

Bethany sent off the P&S, I sent an email to Li Na, and then we continued working. We reviewed financial statements throughout the afternoon without hearing back from either Li Na or her attorney. I didn't know much about the lawyer, Petra Hickman, except that she was a partner at an enormous firm in San Francisco and had a venerable résumé. Bethany said Petra was an asshole, but she said that about most people.

The sky started darkening, and Bethany looked at her watch. "I think we should take a break. We need our IP team to get started on the trade secret transfer documentation. Are you okay with stopping now?"

We'd been working since five this morning. I nodded. "I guess since we haven't heard back from the attorney, we won't hear anything until tomorrow anyway."

Bethany started packing up when her phone buzzed. "It's Petra—she said she's reviewing the documents, and she spoke with Li Na. Li Na's in a meeting, but she'll be in touch with you later tonight."

"Okay. Good." A chill went through me, a mixture of excitement and dread. *Will I get to talk to Hannah tonight?* It had been days, and I had no idea if she was okay. *Is she eating? Did they hurt her? Did they...do anything else to her?*

I willed myself to stop thinking about it, because I would go insane.

Bethany looked as nervous as I felt. "Do you want me to come home with you?"

"No, I'm okay. I'll text you as soon as I hear from Li Na. I'm fine—as fine as I can be under the circumstances. Go home. I promise I'll call you."

I watched as she left, my heart heavy. While we worked, I could almost forget about Hannah and Wes, almost lose myself in analyzing the verbiage of the documents. But as soon as we stopped, even for a moment, the pain and panic took over. It was no different right now. I hustled to get my things together and called Timmy. "Meet me at the car?"

The whole ride home, my phone was silent, unnervingly so. I kept checking it, afraid I'd accidentally hit the mute button and had missed everything, had ruined everything, and that I'd lose the opportunity to talk to Hannah. It was full-on dark by the time we pulled off the exit for Gabe's house.

"You okay, Ms. Taylor?" Timmy asked, breaking my reverie.

"Not at all, Timmy. You?"

He shrugged. "I'll be better when we get your sister home, and when Wesley's okay."

I smiled at my bodyguard, who rarely spoke unless spoken to. "Me too."

My phone buzzed with a text just as I was about to go through the doors. *We received the P&S. Will review. Have your laptop ready in five minutes,* it read. I hustled into the house and put my computer on the island.

"I think Hannah's about to Skype me," I told Gabe. Levi and Ash were out in the field, trying to generate leads to find Hannah. I wished they were here to see this.

Gabe sprang up immediately. "Did you talk to Li Na?"

"We turned in a lot of documents today—I asked to talk to Hannah in exchange for turning this around so quickly." I swallowed hard as I waited for the screen to come to life. "I want to see her."

I grabbed Gabe and held on tight. The screen lit up sooner than I was prepared for, and a picture appeared—suddenly, there was Hannah, sitting listlessly in a chair. Her hair was matted and her blouse was torn at the throat. She looked terrible—clearly in much worse shape than a few days ago.

Someone barked an order, and she looked up at the camera. There was a visible bruise on her cheek, and her eyes were red-rimmed.

The world tilted beneath me. "Hannah! Oh my God, what did they do to you?"

"Huh?" My sister looked at the screen blearily at first, then her eyes focused on me.

"Hannah, *what did they do to you*?"

"Calm down, I'm okay. They just hit me."

I gripped Gabe's hand so I wouldn't fall over.

She managed a small smile. "It's okay, they only did it a few times—after I told them to fuck off. A few times."

I winced. "Hannah…"

"Trust me—they totally deserved it."

It took everything I had to stay calm. "Please tell the guards that if they hurt you again, or if *anything else* happens to you, *this deal will not go through.* Are you listening to me?" I raised my voice so the men could hopefully hear me.

I took a deep breath, trying to calm myself. I couldn't afford to completely lose it. "Their boss wants my company more than she wants anything—and she won't get it if they hurt you! Remind them this is a *very* important deal and that they are low-level pawns. If they do anything else to you, the deal is off! And I will tell their boss that myself!"

Hannah turned around, away from the screen. "Do you animals hear that? You're low-level scum, and if you touch me again, you're dead! Got it? Need me to translate that into first-grade English for you?" She turned back to me and shrugged with what I could only imagine was false bravado. "They're not really that smart. They might not understand."

"Please don't say anything else that's going to get you hurt," I begged. "We're going to get you out of there. Soon."

"I told you not to risk yourself for me." Hannah's voice had a reckless, dangerous edge.

"Gabe had one of his friends, a neurosurgeon, check in with Wes today," I babbled, trying to think of something I could say to make her face change back to normal so she was herself again, not this fearless, dirty captive who looked like she might try to bite the next hand that fed her. "He's doing better. They think he's going to make a full recovery." A fabrication, but I needed to give Hannah a reason to come back to me.

She nodded, her chin wobbling almost imperceptibly. "Good. That's good."

"Of course it's good, but he needs you. So you do what they say, and they're not allowed to hurt you, and I'm going to call Li Na right now—they won't touch you again, I promise."

"Don't make me stupid promises." Hannah's eyes filled with angry tears. "I told you not to negotiate with her—she's a murderer, Lauren, and a liar. If you think she's going to let me just skip out of here someday, you're crazier than I thought!"

I gripped Gabe's hand so hard, it must've hurt. "You listen to *me*. You don't need to worry about Li Na. You just worry about staying safe and staying alive. You worry about coming back to me and back to Wes. He needs you, and so do I. Please don't look like you're giving up, because I can't do this without you."

"Can't do *what*?"

"Anything!" I started to cry, probably the last thing I should be doing. "I can't do anything without you. So stop fighting the people who have you, and keep your mouth shut."

Hannah grimaced, but I thought I saw a familiar spark in her eyes. "There she is. My bossy big sister."

I wiped my eyes and jutted my chin out. "That's right. Don't you forget it—and I have a lifetime supply of bossiness waiting for you back here. Let's concentrate on that."

The guard said something in the background, and before I was ready, the screen went dead. I stared at it. The blank screen reflected how I felt inside, black and empty. I turned to Gabe. "Those animals... Those animals hit my sister..."

The tears came then, along with sobs, racking my body with spasms.

"Oh God. I'm so sorry, honey." Gabe wrapped his arms around me. "She's okay, though—she's alive. We need to focus on that. Hopefully what you said will sink in."

I tried to listen to him. But all I could do was cry, because my heart was breaking.

***

GABE

Lauren sent Li Na an enraged email—documenting the conversation with Hannah and every visible bruise—then curled up into a ball and cried herself to sleep again. I held her until the sobs subsided, and she finally fell into a restless sleep. Then I sat there for a long time, just watching her.

I couldn't sleep. Images of Hannah's bruised face kept coming back to me. Lauren's shuddery breathing pierced my heart. And I kept thinking about Wes, lying in a hospital bed, hooked up to a hundred tubes.

Li Na had ripped my family apart.

I made sure Lauren was settled, then went out to the empty living room. Levi and Ash had come back late from meetings with the police and the FBI and must've gone straight to bed. I grabbed Asher's laptop and fired it up. He'd been unable to ascertain the final digits of the license plate on the security tape. Numbers were my thing, so maybe there was something I could do. I opened up the images from the video feed and started working on an algorithm. I knew that if I could run the different variables, I could possibly match them with a plate from the database Ash had accessed.

By the time the sun came up, I'd figured out the plate number and found a match in the database. I mentally high-fived myself as I went in and sat on Ash's bed, staring at him as he slept. After a minute, he half opened his eyes. "Have you been *staring* at me? That's really rude."

"I figured out the plate number."

Ash sat up, instantly alert, the dark circles under his eyes indicating he'd had only a few hours of sleep. "How?"

"Math." I opened the laptop and pulled up the database. "I found the listing in the database—it looks like the plate was taken from a car at a shopping center in Sunnyvale. Which is only ten miles from Lauren's house. I'm sure they've switched cars since then, but at least it's a start."

Ash hopped up and dressed quickly. "I'm going to get it traced and see if we can find where they dumped it. And then I'm going out with the crew. We'll start searching the area." He nodded at me. "Good work."

"I know. Being a genius has its advantages."

I hustled out to tell Levi what I'd done. Already dressed in a pressed shirt and khakis, he nodded at me over his coffee.

I grabbed a mug for myself. "I figured out the plate number. I used an algorithm and ran the variables."

Levi's eyes brightened. "If you're looking for compliments, you came to the right place. Nice job. Is Ash on it?"

"Yes."

He started pacing, his mind clearly racing. "Excellent. Finally, a break."

"I just hope something comes from it."

"It will."

I sat down with my coffee. "We spoke to Hannah again last night via Skype—she looked like hell. They've been beating her."

"*Jesus.*" Levi curled his hand into a fist, looking infinitely pissed. "I'm going back out there, and I'm going to find her. With the plate number, we have a place to start tracking them. I'm also meeting with the NSA today, to compare intel."

"Good—I hope they have something."

Levi nodded. "Since your tech expertise is coming in handy, I have something else for you to do."

"What's that?"

"I want you to review those two Skype videos more thoroughly with your IT team. You work with the most sophisticated people in the industry—hopefully they can figure something out. Maybe reroute the IP address and track it back to Shenzhen, or something. But there's gotta be a way to get more information about Hannah's location from that interface."

"I'll send the tape from last night to Dave and Leo. If anyone can figure something out, they can. But they reverse-engineered the first session, and the signal was rerouted from a proxy server in Russia—which is what these people do. Li Na has this routine down pat."

Ash came in, fully dressed and ready to go. He nodded at Levi. "I have a call in to the police to find out if this car has been dumped. I'm going to head to Sunnyvale while I wait to hear back from them. I need to do something—if I sit around here anymore, I'm going to go nuts."

I stood up. "I'll go with you."

Ash and Levi exchanged a quick look. "I don't think so," Levi said. "We should leave the fieldwork to the experts. You did a great job tracking the number, and we appreciate the hell out of it, but you should stick to what you're good at."

I ignored him and turned to Ash. "Can I come? I'll go crazy waiting to hear something."

Ash looked miserable. "I think we need to stick with the plan. But I promise I'll text you as soon as I find something. Please tell Lauren I'm going out there, and I'm going to find something, okay? I promise." Nodding at me one final time, he took off.

I stared Levi down. "Why won't you let me help?"

"Gabe—you just helped by finding that plate number. But I don't have insurance to cover your ass out in the field. Ash and I will take care of it with our team. Why don't you go see if Lauren's up, and if she's okay?" he asked, dismissing me.

He might not be doing it on purpose, but Levi was getting under my skin. His nose was going to get broken again—*soon.* Still, I headed to the bedroom without touching his precious, smug fucking face. For now.

Lauren needed me, and I needed to keep my shit together for her sake.

She rolled over, just waking up. "Hey." Her eyes were puffy and unfocused.

I slid into bed and pulled her close, kissing her forehead. "Hey yourself. Would you like some coffee?"

"Yeah—but I need to get up and get going. I have to get back to the office." She sat up straighter, and then she seemed to fully wake up, a look of realization dawning over her face. She shook her head, her eyes filling with tears. "Oh my God. Hannah..."

I held her. "It's okay."

"I can't believe she's...gone. And I can't help her. And those animals... They *beat* her." She sobbed against my chest.

I rocked her against me. "Hannah's tougher than we knew. She is *not* letting these people get under her skin. At least, she's not showing it. She's strong, babe. I never would've thought your sister would handle herself like this, but she's a fighter."

Lauren brushed her tears aside and laughed, a messy jumble of emotion. "She really *is* kind of a badass, isn't she?"

"She takes after her big sister."

"I could never be that brave."

"I don't know about that."

"I do." She shook her head. "When our parents died, I was the one who held it together. Hannah fell apart—she was young, and it was so sudden. It was horrible, but I didn't cry. I thought *I* was the strong one because I didn't let any of my emotion out. I did that for Hannah because she was my baby sister and I was trying to protect her. I was trying to be strong for her."

She wiped her face roughly. "But I can see it now—she's been the strong one all along. She doesn't hold back, and she never has. She lives closer to the truth. She's never been afraid of it."

"It's good that she's strong. She's going to make it through this."

Lauren stared out into space for a minute while she processed. "I don't know... I'm worried she's going to get herself killed because she won't keep her mouth shut. *And* I'm worried she's not going to cooperate because she doesn't want Li Na to get what she wants."

I had the same concerns, but I kept them to myself. "We'll just take it one step at a time. There's *some* good news—we figured out the plate number for the car they took her in."

Lauren sat up straight. "Oh my God! Can they trace the car to where Hannah is?"

"Not yet, but at least we have somewhere to start. Ash went out this morning to start a search. We're going to find her, Lauren, I promise. My brothers are doing everything in their power, and so am I."

Lauren threw her arms around my neck. "I've been alone my whole life, and I've dealt with some big things, but I know for a fact I would *not* be able to do this without you. Thank you."

I kissed the top of her head. "I love you, babe. And we're going to get through this."

CHAPTER 7

LAUREN

Bethany and I met in my office later that morning. It felt like we were living the same day over and over again, a mind-numbing collection of hours running together, filled with despair and financial documents. I told Bethany about my conversation with Hannah.

Her face drained of all color. "They beat her up?"

I nodded and turned away, looking at my computer screen instead. "She had a bruise on her face…her shirt was ripped."

"Oh my God."

"But she seemed okay, as crazy as that sounds. She still has her fight—but I'm worried it's directed the wrong way. She was giving the guards holy hell, but she needs to be saving energy to keep herself safe."

Bethany looked thoughtful. "I don't know. I'd rather have her feisty than petrified."

"But not if it gets her killed. Or…anything else." I shut that train of thought down immediately, feeling sick. I couldn't bear to think about what could be happening to her. If I let myself imagine the possibilities, I'd end up rocking in a corner, a prime candidate for the psychiatric ward.

My phone buzzed, and I lunged for it, like I did every time it made any sort of noise now.

It was a text from Li Na.

*My attorney sent me another update. With a few changes, the P&S is in good shape. Meaningful progress has been made. My guards have updated me, and I've instructed them not to harm your sister—*if* you do what I ask. Once you've finished the materials list and have an update on the IP transfer docs, I am open to arranging her release in exchange for you.*

Will work on those documents today, I wrote back immediately. *I want to do this as soon as possible.* TELL YOUR MEN NOT TO TOUCH HER. *If anything else happens to Hannah, the deal is off!*

You don't need to make proclamations—just send my attorney an update, Li Na texted back. *I'll be in touch.*

My hands were shaking as I put the phone down.

"Who was that?" Bethany asked.

I went to the window and looked outside, my mind racing. "Li Na. She wants us to wrap up the materials list and send it over today. Can we do that?"

I felt Bethany staring a hole into my back, but I didn't turn around.

"Sure. But what happens after that?"

"I'm not sure yet," I lied. "I just know that I want this done as soon as possible. So let's get going, okay?"

I couldn't dwell on what was going to happen to me. I had to get my sister back at any cost...even if the cost was my own life.

I refused to think about Gabe—about how he would feel. About how *I* would feel if I had to say good-bye to him. If I thought about it, I would break. And there was no room for error now.

Hannah's life depended on it.

***

Bethany and I spent the rest of the day getting everything together, and we had several conference calls with my intellectual property team. They were preparing my licenses for transfer, along with contracts for the few patents I'd acquired over the years.

There was so much work to do, I wasn't sure how we were managing it. But the nineteen-hour days Bethany and I were putting in helped make a dent in the process, and my determination to move forward as swiftly as possible kept me on track.

"Babe." Gabe's voice brought me back to the present and the quick glass of wine we were having before bed. "You spaced out on me for a second. What's going on?"

I swirled the red wine around, watching the trail it left on the glass. "I'm just figuring out what's left to do." I shivered. If I did as Li Na asked—if I went to her—there would be nothing else to figure out.

Except how to say good-bye.

I could barely stand to look at Gabe's handsome face, which was lined with worry. I hadn't told him about the earlier texts from Li Na. I couldn't bear to.

We were interrupted by a text from Bethany. *Petra gave prelim approval on the materials list. She made a couple of changes. I'll send you the updates for your review. If you approve, we'll get started on the rest of it.*

I bit my lip and put the phone down. "That was Bethany. She said she's updating this round of docs based on the other lawyer's comments. Then she's sending them back over to me for review."

Gabe scrubbed his hands over his face. "This is happening so fast."

I nodded. "Li Na told me what she wanted, and I'm giving it to her. I'm not going to put up a fight. It's not worth it."

"What's next?"

I took a gulp of wine and looked out the window, searching the stars for Orion, my favorite constellation. "I have to reach out to my investors, and I need to tell the staff that we're winding up the business. Then there's the rest of the documentation, which will be a lot of work. But after that, Paragon will be...gone. It will be part and parcel of Jiàn Innovations, where I'm sure Li Na will promptly run it into the ground."

"What're you going to do about your employees?"

I winced. This part gutted me. "I'm going to give them six weeks' severance, which is as much as I can afford. And that's it."

"I've been thinking about something." Gabe reached for my hand. "Your people can come work at Dynamica. I'm launching some new initiatives, and I need a great team."

I raised my eyebrows. "You suddenly need enough staff for another entire *company*?"

He leaned back and put his feet up on the ottoman, looking pleased with himself. "That's what I said. Put a good word in for me. Tell them I'm a great boss and that we have a very friendly office environment—a huge game room and the best cafeteria in Silicon Valley. I have an on-site sushi chef. Employees from Facebook come to eat at my place, for Christ's sake."

I shook my head, feeling overwhelmed by his generosity. "Gabe. You don't have to do this for me."

His dimple flashed. "It's not just for you—it's for me. I'm going to put your people to work, and I'm going to make you the president of a new biotech R&D division at Dynamica. And then you're going to be happy and productive, and in the office right next to mine, and I'm going to get laid on a *very* regular basis." He put his arms behind his head, making his biceps pop. "Win-win, babe."

My throat constricted as I imagined a future like that. A future that was happy, safe, and secure. A future with Gabe.

A future that might never happen.

He must've seen the look of despair cross my face, because he stopped smiling and sat up. "What." He didn't bother to make it sound like a question.

"N-nothing. I'm just processing."

His eyes flashed. "Did you hear anything from Li Na since last night?"

I nodded, trying to compose my features. "She said the P&S was in good shape, and that she'd instructed her men not to touch Hannah. Nothing else."

The lie hung in the air between us; desperation and regret bubbled up inside me. "I think she just wants to get everything finalized."

My phone beeped again, and I opened my messages. The revised documents were in my inbox. "Bethany just sent me the revisions. I need to work on this. She'll probably come over."

I didn't wait for a response as I rushed to the safety of my computer. I needed to get away from him before he started asking me more questions and I cracked. I hid in his home office and scrolled through the documents on my laptop, knowing I couldn't hide from him much longer. Gabe was the love of my life. I owed him the truth.

I just had to find the strength to tell him, and to ask him for what only he could give me: forgiveness.

And, hopefully, his blessing.

Chapter 8

GABE

Lauren was busy preparing for the sale, but she was also busy hiding something from me.

And I had a very good idea what it was.

So later that night, while she was wrapped up reviewing documents with Bethany, I stole her phone. This constituted a breach of trust, and I knew it. It was also a douche move.

But whatever she was hiding could potentially harm her. I had to know what it was in order to protect her. That was my job, douche move or not.

I scrolled through her messages, finding the one from Li Na almost immediately. Lauren hadn't bothered to delete it. She was a genius, but I swear that sometimes because of that, she didn't pay attention to the normal details of everyday life. I'd lost count of how many times she'd forgotten to eat because she was so wrapped up in her work. She was the CEO of a multibillion-dollar company, yet she couldn't remember to delete an incriminating text message.

I imagined her train of thought: *I should really delete this, but—wait! Shiny new algorithm! This one might cure cancer! Let me see if I can work the convoluted algebraic equation through my perfect, genius brain!*

I would've laughed at the image, but I was too pissed.

I read the text again. *Once you've finished the materials list and have an update on the IP transfer docs, I am open to arranging her release in exchange for you.*

She was preparing to sacrifice herself without even discussing it with me. My blood boiling, I stalked down the hall and found her in my office, hunched over documents with Bethany.

"Lauren."

She looked up, her eyes bleary from staring at her screen. "Huh? What's up?"

I held up her phone. "I need to talk to you. Now."

She opened her mouth to argue but then closed it. "I'll be back soon," she told Bethany.

You hope.

I hustled her into the bedroom and tossed her phone to the bed, pointing at it. "What. The. Fuck."

"I'm guessing you read the text from Li Na." She started pacing. "I got it earlier today. I was going to tell you. I'd already made up my mind to—"

"But you didn't!" I ran my hands through my hair. "You hid it from me! What were you going to do? Tell me when you were on your way to fucking *China*?"

She whirled on me. "Stop! This is Hannah we're talking about! What are my options? Tell Li Na: 'Sorry, I changed my mind—*go ahead and execute my sister*?'"

"No! But you can't sacrifice yourself, and you can't lie to me, goddamn it!"

Lauren suddenly sat down on the bed, as if all the fight had left her. "I was going to tell you tonight. I swear." She raised her eyes to meet mine—she looked hollowed out.

"How can I trust you when you kept this from me?"

"How can I trust *you* when you snooped through my messages?"

The muscle in my jaw popped. "You should've told me."

"I didn't want to tell you because then it would be *real.* And I don't want it to be real. I don't want any of this to be real. You think I want to lose everything?" She looked near tears. "You think I want to leave you?"

I melted a little, but I stayed on the other side of the room. "Then you have to let me help. Between the two of us and my brothers, we'll figure out how to make this work. You're so much safer if you let us in. If you go off on your own, you're dead."

I waited until she looked at me. "It's fucking crazy, Lauren. *No one wants you dead.* Especially not Hannah. If you want to save her, you have to give her a reason to live!"

Lauren jumped up and started pacing again, possessed by another round of anxious energy. "I don't know what to do. I've gone over it and over it, and I don't know how I can circumvent Li Na. How I can get out of this with Hannah alive, without me having to go in her place."

"Stop pacing." I reached for her, dragging her to a halt. "You're exhausted. Go wrap things up with Bethany and then tell her you're going to bed."

She shook her head. "I can't stop working—"

I lowered my face to hers. "You are going to bed. With me. You need to sleep and get your head on straight. No wonder you can't figure out what to do with Li Na—she's got you exhausted and running in circles. Bethany can finish the paperwork."

I ushered her out. "If you're not back in five minutes, I'm coming for you."

I would pick her up and throw her over my shoulder if I had to. Lauren and I needed to work a few things out. Between her and my brothers and everything spiraling out of control, I was about to lose it.

But amid all the craziness, it was still her and me. If *we* didn't make sense, nothing made sense.

I'd calmed down and was ready for her when she came back, ten minutes later.

"You're late." I handed her another glass of wine. "And you look like you need that."

She took a sip, sighing. "You're right about that last part, at least."

"I'm going to show you exactly how right I am." I could feel myself getting hard. "I'm going to take a shower. Once you've relaxed a little with your wine, take off your clothes. When I get back, I want you ready for me. Naked. On the bed, with your legs open and your mouth closed."

"Seriously? Right *now*?"

I glared at her. "I don't think there's a better time for us to work this shit out. Time is of the essence. You're going to start listening to me—once and for all. Now, *do what I say.* Clothes off. On the bed. Legs open and *most* importantly—mouth closed."

"You can't always boss me around." She sounded defiant, but her eyes glittered.

"The hell I can't!"

She crossed her arms. "If I do it, it's only because I'm trying to forget what's happening for a little while—*not* because you're my boss or because I approve of you going through my messages. You're not, and I don't. Are we clear?"

"Duly noted, Your Highness." I stalked off to take a shower. Now I was rock hard, my body yearning to get inside Lauren and leave a deep mark. She made me crazy. I knew how upset she was, but she had to understand—she couldn't hide things from me, and she *sure* as hell couldn't run off to Shenzhen to sacrifice herself.

Did she really think I'd let her hop on a plane so Li Na could keep her prisoner—or worse?

"You can't always boss me around."

My cock throbbed. It couldn't *wait* to show her who the boss was.

In a rare act of obedience, she was waiting for me when I got out of the shower. Lying on the bed, naked and spread-eagle. All I could see was smooth, ivory skin, long blonde hair spread out on the pillow, luscious breasts, erect dusky pink nipples, and her sex open, pure and perfect pink, glistening with moisture.

"At least you finally listened to me."

She gave me a dirty look, but then her gaze drifted down to my dick, as if she couldn't help herself. I started fisting myself, watching her watch me. She arched her back a little, a sure sign that she wanted me.

Well. She was going to have to wait.

Her fingers trailed down her skin, caressing her breasts, pinching her nipples, until they drifted down to her sex. She started stroking herself, moaning.

"Lauren. Stop."

She shot me a filthy look. "You're touching yourself. I figured it's fair game."

"Take your hand away," I ordered. "You're being punished. You're going to do *exactly* what I say if you want to even get close to having an orgasm tonight."

Lauren looked fired up—she opened her mouth to say something, but then she snapped it shut, taking her hand off her clit. She looked like she was muttering and cursing silently, but she didn't make a sound. She must have felt guilty, and she must've wanted that orgasm. I intended to press my advantage as hard as I could, until I was satisfied that she'd learned her lesson. Which, admittedly, was going to take more than one night.

Good thing I was in this for the long haul. Knowing her, this could take a lifetime.

I went to the bed and spread her legs apart a little farther. "I'm going to enjoy this."

She gave me a haughty look, but as soon as I put my face between her legs, kissing and nipping her inner thighs before licking her slit from bottom to top, she shuddered beneath me. I put two fingers inside her, and she clenched around them as I stroked her inside. Then I flicked her clit with my tongue, slowly, languidly, lapping at her delicious body as I fucked her with my fingers.

She didn't say a word. But I could hear her breathing turn ragged. She was getting close, her body coiled and tense. I clamped my mouth over her clit and sucked hard until she grabbed the top of my head and unselfconsciously ground herself against my face.

But I pulled back before she could come.

"What? *No!*" she wailed, grabbing my face and trying to lure me back. "So close...baby...*please...*"

"You like that?"

"I think you can tell I liked it." She was still breathing in shuddery gasps. "I want more."

"So let me be in charge. Do as I say. *For once.*" I leaned back and started fisting myself again. I was so turned on, my erection huge and throbbing.

Lauren licked her lips. "Can I do that for you?"

I watched her get onto all fours and come toward me. She tentatively took the head of my cock into her mouth and sighed with pleasure, as if she couldn't wait to suck me.

My body vibrated with desire. "You like the way I taste?"

She answered by opening her throat and taking me all the way in. *Fuck.* She wrapped her fingers around my shaft and stroked me, her mouth chasing her fingers. The combination of sensations, and the way she kept running her tongue over my sensitive tip, almost made me lose it right there. But I opened my eyes long enough to see that she was grinding herself against the sheets, probably close to having a forbidden orgasm as she went down on me.

"Oh, fuck. Stop."

After a long pull, she reluctantly released my cock and looked at me. Her face was flushed and her lips were pouty, swollen. She looked at me expectantly.

I wanted nothing more than to bury myself in her and take her six ways from Sunday, but then I would come right away, and I had *plans.* "Do you want to try something different?"

"*Tonight?*"

"I have something I've been saving to try with you…to increase your pleasure. And mine." I stroked her cheek gently. "It might help take your mind off what's happening." I rolled over to my nightstand and pulled something out, handing it to her. It was textured glass, smooth and conical, with a knob at the end.

She looked confused. "I don't know what this is."

"I know you don't." I'd been her first, a fact that still made a hot pride bloom inside my chest. I wanted to open the world up for her, show her every pleasure her body was capable of—and tonight, I wanted to try to take her mind off the nightmare unfolding around us, even if only for a few minutes.

After that text from Li Na, I also wanted to show her that I owned her ass—literally. "But I think you'll like it…and I'd like to show you, if you'd let me."

She nodded, running her fingers tentatively over the plug. "Okay."

"Only if you want to, babe. If tonight's not the right time, I understand."

"No, I want—I want to feel something. I want you to make me feel something besides…" She let her voice trail off, but her eyes met mine. They burned with sadness, but also with need.

I grabbed a tube, and I watched Lauren's cheeks flame as she guessed it was lubricant.

I moved to the edge of the bed and sat down. "Lie across my knees and relax," I commanded.

She looked at me, unsure, but then she crawled across my lap. I cupped her ass and squeezed. She wriggled against me, and I spread her open a little, my fingers lightly circling her anus.

Her breath hitched. "What are you doing?"

"Getting you ready."

"For what?"

"Relax, babe." I stopped stroking her for a moment. "Have I ever hurt you?"

"No," she said hoarsely.

"Have I ever let you down?"

"Never."

"Do you trust me with your body?"

She finally relaxed against me. "Of course I do."

"I'm going to make you forget about everything else, at least for a little while. I just want you to be with me. Let me take care of you." I traced the glass plug against her skin, trailing it down her backside.

She shivered. "Is that the…*thing*?"

"It's an anal plug." I teased her open with my fingers and then gently slid the lubricated tip inside her. Her whole body tensed against the cool texture. "I want you to relax—that's important. I'm going to slide this inside you, and you're going to slowly get used to the feel of it."

Her breath hitched. "Okay."

I stroked her ass. "Once it's in and you adjust, I'm going to fuck you very, very hard. I'm going to make you come—but not until I tell you to. I want you to feel me."

I slipped the plug a little farther inside her, and she shivered. "I want you to know that I *own* you. *All* of you."

I took my time, stroking her back, whispering to her, as I worked the plug all the way in. She moaned again.

"Are you okay?"

"It's not uncomfortable, just...*different.*"

I reached down and slowly pinched her clit, rolling it between my fingers. She cried out when I stuck my fingers inside her again, stroking her. Her breath was coming in short, hot spurts. I liked having her across my lap like this. I liked having my way with her, with unadulterated, VIP access to some of my favorite places.

"So wet for me. My little virgin, all grown up." I thrust my fingers in and out, and she arched against me, raising her ass in the air. She was ready—and I was about to lose it.

"On the bed. All fours."

She crawled up the bed, and my cock bobbed after her as I watched the plug glitter between her ass cheeks. I wondered what she was feeling right now.

But when she got on all fours and opened her glistening, wet sex for me, I had a pretty good idea.

I knelt behind her, running my hands down her hot skin and cupping her breasts from behind. She rocked back against me, wet and wild. I ran my erection down her slit, making myself slick.

Lauren ground herself against me with urgency.

I couldn't hold back anymore. I fingered the plug while inch by thick inch, I slowly entered her pussy. The pressure from the plug accentuated the snug fit of Lauren's body around mine. I sucked in a deep breath. I wasn't going to last long.

"Are you still okay?" My voice came out thick.

She moved against me, hot and urgent. "Yes—I want you to fuck me. Deep. Hard. I want to feel you all the way in."

Grunting, I flexed my hips and entered her fully. *Holy fucking tightness.* She cried out as I filled her, my cock sliding in and out. "You're so wet."

"Please," she whimpered. She started to finger herself and to buck against me, but I took both of her hands and held them behind her back, pulling her up onto her knees. At this angle, I could thrust into her very hard and very deep. She was at my mercy, just where I wanted her, *finally.* She cried out as I pumped into her. I felt my balls tightening as they slapped against her.

I was so close. I let go of her hands and pushed her back onto all fours. I thrust into her deeply, savagely, one hand putting slight pressure against the plug, one hand finding her clit. Her whole body tensed, and she whimpered.

"You can come now."

"Oh my God—*Gabe!*" She unraveled against me, completely giving herself over, her whole body trembling with the impact of the orgasm.

Just how I wanted her.

I came then, hard and hot. Her pussy clamped me like a vise. I kept thrusting, out of my mind, emptying myself into her. "Fuck, Lauren. So, so good."

After a few hazy minutes, I removed the plug, and we cleaned ourselves up. Lauren climbed back into bed and snuggled against me. "You were right about taking my mind off things. I almost passed out—in a good way."

I arched an eyebrow. "You want to do it again?"

"Hell no," she laughed. "I can't even keep my eyes open."

I leaned down, pulling her into my arms, kissing her tenderly. I was entirely spent from loving her like that, so hard and fierce.

"I love you," she said. "And I'm sorry."

"I know. I'm sorry I went through your messages. And I love you too. So let me. *Let me love you.*" I couldn't hide the raw quality of my voice. I sounded vulnerable to my own ears.

She looked up at me and stroked my face. "I want to. But I have to save—"

"I know. But let it go for tonight. Sleep, and we'll figure it out in the morning. *Together.*"

"Together," she agreed, and then fell asleep safe in my arms.

Now I just had to figure out how to keep her there.

CHAPTER 9

LAUREN

Before I headed back to the office the next morning, I stopped by the hospital. A different nurse was in Wes's room. She nodded, smiling at me encouragingly. "All of his vitals look good. The doctors are doing rounds this afternoon—they'll run more tests."

"Thank you." I waited until she'd finished with his IV and left the room before I went to the bed. "Hey, Wes."

His big body lay unmoving. The bruises on his face had faded to a sickly yellow.

I clutched his hand and promptly burst into tears.

"Sorry to cry like this, but I just...I just miss you, and I miss my sister, and I don't know what to do. Hannah's being so tough. I talked to her again. You would be proud—she's been standing up to the guards." I squeezed his hand. "I'm actually mad at her about it, but she's holding her own. So that's...that's good, right?"

It probably wasn't fair of me to cry all over Wesley, but I couldn't stop.

"I need to get everything back to normal," I continued, babbling. "For my sake, yours, Hannah's—and for Gabe. I know that sounds crazy with everything else going on, but I'm worried about him. He's having a hard time."

It felt good to release some of what I'd been holding inside. I squeezed Wes's hand again, hoping he'd understand that I was falling apart. "Gabe's trying to hold it together for me, but I know this is killing him. He's used to being in control. He's worked hard his whole life to make things right, and he can't…he can't make this right."

I laid my forehead on the bed, holding on to Wes for dear life. "He cares about you so much, you know? And Hannah. He just wants us all back together and safe. But now I have to sell the company, and Li Na wants me to exchange myself for Hannah…"

I took a deep, shuddery breath. "I can't lose Hannah. It's me Li Na wants. I'll find a way to come back—but I can't let her hurt my baby sister. I've taken care of Hannah my whole life, and this isn't any different. You understand, don't you?"

I waited for a sign from him, but nothing came.

I stayed for a few minutes longer, listening to the sounds of the machines. I forced myself to calm down so I could leave Wes with some positive energy instead of my hysterics.

I dried my eyes and straightened my shoulders. "I'll be back tomorrow. Maybe I'll have some good news." That sounded like a lie, but I had to try to stay positive—for both Wes's and my own sanity's sake.

I hustled back to the lobby, motioning for Timmy to follow. We headed back to my company—or rather, what was left of my company. On the surface, things looked the same at Paragon, but I still shivered as I strode through the doors. How many more mornings did I have left here? Stephanie greeted me as I headed into my office. She'd worked for me for six years, since Paragon's inception—as had most of my employees. What was life going to be like for all of us after this was over?

And would I even be here to find out?

Inside my office, Bethany was already set up at a table, buried in a stack of paperwork. "Good morning. I hope you didn't get into too much trouble with Gabe last night. What was that about, anyway?"

"The text Li Na sent me yesterday. I didn't tell you everything she said."

"I *thought* you weren't telling me something. What's going on?"

I put down my bag and faced my attorney, one of the few people I counted as a friend. "Li Na wants me to exchange myself for Hannah as soon as this round of documents is finalized."

Bethany frowned. "What're you going to do?"

"I have no idea," I admitted. "I'm hoping Levi can deliver on his promise to get Hannah back and somehow keep me safe."

Bethany tapped her pen against her stack of papers. "I can mess around with these numbers, which would make the revisions take longer. Do you want me to do that, just to buy us some time?"

"No. Getting Hannah back is the priority. We need to do exactly what Li Na wants, how she wants it. My sister's in bad shape. I feel like we're running out of time."

Bethany went back to work without another word—she could tell I'd made up my mind.

Stephanie buzzed in a little while later. "I have an Agent Marks on the line for you."

"Thank you." I waited until the line clicked over. "Agent Marks? Do you have news for me?"

"Unfortunately, no. But I spoke with Levi earlier—he informed me that you'd had another conversation with Zhao. Care to fill me in?"

I scribbled furiously on a Post-it and shoved it in front of Bethany. *Do I have to tell him everything?* I didn't want to compromise the agreement I had with Li Na, in case it adversely impacted Hannah.

She shook her head no. *Not unless he can help us,* she mouthed.

I doubted that he had more information than we did. "I really don't know much. We just talked about the sale. I'm in the process of finalizing the documents to transfer Paragon to one of Li Na's companies. Once I do that, she said we could talk about my sister's release."

"Will you please keep me informed about what's going on? I'm only getting monosyllabic answers from Levi."

"Do you have any answers for *us*? Is your division preparing to indict Zhao on any charges, or connect her to the shootings or Hannah's disappearance?"

He sighed. "I thought you understood—beginning a proceeding against Zhao, who is a Chinese national on home soil, is difficult if not impossible. But I'm still involved in this case, Ms. Taylor. I would appreciate the opportunity to intervene, if necessary—and not like last time, when I had to storm an office building with machine guns and multiple agents to rescue you at the last second."

"Of course. I'll contact you if I have any news." I hung up, not knowing what else to say. I looked at Bethany. "I can't believe I just got off the phone with the FBI and *lied* to them, and it doesn't even *faze* me. It's just…a typical day at the office. Is it me, or are things really crazy around here lately?"

She didn't bother to look up from her document. "It's not you. Trust me."

I went back to work, because that was what I did. Work had always been my solace in the past. I just hoped it could save my future.

***

GABE

Last night with Lauren had taken a little of the edge off, but only a little. Things seemed better with us, but I had to watch her—Lauren's big heart and unfaltering loyalty would get her into trouble. I couldn't let that happen.

I headed from my room to get some coffee, my brothers already gone for the day. I enjoyed the rush of caffeine in peace, and then I called Timmy, who'd left earlier with Lauren.

"Good morning," he said. He sounded as if he'd been expecting the call. "I'm at the hospital with Ms. Taylor—she's visiting Wesley."

"Okay, good. Listen, Lauren has been in direct communication with Li Na again. Did you know that?"

"She mentioned it."

"Li Na wants to do the exchange soon. Nothing's been finalized yet, but I need to make sure that unless she's with me, you're with her every second of the day. She's not to go anywhere or meet with anyone unless I've approved of it beforehand. Do you understand?"

"Yes, but...sir? Does Ms. Taylor know we're having this conversation?"

I pinched the bridge of my nose. "Of course not."

"Okay. Hopefully, we won't need to worry about it." Timmy didn't sound convinced.

"If she tries something, you say *no.* Then you call me. You're working for me now, and I just tripled your salary."

I thought he sighed, but I might've imagined it. "Yes, sir." He hung up before I could pester him further.

Levi sent me a text. *Let's meet at the house tonight. We need to catch up on details.*

Fine, I texted back immediately. I wanted to type *Hannah's life is on the line, so you better actually have some goddamned details to catch up on,* but I thought better of it. Instead, I headed to my Spyder, which I drove well over the legal speed limit all the way into work.

Ryan jumped up when I came in. "We've had several phone calls from our partner in London," he said, looking worried. "She doesn't sound happy."

"Olivia? What's the problem?"

"It has something to do with the patch—that's all I know." Ryan backed out of my office, looking wary. "You might want to ask her not to swear at me next time."

I paced for a while before I called Olivia back. She'd been a friend of mine at Harvard, and our paths had crossed professionally again when I'd started Dynamica. She was tough, but she'd never given me any trouble before.

As I picked up the phone, I had a sinking feeling that was about to change.

"Hey, Olivia. My assistant said you called a couple of times—sorry I wasn't in yet. What can I do for you?"

"You can tell me why the hell Lauren Taylor's selling her company to the Chinese, for starters." Olivia's British accent was clipped and angry. "And I'd like to know why I heard this from someone besides you. That's a good place to start!"

Taken off guard, I didn't say anything for a moment.

"Gabe? I'd like an answer, please."

I stood there, reeling. "I'd like to know who you *did* hear this from."

Olivia sighed, which sounded very British and dramatic. "I'm not getting into that right now, but I *would* like to know: is it true? The patch has been selling really well for us over here, and I mean *really* well, but I don't want to get involved with dealing with a Chinese company—"

"Nothing's set in stone."

"But *is* there a possibility? Why does Lauren want to sell Paragon right now? We've just gotten started, and we're selling well over the projected numbers. The patients love the patch and so do the lab techs. Does she just want to get rich and get out? I thought she was in this for the long haul."

"She is. I can't really say more than that right now."

"Well, I need more assurance than that. A large part of our fiscal planning for next year involves our agreement with Dynamica—if things are changing, I need to know."

"I swear, as soon as I know something, I will tell you. You have my word."

She sighed again. "Fine."

I should probably have Skyped her. Historically, she'd always reacted well to my dimple. "Have you discussed this with anyone else?" I asked.

"Not yet."

"You shouldn't. This information isn't coming from my office or from Paragon. It's completely unverified—you should know that, and so should anyone else that you speak with. But I would like you to tell me where you heard it. I brought you in on this deal in the first place—I think you owe me that much."

"I wouldn't call the information 'completely unverified,' but I can't tell you the source. I'll leave it at that. I'm taking a risk by telling you, but I'm doing you a favor—you need to nip this in the bud, Gabriel. We just started distribution and I've always considered Dynamica a friendly partner. But if the patch changes in price or structure, my labs are going to be upset. Everyone's been adapting to the new technology and making plans to convert to primarily using the patch for testing."

I wanted to keep her focused on the upside. "That's good."

"Not if Lauren sells the company! This could permanently damage my reputation and my relationship with my labs, and I won't be happy. Neither will anyone else. The Chinese can be difficult to deal with, and I happen to know that they will raise prices in an instant. No one wants that, especially not me."

"Not me either. Thanks for the call, Olivia. I'll be in touch soon."

I hung up and started to pace, running my hands through my hair.

News of the impending sale had been leaked—which had the potential to blow up the deal. If my international partners got wind of the fact that the cutthroat and aggressively growing Jiàn Innovations might be purchasing Paragon, they would bail out of our agreement in droves. Li Na would *not* be pleased with the potential drop in earnings.

If she found out about this before we got Hannah back, there could be dire consequences.

Who had leaked this, and why? I stalk-paced around my office, considering the options. As far as I knew, Lauren hadn't told her employees yet, just her board of directors. I hadn't shared the news with anyone other than my brothers. Whoever had contacted Olivia was someone close to us, someone who understood that news of a sale to Jiàn Innovations would rattle our partners.

Someone who understood this could potentially implode the deal.

Olivia was upset, and she had reason to be: I hadn't disclosed the possible sale, which meant I'd essentially lied to her. I'd built a massive empire on my own technical expertise, but more than that, I'd built relationships with people. People who believed they could trust Dynamica and trust me, because I delivered.

With everything going on, I hadn't stopped to consider what was going to happen to *my* company's reputation and prospects as a result of Li Na's hardcore tactics. Paragon's sale would cause shockwaves throughout my own ecosphere. I'd never been afraid of starting over, but I had people depending on me, including Lauren's people, because I wanted to give them a safe haven when this was all over. That offer wasn't born of pity; Lauren's team was top-notch. If she became an executive at Dynamica, we could rule the biotech industry together.

But not if our reputations were trashed.

Maybe it *was* time to quit the business, I mused. I had enough money. I could go buy that island we'd visited a few short months ago. We could all live there happily ever after. Me, Lauren, Hannah, and Wesley… I might even let my brothers visit.

I stood by my window and looked out at the parking lot: it was full. I looked around my office, at the original artwork and couches…but the things I owned didn't matter to me. The people I supported, however, meant everything.

I looked back at the parking lot. I could run and hide from the world, but this was my company, dammit, and Paragon was Lauren's. And we'd worked for years to build everything we had. We had people depending on us, people with families and mortgages and car payments and dreams.

More important than all that—and all that was very important—this was *bullshit*. Li Na could bite me. She wasn't going to take my family and everything that I'd worked for away from me.

I just had to figure out how to hold on.

And I *had* to figure out a way to keep Lauren away from Li Na. If the time came, she would sacrifice herself for Hannah. She wouldn't even hesitate. That was part of the reason I loved her—she was fearless, more than she gave herself credit for. But I couldn't let her surrender herself, even though I certainly understood. I would do the same thing, even though both Levi and Asher hadn't brought Hannah home yet…

Ryan buzzed in. "What?" I snapped.

"Your brother Ash is on the phone."

"Put him through."

"We found the car," he said without preamble.

"Where?"

"At the Eastridge Mall."

The mall was a half hour from Lauren's house. "Good work. What's next?"

"This doesn't mean they're hiding nearby, but it's at least a start. We're going to start looking, start canvassing the area. And then we're going to find Hannah, and then we're going to get her out. How does that sound?"

I stared at the full parking lot, my hand gripping the phone. "It sounds like exactly what I needed to hear."

Chapter 10

LAUREN

My brothers want to have a meeting tonight, Gabe texted me.

I'm leaving soon, I texted back.

I took a final look at the patent agreement my team had drafted. "I think this looks good enough to send over," I said to Bethany. "What do you think?"

"I agree." Bethany started drafting an email to Petra. Her gaze flicked to me. "You ready to do this?"

I nodded. It wasn't as though I had a choice.

"I'm going home to have a meeting with Gabe and his brothers—would you like to join us?"

Bethany hit Send and grabbed her bag. "Okay. I just hope they have some news. I'm sure you feel the same way."

The men were waiting for us when we got home. Gabe jumped up when he saw me, taking me into his arms. "Did you hear anything today?"

"No, but we finished the documents and sent them over." *Which means we're closer to a showdown.* I looked away, not wanting to see his expression.

His grip around me tightened, which told me everything.

"Lauren, thanks for being here. I know you're extremely busy," Levi said. "I want to update you. You know we traced the plates to the vehicle that Li Na's men stole. We found that car at the Eastridge Mall today—and Ash tracked down the owners."

My pulse quickened. "Did you find anything that leads to Hannah?"

"Not yet, but this car was stolen from San Francisco, from a neighborhood that experiences a pretty high level of crime. I'm guessing they knew that—I think the people who did the job could be locals. Which is both good and bad. Good because they might be comfortable enough to stay in the area, and bad for the same reason. They could be very well hidden."

"So what's next?" I asked.

"I've been consulting with the FBI and the NSA, so I'll follow up on this lead with them," Levi said. "They might have something useful with the neighborhood—we can cross-reference their databases to try to find the men we're looking for."

Ash leaned forward. "And I'm taking the crew to go out and do a search. We'll start at the mall, checking neighborhoods around the area. We're also looking into every stolen vehicle that's been taken from the area during this timeframe. It's going to take a while, but at least we'll be doing something while we wait for their next move."

"That's great—it's progress. Thank you."

Ash nodded. "Hopefully, we'll turn up something."

I swallowed hard, dreading what I needed to say next. It wasn't going to go well, but we *had* to talk about it. "I think Li Na's next move is to arrange the exchange—as soon as the paperwork's approved. I got the sense from her that she wants me sooner than later."

Gabe tensed next to me. "Babe—"

"Hey." I put my hand on his thigh and squeezed. "We need to discuss this, okay?"

He opened his mouth to start arguing, so I turned back to Levi. "If she wants to set up an exchange, is there something we can do? To...disrupt it?"

I didn't want to become Li Na's prisoner, but I wasn't sure what, if any, options I had.

"It depends on the setup," Levi explained. "But we'll do everything we can to keep you away from her."

"And get Hannah back," I said. "Because that's the important thing."

I stared at Levi as Gabe stared at me.

"Doing 'everything you can' isn't specific enough for me," Bethany chimed in. "If my client's life is going to be put in danger, I would like more assurance than what you're offering, which sounds suspiciously like a campaign promise."

"I second that." Gabe sounded both miserable and pissed.

Levi rolled his eyes. "I can't make promises without more information. Of course I'm going to keep Lauren safe and get Hannah back. That's the whole point."

There was an uneasy break in the conversation as we considered what lay ahead.

"What can we do tonight?" Gabe asked.

"I'm going to take the crew out to start surveillance on the area," Ash said. "You're welcome to come."

Levi shot Ash a look, but Gabe ignored it, jumping up immediately. "Sounds great. I'll be ready in ten minutes." He hustled from the room, not giving any of us a backward glance, in case I complained or Levi rescinded Ash's offer.

"What're you doing?" Levi asked Ash warily.

Ash shrugged. "He wants to help. It's not like we're going to do anything exciting." He got up and left before Levi could tear into him.

Levi turned back to me and Bethany. "Let me know when Zhao contacts you again."

"Of course. Also, Agent Marks called me today looking for an update. I didn't get into specifics."

"That's fine—he's not much help these days. I'll check in with him again tonight, but I have another buddy over there who's much more useful."

We sat in awkward silence for a moment. There was nothing left to do but wait for Li Na's next move.

"Would you both like a drink?" Levi asked. "I'm pretty sure I'm overdue."

I raised my hand. "I have to face Gabe—of course I'd like a drink. Bethany?"

"Sure?" She sounded skeptical.

Levi handed Bethany a glass of wine. "I can tell you more about what we've been doing and my background—you seem like you still need some convincing that my company's legitimate."

"All the convincing I need is for you to actually get something *done* on this case."

"I appreciate you not mincing words." He raised his glass. "Cheers."

Bethany arched an eyebrow. "I'm not sure there's much to be toasting, yet..."

I grabbed my own wine and snuck out, leaving them to their pissing contest.

Gabe was in the bedroom. He'd changed into a dark sweatshirt.

I sank down on the bed. "Is what you're doing tonight going to be dangerous?"

"Are *you* seriously asking me that?"

"I haven't done anything." *Yet.* I jutted my chin out. "And I can't fight with you about what I haven't done. I can, however, worry that you're about to get yourself shot."

He sighed and cupped my chin. "We're just doing preliminary legwork. I guarantee you we won't find anything tonight—the only lead we have is where they dumped the car. Looking for Hannah from there is..."

"Is what?"

A glimmer of sympathy lit his eyes. "It's like looking for a blonde needle in a haystack."

I nodded. I either refused or was unable to cry at this point; I wasn't sure which.

"I forgot to tell you something," he said. "I had a call from my vendor in London—she heard about the sale."

"*What?* Heard about it how?"

"She wouldn't tell me that."

I stood up and started pacing. "Who would've leaked that news, especially to one of your partners? Everyone who knows is aware it's confidential!"

"I don't know, but I don't like it."

"Li Na won't like it either—and I can't let that be a problem. Did you tell your brothers?"

"I mentioned it. I didn't want to tell you and make you upset, but I also didn't want to hide it, because...you know. We aren't doing that." He stopped me from pacing and tucked a lock of hair behind my ear. "But I want you to know that I'm going to handle it. You have enough on your plate right now."

"I appreciate that, but please keep me posted. And just so you know, when Li Na does get in touch about the trade, I promise to tell you *everything*."

"Good—that's reasonable."

"In exchange, *you* have to be as reasonable about what she wants, given the circumstances."

"I promise to be reasonable. As long as she doesn't touch a hair on your precious blonde head."

"Gabe!" Ash called from down the hall. "Let's go!"

I pulled away from him reluctantly. "Why are you doing this tonight? Is it going to be dangerous at *all*?"

"It won't be dangerous at all—only dangerously boring. But I can't stand sitting around here, not doing anything. I talked with Leo and Dave today, and got them to look at the new Skype feed, but they can't come up with anything. We're at a dead-end. And then I get this call for my vendor... Going with Ash tonight will give me something to do besides just go crazy. Does that make sense?"

"Yes. Of course."

"What will you do while I'm gone?"

I forced myself to smile. "Keep working. And worrying."

He kissed the top of my head. "I love you, babe."

"I love you too."

I followed him to the door, wanting to beg him to stay. "I went to visit Wesley today. The nurse said his vitals look good, and that the doctors would be in this afternoon. I'm going to call the hospital to see if there's any update."

"He's a fighter, like your sister. They really are perfect for each other."

"I just hope they're both going to be okay."

Gabe came back and swept me into his arms. "They're going to be okay. I promise."

That wasn't his promise to make, but I still clung to it—and him.

He kissed me one last time as he headed from the room. "I'll call you later. Try to get some sleep."

After he'd gone, my phone beeped with an email notification. It was from Petra, saying she'd received the documents and would be in touch shortly.

Good. Things were moving forward, for better or for worse.

I went back into the bedroom and closed the door. Then I did something that I'd never done before that night: I got on my knees and prayed. I prayed for everything to somehow fall into place. I prayed that I could find a way to get Hannah back.

And I prayed that somehow, I could manage to stay alive.

Chapter 11

GABE

"Gabe, this is Philip, Ian, and Greg. Guys, you remember my brother. He's coming with us tonight, riding with me. Don't let him shoot you or bother you too much," Ash joked.

"Ha-ha." I looked at the men. "For the record, I've kicked Ash's ass on a regular basis for his entire life."

I gave Ash a nasty smile as we slid into his car. "And here I thought you were my favorite brother."

"You know it's not Levi," he said under his breath.

We headed toward Eastridge Mall, where they'd found the stolen car. We'd reviewed the mall security videos, but had been unable to get a clear shot of whoever had left it there. The police were assembling a list of all vehicles stolen from the area in the last week, to try to narrow down a list of possible cars the assailants had taken after they dumped the first one. While we waited for that information, we planned to search the surrounding neighborhoods and office parks for signs of suspicious activities or anything else that caught our eye. We didn't have much to go on, but at least it was something.

The neighborhoods surrounding the mall were largely commercial, with strip mall after strip mall filled with higher-end chain restaurants and stores. Ash diligently pulled into every parking lot, and although I wasn't sure that we had a reasonable expectation of finding any clues of Hannah's whereabouts, it made me feel better that we were looking.

After a couple of hours, we drove out farther, to the closest adjacent residential neighborhoods. Ash was thorough and slow, checking every car and every house. "You can't drive through every neighborhood in Northern California. You know that, right?" His unscientific approach was starting to bother me as the hours ticked by.

"Listen, Mr. Algorithm, sometimes surveillance work has to start with a gut feeling."

"Do you have a gut feeling about this neighborhood?"

Ash grimaced. "No. But it's better than sitting around. Poor Lauren..."

"I know." I hoped she was sleeping.

We spent the rest of the night driving through different neighborhoods. The sun was coming up as we headed back to the house. "Do you feel like that actually accomplished anything?" I'd seen nothing to give me hope.

"I didn't see anything interesting—which tells me that where we searched is clear."

"But you can't be sure."

"I can't be sure, but I feel pretty certain that concentrating strictly on this area would be a waste of our time."

"*You* just wasted our time."

"It wasn't a waste. We know more than we did last night."

"What do we do now?"

Ash kept his eyes on the road. "We find Hannah."

***

We stopped for breakfast. "So, what did you think? Security's not as exciting as you'd hoped, right?"

"Of course it wasn't exciting," I said. "Most work isn't exciting."

Ash stabbed a forkful of pancake. "Do you still feel like you're missing out on something?"

I stirred my coffee around for no reason—it was black, just like my mood. *Did* I feel like I was missing out on something by not being in the family business? In some ways, yes. But I would never leave my world behind. "It just makes me wonder what might've been. If Dad hadn't forbidden me..." I let my voice trail off.

I'd promised my dad I'd do something big with my life—and that promise was a choice that *I* had made. "I think having you guys out here and the fact that this case is so personal—it's just bringing this stuff up." I shrugged. "I'm over it."

Ash smiled at our cute, auburn-haired waitress as she brought the check and then focused on me. "Good. Because you've got a pretty good thing going. Levi and I have been talking about relocating the business out here... I think there's a serious need for high-end security in your industry. What do you think?"

"I think you're absolutely right—your business would grow exponentially if you made the move. But what about Mom?" My mother and her fiancé, Alexander Viejo, were firmly rooted in Boston. He was a professor at MIT, and all their friends lived in the area. She would have an absolute *fit* if all three of her sons were living on the West Coast.

"I don't know. Alexander's pretty old, though. He's gotta be about to retire. Then they wouldn't have to stay in Boston."

"Are you saying that *Mom* might move out here too?" I'd been in Northern California by myself for a long time. I loved my family, but I also loved them not breathing down my neck.

Ash smiled and shrugged; I couldn't tell if he was just fucking with me. "She's really pissed that she hasn't met Lauren yet. You need to do something about that."

"I'm bringing her to the wedding. We *are* sort of in the middle of a crisis out here, you know?"

"I know, and Mom knows, but that doesn't mean her feelings aren't hurt..."

I groaned. My mother and her feelings were sometimes labor-intensive. "I'll call her."

"You better. Otherwise, you'll never hear the end of it."

I drove home while Ash checked his email. "Hey—I got something from the police. A list of all the vehicles stolen in the past week."

"Are there a lot?"

"No," he said, scrolling through the email. "But there's enough that we can split up the team and track each lead down. There's no guarantee that these guys stole another vehicle from the area, but it's something—and that's all I need."

***

I crawled into bed, wrapping my arms around Lauren's warm body, and immediately fell asleep. An hour later, Lauren's phone buzzed with a text message, waking us. She sat up and read it immediately, her eyes wide, and then handed me the phone without a word.

Meet my men at the office park near Oakland Airport. Building 900, Langham Landing. Wednesday at 3 p.m. They will have Hannah.

Lauren, you will need your passport, your remote access codes, clothes, etc. No cell phone. No security. You drive yourself to Oakland, and your sister can drive your car home.

No exceptions.

If you are followed to the exchange site, or if anyone else is notified of or involved in this transaction, the trade is off. As are all promises.

Wednesday was four days from now.

"No." I threw the phone on the bed. "No fucking way."

Lauren stiffened, but she didn't look at me. She stared at the pattern on the comforter, her jaw set. "I know this isn't what you wanted to hear...but the instructions are pretty clear."

I wanted to argue, but I needed to go about this the right way, before things—me—got out of hand. "Get dressed. We need to show this to my brothers."

Levi was mulling his coffee when I jammed the phone into his perfectly pressed dress shirt, unable to form a coherent introductory sentence.

"It's a text from Li Na," Lauren explained.

He read the message, his face impassive. Then he put the phone down and stared out the window.

Ash came in, and Lauren handed him the phone. He read the text, his brow furrowed.

"So?" I asked, when neither of them said anything.

Levi turned to me. "*So.* This is pretty clear. We'll follow these directions to the letter—except for the fact that my team will be there. We'll get Hannah out."

But he'd missed the most important point. "What about Lauren?"

He squared his shoulders. "*I'm* not going to let anything happen to her."

Tension snaked through my body as I stepped toward him. "That's not good enough." My face was inches from his. "I need to be there. To protect her. I'm not letting her go alone."

"She won't be alone." Levi's eyes flashed at me. "But you read the text. You *can't* be there, and we've already talked about this—"

"Easy. Easy, guys," Ash said, inserting himself between us as we glared at each other. "We have a limited amount of time to make a plan. Let's not fuck it up because we're in-fighting."

"Fine," Levi said.

"Fine," I said, though I was anything but.

Ash held up the phone. "If she's meeting us in Oakland, there's a good chance that Hannah's still in the area. I think we should make our priority trying to find her before Wednesday. If we have to take her from that parking lot, we can, but it would be cleaner to try to get her before." He looked at Levi. "Any ideas?"

"You already went out on surveillance—you know what we're up against. She could be anywhere. A hotel. An office that Zhao owns. A condo she's rented. There's so much real estate being sold around here to cash buyers these days, she could be anywhere."

Ash nodded. "I'm going to start looking into the latest batch of stolen vehicles."

Levi nodded. "Definitely—get going *now*."

"What else?" I asked.

"We're going to get ready for this. I'll put my best field team together. We'll go over to the address today and start blocking things out," Levi said.

I grimaced. "I *don't* want Lauren going to the exchange alone. It's not safe. What if they grab her?" *Or worse?*

"I'm going to protect her." Levi looked like he was trying to marshal what remained of his patience. "Let's not get ahead of ourselves, okay?"

Lauren said nothing. She just stared out the window, her mind clearly racing. I went and put my arms around her, trying to calm myself and comfort her. I wished I could hold her right in this spot forever, so she wouldn't try something dangerous.

"I'm not going to fight with you." Her voice was quiet.

"Good."

She turned and looked at me. "That doesn't mean I'm going to do whatever you say."

"I know."

She arched an eyebrow and then went back to staring out the window, showcasing her intelligence: she wasn't going to argue. Not now.

I held her close, wishing I could keep her with me like this forever. And that somehow, we could still manage to bring her sister home.

Four days isn't a lot of time. Will it be enough?

CHAPTER 12

GABE

"I'll get in touch with the FBI," Levi said. "I need to let them know that Zhao's made contact again. They haven't been good for much, but they're good enough to back us up."

I clenched my fists. "But they can't be there—not if they're going to try to take over at the site. We can't do anything to compromise this."

"Except for *you* showing up, right?" Levi shot me a look.

Ash looked up from his laptop. "It's the FBI. I'm pretty sure they can handle themselves."

"How does that work?" Lauren asked. "Your company and the FBI? The police?"

"We don't break the law, and they stay out of our way," Levi explained. "If we have knowledge of illegal activity, we share that information with them. If we come across a person of interest, we turn them in. I'll call Agent Marks and let him know what's happening."

"It's a symbiotic relationship," Ash said. "Sometimes they're actually our client."

"Okay. Good to know." Based on Lauren's expression, the information was cold comfort. She started pacing. "I guess there's nothing else we can do right now..."

"I'm going out there to look for her," Ash said, closing his screen. "Some of the guys are already tracking down those plates. I'll check in with them, and I'll check the residential areas near the airport. If we could find her before the meeting… that could change everything."

"Do you want company?" I asked, anxious to be useful.

Ash shook his head. "Not this time. Take care of your own business for right now—I have a feeling the rest of this week is going to be busy."

"I'm going to meet with Agent Marks, my other contact, and also check in with my friend from the NSA," Levi said. "I need everything they've got on Li Na's operations. I'll check in with you later—keep security with you, and stay safe." He and Ash headed out.

I turned to Lauren. "What do you want to do? Are you going to head to the office?"

Lauren's face was pale, with two hectic spots of color dotting her cheeks. "I should. I need to tell my people about what's going on…about the status of the sale."

"Have you thought some more about my offer? Because it still stands."

She reached out and took my hand. "If you'd be willing to give my people a home at Dynamica, that would mean everything to me."

"What about you?" I smiled, trying to lighten the mood. "I'd love to have you in the office next to mine for…reasons."

"Ha." But she knew I meant it. "I'm thinking about it, and I want you to know how much it means to me. But I can't make a professional commitment right now. I don't feel capable."

I pulled her into my arms, feeling anxiety rolling off her in waves. She was wound taut, close to fraying. "Take your time. When you're ready, make plans for the future—for *our* future."

She buried her face in my chest. "I will. Just let me get through the end of this week, okay? I have to deal with this one step at a time."

I kissed the top of her head. "Of course."

Since there was nothing left to do at home but wait, we both decided it would be better to be busy at work. I went to Dynamica, and Lauren went to Paragon—with Timmy and three other security guards, at my insistence—and she promised to check in later. I called Olivia, my disgruntled London partner, when I got to the office. "Our conversation's been on my mind. I know you don't want to reveal your source, but I need to know who gave you the information about Paragon. It's important."

"You're putting me in a bad spot," she said.

"I'm still asking."

"I'm really not at liberty to say, which I know is going to bother you. But I *will* tell you that you need to watch your back, and so does Lauren."

"What the hell does that mean?" We were already busy watching our backs—and trying to pull Li Na's preexisting daggers out.

"I can't tell you, because I can't have this coming back to me." Olivia sounded firm. "I might need more information from this person, so I'm not burning the bridge."

"Even if it means you're burning a bridge with *me*? I know business is more important than friendship, but we *have* been friends for a long time, Olivia."

"I know. So trust me when I say that you really don't want to know who told me."

"Call me when you come to your senses." I hung up before I started yelling.

I spent the rest of the morning drinking coffee, feeling distracted, annoyed, and wary. Someone had compromised our confidentiality—someone who was looking to undermine the sale of Paragon to Jiàn Innovations. But the circle who knew about the impending transaction was small, and it was tight.

I swallowed a bitter taste in my mouth. I knew the person who'd done this was close to us. I'd get to the bottom of it. Whoever I met down there had a lot of explaining to do.

I pushed the issue to the side—I would have to deal with it later. If I was offering Lauren's people positions, I needed to make sure everything at Dynamica was in order. I spent the rest of the day going through compliance reports, meeting with my department heads, and checking in with the rest of my international distributors. There was no sign that information about the sale had been leaked elsewhere, but what was happening in London hadn't taken place in a vacuum. I had to isolate the problem and deal with it quickly.

And when I said deal with it, I meant exterminate it—before Li Na learned that people wanted out of the sandbox before her grubby paws got into it.

***

I sent Lauren a text as the late afternoon turned into evening. *Meet me at the Stanford hotel? I think we could both use a break tonight.* She'd been so tense at the house. I wanted to do anything I could to cheer her or distract her. She'd mentioned The Stanford before—it was one of Hannah's favorite places in the city, but we'd never taken the time to check it out.

She called a minute later. "What's up?"

"I just thought we could use the night away for just us, before we deal with… everything else this week. Does that sound okay?"

"That sounds perfect."

"I'll meet you there. I can't wait."

Before I left, I remembered what Ash had said about my mom. I needed to speak with her anyway, so I hit her number quickly as I headed to my car. "Hey, Mom."

"Well, the prodigal son finally remembers he has a mother! How are you, honey?"

"I'm fine. Mostly. It's been sort of…hectic out here."

"That's what Ash told me—it's terrible about Lauren's sister. I would love to call her, but as I haven't actually had the privilege of *meeting* her yet, I thought I should wait. Can I send her a card?"

"A card?" Did people still do that? "Sure."

"It doesn't seem too formal to you? I feel like *since I haven't met her*, it's the only appropriate way to reach out, without overwhelming the poor girl…" She sniffed.

I groaned and hoped she didn't hear me. "I'm bringing her to the wedding." *That is, if she doesn't defect to China as Li Na Zhao's prisoner.*

"You'd better," she said.

Time to switch gears. "How's everything going? How's Alexander?"

"He's great!" Distracted, she chatted happily for a few minutes about her fiancé, Alexander Viejo, and his latest semester at MIT. "He said that Lauren was one of the best students he ever had," she continued.

My mind was somewhere else. "Uh-huh."

"Gabe, are you even listening to me? Why did you call anyway? You never call."

"I need to ask you for something."

There was dead silence on the other end of the line. She probably couldn't fathom what I wanted—I was a self-made billionaire who never asked for anything.

"Are you okay, honey?" My mother's first instinct was always to panic.

I groaned. "I'm *fine.* I just need something."

She went quiet for a minute. "What?"

We'd only talked about this once, years ago, but I knew she'd figure it out. "You know...that thing we talked about in the kitchen at Christmas a few years back..."

"Oh my God!" she yelped after a moment, realization finally dawning. "Are you *serious*?"

I couldn't keep the grin off my face. "I've never been more serious in my life."

"You don't want something...different? I know you could afford it."

"Wouldn't be the same."

"Aw, honey," she said, and I could tell she was crying. "You always knew how to make your mother proud."

CHAPTER 13

LAUREN

It was so sweet of Gabe to remember that Hannah loved The Stanford. She'd been to the hotel bar with a date, the guy she'd gone out with before Wesley, and had raved about it. "It is *the* hot place," she'd told me a year ago.

I'd rolled my eyes at the time. "Thank you for sharing that information, because it's so pertinent to my exciting lifestyle." That was back before I'd met Gabe, when Hannah used to force me to vicariously live through her Silicon Valley exploits. My gut twisted as I thought of her. I wondered what'd happened since we'd talked—had she kept her mouth shut and behaved? Had her captors hurt her further, despite Li Na's orders? Or had Li Na fooled me again, pretending to call off her guards, when it was just a ploy to get me to cooperate?

The questions swirled through my mind as Timmy and my driver took me downtown. It was dark now and the buildings were lit up, beautiful in their own urban, man-made way. But my heart was too heavy to enjoy the scenery. I kept running over Li Na's instructions in my mind. If she discovered Levi's team and the FBI were planning on coming to the exchange, Hannah would suffer for it.

My gut instincts were to follow Li Na's instructions to the letter. I'd dealt with her long enough to know that she didn't care for improvisation. But Gabe would never allow that, and neither would his brothers. They believed they could save Hannah and get us both out of the exchange alive.

But what if they were wrong?

I wouldn't even think twice about giving my life for Hannah's. She was young, innocent, and full of life. She had everything to live for, and Wesley needed her. None of this was her fault—the blame lay squarely at my feet. Paragon was my company, the patch was my invention, and Li Na wanted what I had. Hannah was an ancillary victim of my actions. She never would've been kidnapped if I hadn't defied Li Na in the first place by successfully launching the patch behind her back.

Li Na was making me pay an unbearable price for my victory.

I knew where I stood. Hannah had to be rescued; I couldn't excuse any act of selfishness on my part. I would follow whatever plan Gabe and his brothers constructed, but if it came down to it, I would sacrifice myself for her. I would find a way.

I knew Gabe would never forgive me...and I understood. But my love for him, the ache that filled me every time I thought about leaving him—I couldn't let myself dwell on it. Hannah was my sister, and she was in mortal danger because of *me*. That was the cold, hard truth I had to face.

Jarred from my reverie as the driver pulled up in front of the hotel, I laughed when I saw the opulent, spectacular façade.

Timmy turned his beefy neck around. "This is The Stanford."

"Of course it is. Hannah loves this place." I smiled to myself, even though it hurt to think about my sister in her carefree days. Still, she'd be thrilled I'd finally made it here—The Stanford was a "Hannah-approved" institution.

Gabe had texted he was running late. I went and checked in, making sure Timmy's adjacent room was ready while gawking at the lobby. Everything was designed in clean, modern lines, but the hotel boasted ornate touches of floor-to-ceiling marble, crystal chandeliers, red velvet banquettes, and pillars enameled in gold. It was Silicon Valley meets mid-century Paris. I made a reservation for dinner, even though I had no appetite. Gabe should at least eat.

I laughed again, delighted, when I got up to the room. It was just as over-the-top as the lobby, with a minimalist, modern design punctuated with lush details—red tapestry curtains, oil paintings, and more crystal chandeliers. I supposed that other Silicon Valley CEOs might frequent a trendy hotel like this, but I never would've known it existed if it wasn't for Hannah.

Hannah had great taste and style. She would make a much better billionaire than me.

I sank down on the bed, thinking more about my sister. Financially, she was doing extremely well. Her stake in Paragon had earned millions since we'd gone to market. I needed to get her back so she could start spending some of the money. *Barneys' shoe department and the economy at large need her, dammit! And so do I!*

Wesley needed her too. Hannah had always enjoyed a throng of admirers and a steady stream of boyfriends, but she usually didn't take her relationships too seriously. I wondered if it was different with Wesley.

I wondered if I'd ever find out.

I stayed on the bed, sitting and staring out at the city lights as the sky darkened. I couldn't see the stars. My vision was being blocked, I mused. There was too much light pollution for me to see what was out there—the true answers, the true sky. If I could just get to the end of the week and finally see Hannah—finally reach out and touch her again—I would be able to think and see clearly. Because she was the real light of my life.

There was a knock on the door, bringing me back to earth. I got up and let Gabe in.

"Hey." He looked exhausted but also incredibly handsome in a T-shirt, blazer, dark jeans, and a pair of black Chuck Taylors. He was the epitome of Silicon Valley style—another thing I never would've known about without Hannah.

He pulled me in for a tender kiss. "Hey yourself. I'm so glad this sounded good to you. I thought we could use a little vacation."

I gave him a wan smile. "I'm not sure I deserve a vacation right now...or anything else."

Gabe wrapped his arms around me protectively. "Come on now, Your Highness—let's not indulge in self-flagellation tonight. Let's just pretend that everything is okay and enjoy our time together." He kissed me hungrily, and my body immediately responded, lighting up beneath his touch, in spite of my sorrow.

I pulled back, breathing hard. "We have dinner reservations in ten minutes."

"They'll live without us." He rubbed his erection against me and grinned, flashing his dimple. "We can eat at the bar when we're done—*if* we're ever done."

He kissed me again, and although it felt wonderful, part of me felt strangely detached. Whenever we made love, Gabe and I were completely connected. But as he ran his hands down my back and pulled me closer, I felt a distance between us, even though our bodies were intertwined.

He stripped off my clothes, and I removed his quickly, eager to feel his skin against mine. He took my face between his hands after he laid me back on the bed, a worried look in his eyes. "Babe? Are you okay?"

"I'm fine," I lied. "I just want to feel you. All of you." I grabbed his firm ass and pulled him against me.

He brushed the hair back from my face. "Now?"

"Now."

He entered me all at once and I cried out, grateful to be filled by him and frustrated by the fact that I couldn't lose myself in his embrace. My mind wandered elsewhere, on the sadness and fear I couldn't forget. Still, I moved against him hungrily, desperate for the release that only Gabe could give me.

Unfortunately, it never came.

"Babe?" he said a few minutes later. "I'm close..." The strain was clear in his voice.

"So am I."

He pulled back and looked at me. "You think I can't tell you're lying?"

I wrapped my arms around him, kissing him desperately. I wanted to feel him come inside me, to be comforted by his body's pleasure, even if I couldn't join him. "Please," I whispered, "*please*."

Gabe gently rolled off me. "I can't." He let out a flat laugh. "You've ruined me. I can only come when you come. You'll never get rid of me now."

I laughed, and then I realized I was crying.

He pulled me onto his chest and stroked my hair, letting me get it out. "I'm sorry—this was a bad idea." He sounded miserable. "I was being selfish…I wanted you all to myself."

"N-no. It's me. *I'm* sorry I'm ruining our time together."

He tightened his embrace and kissed the top of my head. "Shh. You don't have anything to apologize for."

I forced myself to calm down. Everything Gabe did, he did for me—a fact I was well aware of. No other man could handle me, or would've had the patience to wait to lure me out of my ivory laboratory, divest me of my virginity, and handle every other crazy thing that'd come our way since.

"I love you," I said.

"I know." He kissed my nose. "And I love you too."

"Even though you have…blue balls?" I laughed, trying to lighten the mood, although my face reddened at the topic.

Gabe looked at me, startled. "Lauren Taylor, where on earth did you hear such an expression?"

"High school AP chemistry," I admitted, and laughed again. "We were doing a section on cryogenics. The boys in my class passed me a note about it—they used to call me 'The Ice Queen.' They said I was the freezer of all balls. They wouldn't stop laughing."

Gabe grimaced. "Do you remember who they were? They might need a visit from your big, bad, vendetta-loving boyfriend."

"Oh, I already took care of them. I got an A-plus in that class, beat them all out for the last remaining spot in the National Honor Society, and I also compromised the integrity of their test tubes so they shattered during our next experiment." I smiled at the memory. "After I started Paragon, one of them had the nerve to try to add me to his LinkedIn. I blocked him, of course."

"Nice." Gabe sounded impressed.

"It seemed appropriate. The Ice Queen doesn't let shit like that go."

Gabe pulled me against him. "That's why she's the boss."

I clung to him. I never thought I'd meet a man who understood me, let alone embrace me for who I was. "Thank you for...loving me. Me, the giver of blue balls."

He patted my hand. "Me and my balls love you—a *lot.* We're good, babe. But we should try to get some rest while we can—are you okay?"

I relaxed against his chest. "I'm okay." And for that brief moment in his arms, I actually meant it.

***

After a quick nap, we left our suite for the lounge. The bartender put menus in front of us, and I struggled to concentrate on the words. I kept thinking about Hannah, about how time was moving—too fast and not fast enough. I wanted my sister back, but I didn't know what was going to happen...to me.

I clung to Gabe. *Four days. What if I have to say good-bye to him?*

I shuddered, and Gabe gave me a questioning look, his hand roaming dangerously up my thigh. "We should order, huh?" He threw the menu open one-handed and looked at it as he squeezed my leg again, making me ache for him.

Hannah and Gabe. Gabe and Hannah. The two people I loved the most—one I might get back, the other I might have to leave...

Sighing, I closed the menu without reading it.

"You need to eat."

"I'm not hungry."

The bartender came over, and Gabe ordered for me anyway: marinated artichokes, pan-seared scallops, and a martini.

"I can't really argue with that," I admitted.

"Good." He squeezed my thigh again.

I took a shaky sip of my martini. While we'd been resting upstairs, I'd had a thought. An idea...about how to fix our non-orgasming intercourse. If we only had four nights left together, I sure as hell wasn't going to waste this opportunity.

I needed to be with him, the way only we fit together. If I had to leave him, I wanted to have the memory of his hands on my body.

But I didn't know how to tell Gabe what I wanted. I didn't even know how to admit it to myself.

We finished our dinner and drinks in record time. It was as if there was a large clock near us, counting down the hours until the exchange. Neither of us mentioned it, but we both felt the urgency, the stress. Gabe practically threw me over his shoulder on the way upstairs. The distance between us from earlier seemed to have receded. A hot desire burned between my legs as I remembered our sex from a few nights ago—with the plug. *"Make you forget. Take your mind off things..."* Gabe's words echoed in my memory.

That was what I wanted. I wanted him to make me forget, the way only he could.

I was glad Timmy wasn't in the elevator with us, because it gave me the opportunity to press myself against Gabe. I stroked his erection through his jeans, desperate to salvage the evening.

"Jesus, babe—stop. I want to actually be inside you when I come."

A thrill went through me, and I rubbed his crown one last time before letting go. "I think I'm...feeling more like myself."

"You mean, you want to go look at cellular slides? Or did you have something else in mind?" He gave me a teasing grin.

"Something else." I licked my lips. "I want you to do all sorts of things to me right now." The words came out fast and hot, before I had the opportunity to censor myself.

Gabe arched an eyebrow, his eyes glittering. "What sorts of things? I'm very curious."

"I don't know..." I let my voice trail off as the elevator got to our floor, then grabbed his hand and hustled him to the room.

"You seem to have *some* sort of plan."

I'd been distracted and holding back before, but now, my need was urgent, consuming me. There was a sharp pang between my legs. I needed Gabe to fill me, to make me forget, but also to remember that I was here, right now.

With him.

I couldn't share my fears—that I might be taken from him this week. I didn't want to say it out loud, because Gabe would lock me up. I clung to him, on the edge of tears, emotion churning through me.

We locked the door behind us, and I kissed him deeply, our tongues lashing, my heart racing.

I wanted to feel something sharp, something jarring that would make me never forget this moment, and block out all the other troubling thoughts I was barely managing to keep at bay. Once we pulled apart, I looked into Gabe's eyes. "I want you to…spank me. Before you fuck me." My breath came out in a rush. "*While* you fuck me."

He took a step back. "You don't need to be punished, Lauren. This isn't your fault."

"I'm not asking to be punished. I just want to…feel something. Something bright—something *sharp*." Something that would make me feel an emotion other than loss, a loss I couldn't bear to face. "Like the other night…with the plug. You made me forget. I just want to feel something *big*, to block everything else out."

"Was earlier too…vanilla for you?" He looked wounded.

My shoulders slumped. "Of course not! No one's more vanilla than me!" I reached out and grabbed his hand. "But I want something…more intense. I just want to feel your hands on me. I want you to take over…be in charge of my body… make me feel alive, the way only you can."

The muscle in his jaw jumped. "I'm not going to hurt you, babe. I don't have that in me."

I shook my head and moved closer to him. "I'm not asking you to hurt me. I'm asking you to make me feel something bigger than the pain I'm feeling inside right now. I want you to make me forget. I want you to just make me feel. Just feel *you*." I reached for him, my heart hammering in my chest. "I want this—just for now. Will you do it?" I reached down and stroked his cock through his pants again. "For me?"

His eyes darkened. "You're not playing fair."

I squeezed the head of his erection. "I'm not playing."

Without another word, I went into the bedroom, stripping off my clothes as I went. Once I was naked, I got on all fours so my ass and my sex were open for him, waiting. I shivered in the cold room even as heat gathered in my body.

He followed me. "You know I would do anything for you." His voice was thick with emotion.

"Then do what I asked." I reached around and spread my ass cheeks apart so he could see me, see how I wanted him. "Please."

Gabe groaned—either because he wanted me too, or because I was torturing him, I couldn't tell which.

"I need you." I started to stroke myself, unable to bear the burning need.

"Take your hands off yourself. Let me do that, for Christ's sake." I heard him undo his belt buckle, then he kicked his pants off. "You know," he said, as he came to the bed and slowly, deliberately fingered the wetness between my legs, "for someone who was a virgin not that long ago, you're pretty bold."

I moaned as he stroked me, giving myself over to the sensation. "Maybe it's years of pent-up frustration finally coming out. Or maybe it's just you—*you* make me bold. You make me want all sorts of things I never even knew about."

His hand worked his way up to my clit, and he circled it slowly, making all the muscles in my body ripple in pleasure. "I think it's innate. It's definitely you, babe." He moved behind me, climbing up on the bed and testing me with his fingers. He grunted, satisfied I was ready, and then slid his cock all the way into me, suddenly and completely.

My body stretched to accommodate his, and I groaned in satisfaction.

"Is that okay?" His voice was soft, but there was a hard promise behind it, and *that* was what I wanted to get at.

"Yes. Give it to me. But don't forget—"

"It's not like I could forget."

He thrust into me, and I shut up, the feeling of fullness eclipsing everything else. He was in deep this way, behind me, and I loved it. My body contracted around his, and he grunted as he continued to pump into me. His cock was large and thick, and my body gripped it greedily, waves of pleasure coursing through me.

And then he stopped.

I looked over my shoulder, breathing hard. "You okay?"

He nodded. His eyes were laser-focused on mine. "Are you sure you want me to do this?"

I licked my lips. "Yes."

He pulled out and smacked my bum a little.

"I feel like you're swatting a fly," I complained, "and it's a fly you really like."

Gabe sighed. "I do really like it."

"Do it harder. Please. I want you…" I gathered the courage to tell him about the image in my mind. "I want you to do it hard, so it stings." I shut my eyes. "And then I want you to fuck me. Hard. And I want you to do it again and again."

He didn't say anything. I couldn't tell if that was a good sign or a bad one.

I opened one eye and peered at him. "Haven't you ever done this before?"

He scoffed. "No, babe, I haven't." He went quiet for a second. "Have *you*?"

My cheeks flamed. "Don't be ridiculous! Of course not!"

Neither one of us said anything for a moment, and I worried that the mood had been shattered.

"If this is what you really want, I'll do it," he finally said. "But if it hurts too much, you have to swear you'll tell me."

"I swear." I turned to look back at him. "But I don't want you to do it if it makes you uncomfortable."

He gave me a wry smile that made his dimple flash, simultaneously calming me and making me swoon. "I already told you, I would do anything for you." He ran his hand down my back, making me shiver. "If this is what you need right now, I can do it. And if it excites you, I'm sure it will excite me."

His hand reached my bottom, and he cupped it, looking at my body worshipfully. "Are you ready?"

I nodded, and suddenly, he slid up beside me, pulling me in for a kiss that made me woozy. His tongue searched for mine. I sighed in pleasure as he cupped my breast, and I felt his erection brush against me. Then he was behind me again, rubbing his cock against my wet slit.

Then he pulled back and smacked my ass.

I sucked in a deep breath. It stung a little, but not much. "Do it harder."

He rubbed my cheeks first, priming them, and then gave me another sharp crack. I shuddered in pleasure.

"Spread your legs open a little."

I did as I was told and cried out in surprised pleasure when he put his face between my legs, licking my sex until I wobbled beneath him.

Then he pulled back and slapped my exposed sex. Softly.

I let out a short puff of breath. *That* was what I wanted—what I hadn't known I'd wanted. "Do that harder. And then fuck me." I spread my legs open farther, and he first spanked my ass cheeks, harder this time, causing them to sting. Then he spanked my sex, making it burn—sharp and bright, just like I wanted.

Then he notched his cock into me and fucked me, hard.

I relished his brute strength as he gave me what I wanted, his strong hips bucking against me. He held my ass and pulled me against his erection, filling me almost painfully, and then he stopped again.

"More," I begged quietly. "I want more, and then I want you to come in me, *hard*."

He let out a strangled groan and then buried his face in my sex again. He took my clit in his teeth and nibbled at me, and I almost came all over him, but he stopped before I could. He got up on his knees and spanked me, so hard I yelped, and I fucking loved him for it. *That's it. Make me feel. Let me know that I'm alive, and that every part of me is yours.*

"Again," I said.

He struck me again and again, and my body quivered under his heavy, rigid hand. My skin burned, but I could feel my pussy clamoring for him. "Now—*now!*"

As soon as he entered me, I shattered around his huge cock.

I felt him go rigid as my body undulated around his. "Oh *fuck*, babe." He came in me hotly, hips pumping, filling me with his seed.

I only realized later, after we'd collapsed on the bed and I could think straight again, that he'd managed to do the impossible: make me forget about what was happening, at least for a little while.

"I love you," I murmured before falling asleep.

He grunted and then opened one eye to look at me. "That means I love you too. In grunting."

He wrapped me in his arms and pulled me against his chest, right where I belonged. And for the first time in weeks, and maybe for the last time for a long time to come, I fell into a dreamless, untroubled sleep.

CHAPTER 14

GABE

The next morning, I stretched luxuriously, my limbs loose and relaxed. And then I remembered: there were only three days left before we had to meet Li Na's henchmen. I rolled over and found Lauren curled into a ball on her side, in a deep sleep. My heart clenched, seeing her like that—peaceful, oblivious.

My phone buzzed with a text from Olivia. *Call me when you have a second*, it read. *We need to talk.*

I slipped out of bed and went into the suite's main living space, calling her immediately. "What's going on?"

She sighed. "I really don't want to get into specifics, but I don't feel right keeping this from you. I couldn't sleep. Some of the other distributors know now…and I wasn't the one who told them."

I steeled myself for the worst. "I'm listening."

"If I tell you this, I need something in exchange…something to protect myself and my company if this comes back to me. Can you do that?"

Of course, she wanted something. Olivia wasn't someone who played nice without some benefit to herself. "What are you looking for?"

"You can't make promises about the patch right now, but I know you're working on some new initiatives. I want to know that I'll get exclusive distribution rights for those in Great Britain."

"You're asking me for speculative distribution rights? On technology I haven't even created yet?"

"Yes. I know that Dynamica will still be working with Paragon in the future—or at least, with Lauren Taylor. That's all the guarantee I need to know it will be great."

Her Highness's magic had struck again. All Olivia wanted was the imprimatur of Lauren's brilliance—that was enough. "Done. Now tell me what you know."

"I can't give you a name. But I *will* tell you that my source was someone internal—someone at Paragon."

I felt my blood pressure spiking. "You're going to have to be a little more specific than that."

"Someone on the board. That's all I can tell you for now."

I gripped the phone so hard, it should've shattered. "That's a good enough place for me to start. Thank you, Olivia. Who else knows?"

She sighed. "The rep from Belgium called me, and Doug from Australia. They aren't happy with the news."

Just fucking perfect. In addition to the personal crisis we were experiencing, a global one was about to hit.

I gathered myself together. "I'll have my legal team draw up an exclusivity agreement for forthcoming intellectual property rights in the UK."

"I appreciate that."

I'm sure she did. People wanted any association with Lauren that they could brush up against. I hung up and paced the room, seething. Someone on her board had betrayed Lauren. Probably in an attempt to thwart the sale and hang on to the company, but still, it was an unauthorized attempt.

I was going to have to call a board meeting, and I might have to employ some questionable tactics. The list of people's asses I needed to kick was growing. Good thing I had plenty of pent-up rage—it'd probably come in handy.

"Gabe." Lauren shot out of the bedroom, looking agitated. "Who was that?"

"Do you remember what I told you about my UK distributor? That someone had leaked news of the sale?"

Lauren nodded, seeming distracted. "Yes, of course. What about it?"

"She just called me. It was...someone from your board."

She cursed and dropped into a nearby chair, her hands curling into fists. "This is literally the last thing I need right now."

I went over and rubbed her shoulders. "I can handle this, if you want. It's Dynamica's problem too."

She nodded shakily. "Okay...okay. I appreciate that. I can't take on a single other thing right now." Her gaze flicked to mine briefly. "Just keep me posted, okay?"

"Of course." The fact that she wasn't fighting me set off an alarm in my head. "What's going on?"

She put her face in her hands. "Li Na just texted me. She said she wants to do the exchange *today.* I need you to call your brothers."

"Okay," I said automatically—even though I felt like the floor was spinning beneath me and that nothing at all was okay, and never would be again.

In a haze of dread, I texted my brothers and drove well over the legal speed limit on the ride home. We were moving fast, but everything felt slow, as if I were having a nightmare I couldn't wake up from. Our brief break from reality was ending too soon. Lauren had been silent since we'd packed up, her lips pressed together in a grim line. I put my hand on her thigh, already apprehensive about the possibility of being separated from her. "Why is she doing this? Why is she changing the timeframe?"

Lauren fidgeted next to me. "I don't know—maybe she doesn't want me to have enough time to prepare, or to get backup prepared."

"What'd the text say?"

"She just gave me the address in Oakland again, and she reiterated that I have to come by myself." She stole a glance at me. "Do you understand that I need to follow her instructions?"

Anxiety rolled through me. "I understand that we need to get Hannah out of there, and that you need to be safe."

She put her hand over mine. "Are you going to be okay?"

I kept my eyes on the road. "Of course. Because nothing bad is going to happen."

"Everything is going to be okay because Hannah is coming home today," Lauren said, "and because I love you. You know that, right?"

I tore my eyes from the road just long enough to glare at her. "Don't do that."

"What?"

"Act like you might not come back. I will lock you up before I let that happen, babe."

"You have to stop threatening me—you need to be an adult about this. I will do everything in my power to make this go smoothly. But Hannah comes first." Her voice broke. "Do you understand?"

"I understand. Do *you* understand that I can't live without you?"

"I can't live without you either."

"Great. Then it's settled—you're not going."

"Yes, I *am*—"

My phone rang, interrupting us. Levi's voice boomed through the Bluetooth speaker. "Are you guys almost here? We have a lot to go through."

"Lauren's not cooperating," I said.

"Gabe's not listening to me, and you need to do something about it!" Lauren snapped.

"Let's get one thing clear," Levi said, sounding as if he were an exhausted parent about to ground the both of us. "I am running this operation today, and you both need to do what I say. And right now I say, *shut it*. This is a big day, and I understand that there's a lot of anxiety—but we're going to bring Hannah home and give you both some options for dealing with Zhao going forward. So stop fighting and get back here."

He hung up and I got off the exit, closing in on home. "I don't want to fight with you."

"So don't." Lauren's voice was hoarse.

Was it only hours ago that I'd held her in my arms, our bodies completely entwined, as close as I'd ever been to anyone? And now, the space between us felt impenetrable, as though she were in another country rather than sitting right next to me.

I put my hand over hers, trying to close the distance.

***

LAUREN

I got another text from Li Na as we pulled up to Gabe's house.

Please remember to bring your passport, clothing, computer, and passcodes, it read. *NO WEAPONS. No other electronics. If anyone else is at the site, this transaction will not occur.*

My nerves, already stretched thin, were fraying. "I got another text."

Gabe threw the car into Park and reached for my phone. He read it silently, the expression on his face tightly controlled. He handed the phone back to me and stared straight ahead.

"Gabe. Please, look at me."

He didn't move. "I can't do this."

"Just come inside. Let's go talk to Levi...everything's going to be okay."

He nodded, clearly not wanting to fight. He even held my hand as we walked inside, but it felt leaden and cold beneath my fingertips.

I didn't want to do this to him—to us. But my sister...

Levi and Ash were inside, as antsy as I'd ever seen them. "I didn't get any leads last night," Ash said immediately. "I didn't have time. So we're going into this cold, which is fine, but it isn't what I wanted."

"It's okay," I told him. "I appreciate that you tried. Li Na just texted me again." I gave him my phone.

Levi and Ash read the text from earlier and the most recent one, then glanced at each other. "It's Sunday, so the office park we're meeting at is closed today. Today might be a better day."

The look they exchanged told me it could also be a worse one, but I didn't say anything.

Levi put his hands on my shoulders, gently. "Your job today is to get Hannah into your car and get out of there. I'm going to have a dozen armed men watching—we'll have your back."

I nodded, pretending I wasn't scared shitless. "Okay. Got it."

Levi turned to Ash. "Call Agent Marks and let him know what's going on. Ask him to meet us there soon—I don't want to wait too long, in case there's some sort of surprise." He turned back to me and Gabe. "We're going to get packed up and head to the site. I want to go over the directives with you before I leave. Do you want to come with us, Gabe? I can't have you at the actual site, but you can stay nearby."

Gabe didn't blink. "I'm going with Lauren."

"You *can't*," Levi said. "You read the texts. We can't compromise Hannah's safety."

I reached out and covered Gabe's hand with mine. "Go with your brothers—which is more dangerous than I can even stand. If I had my way, I'd have you go into the office today."

"You're talking to *me* about danger?" Gabe pulled away. "There's no way in hell I'm letting you go by yourself!"

"We need to get going." Levi, clearly uncomfortable, stood to go. "Lauren, I'll call you from the site and we'll go through every detail. Gabe—you sure you don't want to come?"

Gabe didn't look at him. "I'll call you in a little bit."

I waited until Levi had escaped to start yelling. "Gabe, you can't do this."

"I *can't* let you get kidnapped is what I can't do!"

"That's not going to happen—I won't be by myself, and you know it. Levi and Ash will be there with a whole team. And the FBI." My stomach rolled when I thought about how far we were straying from Li Na's directives. "We're already compromising Hannah's safety. Please let this go."

"You think I can just let *you* go? And hope you live long enough to get dropped off at home afterward?" He leaned back against the counter and glowered at me. "You're not doing this to me again."

"You're right—I'm not!"

"We got lucky in Menlo Park—lucky that Timmy was strong enough to break that guard's neck!"

"Stop. Just…stop." Exasperation bubbled inside me, and I fought to calm down. I didn't have the strength to fight him at every turn. "I'm not doing anything, except exactly what *your* security team's telling me to do! I know you just want to protect me, and I love you for it. But love me enough to trust me. *Please.*"

"I've gotten burned by that before. Several times, babe." His voice had a dangerous edge.

He wasn't budging an inch, and it felt as though I were slamming my head into a brick wall by continuing to argue with him. "I understand your position," I finally said. That was as close as I could come to a compromise.

"Then accept it. I'm not staying here while you go meet with Li Na's armed guards. Not. Going. To. Happen."

I considered slamming into the Brick Wall of Gabe one last time, but I needed to conserve my energy for Hannah's sake. "Fine. You can follow me to Oakland—but only if that's okay with Levi, and only if you pull off way before we get to that office park. Wait for me there. And you have to bring guards." The last thing I wanted was Li Na's henchmen getting their hands on Gabe.

He scrubbed his hands against his stubble. "That's not good enough."

"It's going to have to be good enough! Your brothers and a whole SWAT team are going to be there, watching, waiting for something to go wrong. I'm already compromising Hannah's safety. You can't keep pushing me." I buried my face in my hands, shaking with anger. At Gabe. At myself. At Li Na. *Fucking Li Na.*

Maybe I *would* be able to live with myself if I ordered a hit on her.

Gabe came closer, pulling me to him. We were both angry, but we still clung to each other.

"I'll call Levi and talk to him about it. But you have to promise me, Lauren."

I buried my face in his chest. "Promise you what?"

"That you're going to be in that car when it comes back." He tilted my face up farther toward his. "Say it."

I took a shaky breath. "I promise." The last thing on earth I wanted was to lose Gabe. But my sister… If it came down to it, I would never leave her.

I looked at the man I loved. He was trusting me, again, to come back to him.

And I could see in his face it was against his better judgment.

"Call Levi. If he says yes to this, fine. Otherwise, go meet them now."

Gabe went to call his brother. The phone call was brief. "He said it was okay, but I have to stay at least a mile away."

"Did you agree?"

"I'm not happy about it, but yes."

I wasn't happy about it either—for a different reason—but I kept my mouth shut.

The rest of the morning passed in a slow blur. There were phone calls from Levi and Ash, maps to review, contraband weapons to pack. Fears to ignore. Finally, it was time to go. Timmy and the rest of our security team headed outside, assembling the vehicles and finalizing plans.

"Ms. Taylor." Timmy nodded at me. "Please be safe."

Touched, I patted his hand. "I will." I moved closer. "Please try to keep Gabe in line."

Good thing Timmy wore his wraparound sunglasses—he probably rolled his eyes.

I got into the driver's seat of my sedan—an odd sensation. I could drive competently, but I'd become accustomed to having someone else behind the wheel.

Gabe closed the door for me, then leaned down. "I'll be waiting for you. You be in that car. You come back to me."

I grabbed the back of his neck, pulling him close. "I'll always come back to you. You have the best wine. And the best—"

"Push-button fireplaces, I know." He smiled at me, and for a moment, the dark worry abated and his eyes sparkled with their normal warmth and humor. "Not to mention that you love me and can't live without me."

Our eyes locked. "I do love you."

He cocked an eyebrow at me, clearly trying to lighten the mood for a moment. "I know. You especially love me for my body."

"Gabe," I hissed, looking around, "*stop.*"

"Fine, but you know it's true. By the way, babe—I love you too. And not just for that hot little body of yours." He kissed me, briefly and intensely. It made me dizzy.

When he stood back up, all the humor drained from his face. He was strictly business, pale but still incredibly gorgeous beneath his scruff. "Stick to the plan, Lauren. Get Hannah to the car, and then let Levi take care of the rest. The only reason I've agreed to this is because I trust my brothers. They're the best. I trust them with your life."

I nodded. My palms were slick with sweat against the steering wheel. "I'll see you soon. With Hannah."

He looked miserable. "Come back to me."

"I will. I promise."

Gabe nodded and took a step back, his gaze never leaving mine. I finally turned away, hating to leave him, and put the car into Drive.

CHAPTER 15

LAUREN

Gabe, Timmy, and the rest of the security team followed close behind on the way to Oakland. There was only light traffic on the freeway. I could see Gabe's Spyder in my rearview mirror. If Gabe followed the plan and pulled off well before the meeting point, we wouldn't be in direct violation of Li Na's terms. Whether that would be good enough for her, I didn't know. But it was too late now—either way, I was about to find out.

My phone rang, making me jump in my seat. I hit the speaker button without taking my eyes off the road.

"Lauren. It's Levi." He sounded very clipped. "Our team's in place. Is Gabe behind you?"

"Yes. He's with a guard, and there are two other cars. There are five men total in his security detail."

"Does he have the address for where he's going to wait?" Levi asked. Levi had spent more than an hour on the phone with me earlier, coaching me and running over the final details. But Gabe hadn't spoken with him—probably so Levi couldn't try to talk him out of following me.

"Once we get to the airport exit, he's going to turn into one of the first office parks. He promised."

"He'd better do it." Levi grunted. "The area is clear so far. The FBI checked in. They set up at an alternate site. They haven't seen anything suspicious—there's no sign of Li Na's crew yet."

My mouth had gone dry. "Okay."

"I'm not going to let anything happen to you or your sister. You need to get her into the car, okay? Just like we talked about."

I swallowed hard. "I know. I will."

"Let's run through it one last time," Levi continued. "As soon as Hannah's inside the car, tell Li Na's security that you have the keys in your pocket, that you forgot to leave them for her. Show them the keys so they believe you. And then walk to the driver's side to approach your sister. If they try to get her back out of the car to get the keys, give them hell. Tell them you don't want her to be vulnerable. That's when we'll come out. As soon as you see us or if you hear gunfire, get in that car with Hannah and get the hell out of there. Don't even look back. We'll have a team waiting to follow you out. Get to Gabe, okay?"

I nodded, mostly to reassure myself. "Got it. Have you been to the actual office park yet? Is anyone there?"

"We're here. It's empty. The offices are closed today, so the parking lot's vacant. The FBI's around, like I said, but they set up their own surveillance spot. They haven't seen anything either."

I gripped the steering wheel, my palms sweaty. "Okay. I'll see you soon."

"If everything goes according to plan, you won't see me until we're back at your place, having a celebratory drink with your sister."

He hung up, and I checked the GPS. Twenty more minutes—almost there.

Fifteen minutes later, my phone rang again—it was Levi. "They're here. I'm not going to get in touch again, because I'm going to be on the ground. There're two cars. Two armed men, that I can see."

"And Hannah? Can you see her?"

"They haven't brought her out. Stick to the plan, Lauren. You won't see me, but I'll be out there—don't be afraid."

I followed the signs to Oakland International Airport. I checked my rearview mirror and could still plainly see Gabe's silver sports car, flanked by the rest of his team. By the next time I checked, they were gone. I took a deep, shaky breath as I maneuvered the car down the road to the airport, carefully reading the signs, looking for Langham Place.

Before I felt ready, the exit came into view. I pulled into the massive, mostly empty parking lot and headed for Building 900. Two cars were parked in the lot over to the side. Heart pounding, I headed for them. I checked my mirrors again. Gabe had kept his word. He wasn't following me. And as promised, Levi and his team were completely out of sight.

I didn't know whether to laugh or cry.

Two men stood outside the parked cars. Both were tall and thickly built. I squinted at the cars as I stopped and shifted mine into Park, desperate to get a glimpse of Hannah. The tinted car windows prevented me from seeing anything inside. *Dammit.* Was she even in there? Was this a trap?

I parked and jumped out of my car, far enough away from the men that I had to raise my voice. "Where's Hannah?" My voice was shaking, my whole body thrumming with the rush of adrenaline.

One of the guards, who had a reddish beard, jerked his thumb toward the cars. "In there, Ms. Taylor. You need to get in too."

I shook my head. "Not until she's out of there and safely in my car. That was the deal I made with your boss." Li Na hadn't specifically agreed to anything, but I refused to accept anything less. "Before I leave with you, she needs to be driving out of here. Alone."

The bearded guard nodded at the other one, who opened the car door. He pulled my sister out. I watched as she fought his touch, clearly trying to get his meaty hands off her.

"Hannah!" I yelled. "Stop!"

Our eyes met for a split second—but then she ignored me, trying to push the guard away. He grabbed her roughly. Then he took out his gun and shoved it against her rib cage.

That didn't slow Hannah down a bit. She struggled against him, an enraged look on her face. "Get off me!" she yelled.

I watched as the guard pulled her against him, ramming the gun into her side.

"Stop it!" I screamed. I didn't know if I was yelling at her or at him.

Hannah stopped fighting the guard, but she still gave him a filthy look. He pressed the gun firmly against her, not budging, looking as if he'd be thrilled for an excuse to pull the trigger.

"Let her go!" I shrieked. "Let her come to me. That was the deal."

"You have to come here first," the guard with the red beard called. "Step away from the vehicle."

"Don't you dare!" Hannah yelled at me. "Don't do it, Lauren!"

I shook my head at her, hoping to shut her up, and took several wobbly steps toward them. Hannah watched me, that same furious look on her face. Her blonde hair was matted, hanging over her shoulder, and her normally impeccable clothes were torn and dirty beyond recognition.

"Are you okay?" I asked.

"Not if you come any closer," she said fiercely.

"Let her go," I told the guard who was holding his gun to her. "Let her go, and Li Na can have what she wants. Me."

"Hold on," Big Red said. He came toward me and thoroughly patted me down. "She's clean." He nodded at his partner.

The guard shoved Hannah toward me.

She stood there, not moving, watching me warily.

I held out my hand. "It's okay, Hannah. Come to me. We're going to get you out of here."

She jutted her chin out defiantly. "No."

My eyes filled with tears as absolute panic descended on me. *I have to get her into the car.* "Please. It's okay. They're not going to hurt you."

She nodded. "I know they're not. But they're not going to hurt *you* either. They shot Wes already. I'm not having another person get hurt to protect me—especially not you. I'm not worth it." Her voice shook.

"Wesley is *alive*, he's doing better, but he needs you. *You.* Because you are important, and you mean everything to him. And to me." I took a step toward Hannah, noticing that the guard still had his weapon trained on her. "It's okay. It's going to be okay. Just come to me and get in the car. *Please.*"

Hannah didn't budge. I suddenly remembered a time when we were little, when she'd found a bird about to die in the woods. Even though it was getting dark and we were going to get in big trouble, she wouldn't leave it. I'd cried, and I'd begged her, but she wouldn't move. I remembered the wild panic I'd felt as I'd watched the sky darken. A child's terror, stark and overwhelming. I was older, but I felt the same way right now. I couldn't leave her. She was so stubborn—and if she didn't do what I said, we were both going to be lost.

"Hannah. Listen to me." Except I had nothing to say. I couldn't tell her Levi and his team were waiting nearby. I'd ruin everything. "Li Na wants me alive. She's not going to hurt me. I talked to her. We've figured it all out. We have a deal."

Hannah shook her head, tears coursing down her face. "It's a trap, Lauren. I meant what I said."

I clenched my fists. I could feel the guards watching us. "Just get in the car."

"I'm not going to let you sacrifice yourself for me. I told you, I'm tired of that Mother Teresa act." She smiled at me through her tears and took a step back, turning to the guard. "There's not going to be a trade. But would you consider letting us both go? We could pay you." She jerked her thumb at me. "My sister's a billionaire, and her boyfriend's a mega-billionaire. We could *totally* make it worth your while. We can triple whatever it is you're being paid—or more. Cash. And you can both walk away, no questions asked."

Hope kindled in my chest because Hannah *finally* sounded like herself, attempting to throw money at the problem.

The guards looked at each other. Big Red looked as if he were considering it, but the other guard grunted. "No deal—I don't trust them. We have strict instructions. You go, she stays. If that doesn't happen, we're bringing you back." He looked up at me. "Both of you."

Hannah ran at him. "No! You can't!"

He shoved her off and turned the gun on her.

"Hannah!" I screamed hoarsely.

She sank to her knees in front of the burly guard, her eyes never leaving his face.

"Just do it," she said. "Shoot me!"

"Hannah!" I screamed again. "*NO!*"

Hannah looked at the guard, her hands clasped together, begging him. "*Please.* I don't want to be a liability anymore."

"Get up," the guard growled at her. "Let's go."

"You too." Big Red pulled out his gun and pointed it at me. "Get in the car, ma'am."

"Don't do it, Lauren!" Hannah yelled, her voice shrill in the empty parking lot. "She's just going to use me against you. You were meant for great things. Don't let her take that from you!"

"Shut *up*," the guard said, disgusted. He grabbed Hannah by the shirt, dragged her to her feet, and shoved her back inside the car. He nodded at Big Red. "Get the other one. I'm done with the drama. Let's go."

Big Red kept his gun trained on me. He motioned to the other car, and I went, holding my breath the whole time, praying that Hannah kept her mouth shut and stayed alive.

There was a driver waiting inside the car. I hadn't even noticed him. *Where is Levi?* I wondered, climbing shakily into the backseat.

Big Red hopped into the passenger seat, and the driver sped off.

Another question pierced my heart. *Am I ever going to see Gabe again?*

But all thought soon ceased. We didn't even make it to the freeway. Everything happened at once. I heard something loud, something I couldn't place. Then the windshield shattered. The driver slumped over, and the car spun wildly in a circle, out of control.

Big Red reached for the wheel, but I felt us slam against something, and the car screeched to a stop.

"Lauren! Get down!" someone outside bellowed, and then Big Red started shooting. I covered my head and hit the floor in the back.

The gunfire went on for what felt like forever. I stayed down in the backseat, cringing. But Big Red suddenly stopped—a spray of gunfire came in through the windshield, and I heard him slump over. I stayed down and kept my hands over my head. It went quiet for a moment, except for my own ragged breathing.

He must be dead. He and the driver both must both be dead.

There was more yelling but no more shooting, so I cautiously sat up. I held my breath, looking wildly around the scene for Hannah. There was no sign of the car she'd been taken in—just a van.

Big Red and the driver were both slumped over in the front seat. I shut my eyes and turned from them, wincing.

The back door opened, and Levi pulled me gently but firmly from the car. "Get in the van. Now." He waved his team over as he looked at the bodies in the front seat.

Smoke rose from the hood of the car; we'd slammed into a concrete barrier. "Where's Hannah?"

Levi wouldn't look at me. "Ash went after her. They had a head start, though. I don't know if he'll be able to get to them."

"Where were you? They almost *shot* her," I spat.

He turned to me, his jaw taut, reminding me very much of Gabe. "I couldn't get a clean shot, and I didn't want your sister taking a bullet in the head. What the fuck did she pull back there, anyway?"

I wrapped my arms around myself. "She didn't want me to get hurt. She was trying to sacrifice herself."

Levi shook his head. The forced gentleness was gone, and he looked infinitely pissed. "When we finally get her home safe, she's going to hear it from me for that little act. She almost got herself killed."

"She was trying to be brave," I said, defending Hannah. If I ever saw her alive again, I planned to smack her. But that was *my* job.

It had been Levi's job to rescue her, and he'd failed.

He jerked his thumb at the van again. "Go. We'll clean up the scene. I want you out of here before the police and the FBI show up."

I didn't move. "Why? Aren't they going after her too?"

Levi's eyes flashed. "Don't ask any more questions. Just get in the van!"

A car squealed onto the scene then, and I saw Agent Marks in the passenger seat. He was yelling into his cell phone and gestured at the smoking car. His angry gaze settled on Levi.

Levi pointed to the van. "*Now*, Lauren—don't make me say it again!"

I hustled into the van, where I proceeded to interrogate the driver as he immediately threw the vehicle into Drive. "Have you heard from Ash? Does he have Hannah? Can we follow them?"

The driver sped out onto the freeway, shooting a quick look at the guard riding in the passenger seat. "Can you get her to stop asking questions? I gotta drive."

The other guard turned to me. "We don't know anything else, Ms. Taylor. We're under strict instructions to bring you home. No more questions, please. Let us do our job."

He didn't look my way again. Dismissed, I turned from them and scanned the freeway. There was light traffic, no signs of anything amiss, no sirens.

We were abruptly back in the real world. And I had no idea where Hannah was, again.

The guard in the passenger seat must have gotten a text, because he looked at his phone and cursed. "Pull over," he told the driver.

"What? We're under direct orders to get back to the Betts property ASAP."

The guard held up his phone. "Gabriel Betts just texted me. He said to pull over or he's going to run us off the road."

The driver swore under his breath as he maneuvered the van to the side of the highway. A moment later, Gabe's Spyder skidded to a stop in front of us. Gabe jumped out and stalked around the van. He threw open the door and grabbed my wrist. "Let's go." He turned to the guards. "We'll see you back at my place. Stay close. I think I lost my security team back there because I was speeding so goddamned fast to catch up with you."

Gabe marshaled me to the car, opening the winglike door and practically stuffing me inside. He didn't say a word until we were back on the freeway, flooring it toward home. From his demeanor, I felt certain that Levi had already caught him up on the details of the botched exchange.

His knuckles were white as he changed lanes, flying above the speed limit. "What the fuck was that back there, Lauren?"

"Hannah wouldn't come to me. She didn't want to...trade herself for me." My voice was hoarse.

The Spyder was going well over a hundred. Gabe passed three cars in a row, weaving in and out of the lanes so quickly that I felt dizzy. "So you volunteered to go too?"

I closed my eyes. "If you're so interested in keeping me safe, do you think you could slow down a little?"

I felt the car slow, coming closer to the speed limit. I opened my eyes and stole a glimpse at him, but he looked the same—pale, jaw taut, hands clutching the steering wheel.

"Hannah wouldn't exchange herself for me. Then she offered the guards money to let us both go, but they refused." I paused for a beat, trying to calm down so I could tell him the rest without bursting into tears. "*Then* she asked the guard to shoot her. She said she didn't want to be...a liability anymore."

"Hannah has a flair for the dramatic," Gabe said tightly.

"She's so stubborn. It almost got her killed back there. I don't know what they're going to do to her now." My eyes filled with tears, but I willed them away. I had to stay strong, and I had to get her back before she did something else crazy. "Levi said he couldn't get a clean shot at the guards without harming her, so that's why he let them drive out of there. He killed the men who had me, but Hannah's car got away. Ash is chasing them."

"I know. Ash'll find her." Gabe sounded certain. "I told Levi that you were the number-one priority. He wasn't allowed to leave you alone."

I bristled. "My *sister* is the number-one priority. You don't have the right—"

"Yes, I absofuckinglutely do." Gabe cut me off. "You're *my* number-one priority, and Levi works for me. I love Hannah too, but I only let you go today because you promised me you'd follow Levi's instructions."

"It wasn't my *fault*—"

"I don't want to hear it, Lauren." His tone was final, unyielding. "You're not going to be put in a situation like that again. Levi fucked up because he let you get in that car in the first place. He's going to have hell to pay when I get my hands on him."

Panic tightened my chest, and not because of what Gabe had planned for Levi. "He didn't want to shoot Hannah in the goddamned *head*. Please stop! I have no idea what Li Na's going to do to her now that this got so messed up."

He surprised me by immediately putting his hand over mine. "She's not going to hurt her. That's her play. Hannah's the only thing you'd be willing to bargain for. She's worth nothing to Li Na if she's dead."

I squeezed his hand, relishing his touch even though we were both angry. "I know—the problem is, Hannah knows it too."

"She won't do anything to herself." The furious tone drained from his voice. "She loves you too much."

"That's what I'm worried about."

I appreciated that Gabe had set aside his anger, but his words couldn't soothe me. I'd been so close to Hannah just now—close enough to touch her—and she'd slipped through my fingers. I vowed if I ever got her back, I would never let her go.

But in order for that to happen, we had to find her again.

CHAPTER 16

GABE

"What do you mean, you *lost* them?" Lauren yelled at Ash. She paced back and forth across the kitchen. "How did that *happen*?"

Ash winced. "I lost them on the highway. They might've gotten off and gone to a residential neighborhood close to the airport. We searched around there, but I didn't find anything. They could have switched cars—or maybe they pulled into a garage. I have a team out there, tracing the area. But we haven't found any signs of the vehicle yet."

"We'll check it out further with the surveillance team. They've definitely dumped the car, though—we'll have to start fresh," Levi said. "We can also start pulling recent real estate transactions in that part of the city. Maybe we'll find something. The police and the FBI are looking too, for what it's worth."

Ash nodded and opened his laptop, hiding behind it.

Lauren turned her hell-bent spotlight on me. "You *said* he would find her."

I scrubbed a hand across my face. "He will."

"What do you think they're going to do to her in the meantime, huh?"

Lauren's phone buzzed against the island, and we all jumped. She grabbed for it. "It's Li Na."

She shoved the phone at me after she'd read the text, her hands shaking.

Li Na: *Your sister is almost as much of a pain in the ass as you are.*

I handed Levi the phone, and he quickly read the text.

"Bring it back to Paragon," Levi instructed Lauren. "We need to keep her focused on the outcome."

Lauren nodded almost imperceptibly and started typing as we read over her shoulder. *Is Hannah okay?*

Li Na: *For the moment.*

Lauren: *I'm sorry things didn't work out as planned today. I've started arranging the supporting financial and patent documents necessary for the sale. I still want to proceed.*

Li Na fired back a text of several emoji who were laughing so hard they were crying, and then wrote, *You're kidding, right?*

Lauren: *No. What happened today was unfortunate.*

Li Na: *Your security team wasn't supposed to be there. They killed my men. That wasn't unfortunate—it was an act of hubris. You don't care about your sister? Maybe you're not as boring as I thought!*

Lauren: *Hannah's the most important thing in the world to me. But she was trying to protect me, and so were my people. I'm sorry—it was out of my control.*

Li Na: *I thought you were the one in charge.*

Lauren: *Sometimes the people around me like to think it's them.*

I stiffened and shot Lauren a look, but she ignored me.

Li Na: *I'm going to let her think about what she's done. And you too. Prepare an agenda for the closing and send it to my counsel. Do it by tomorrow, and your sister lives for another day. But not if she pulls anything else.*

Lauren: *You're never getting Paragon if you hurt her.*

Li Na: *It's amusing that you choose *now* to act like you're calling the shots. You should've done that earlier—we wouldn't be having this conversation and your sister would be safe.*

Lauren typed a furious response. Anxiety rolled off her in waves.

Lauren: *I was trying to save her. That's all I want.*

Li Na: *Next time you cross me, it's the last time. You've been warned.*

Lauren stared at the phone miserably, waiting, but there was nothing further.

"I'm going to call Bethany," she said when it was clear that Li Na had ended her rant. "We need to get started on the rest of those documents."

I squeezed her shoulder. "I think you should."

"I'll be back." She grabbed her phone, going outside to talk to her attorney in private.

I texted my assistant, Ryan, to coordinate with Lauren's assistant, Stephanie. We needed to set up a meeting with Lauren's board for tomorrow—if Li Na got wind that Paragon's overseas partners were getting cold feet, our trouble would only grow. There wasn't a lot I could do to help Lauren right now, so taking any sort of action to protect her would feel good.

I turned to Levi. He was staring out the window at Lauren. "I'm seriously pissed at you."

"I fucked up today," he admitted. "But it's not really any of your business."

"That's bullshit and you know it. Lauren could have *died* back there. Because not only did you fail to get her away from those guards, you shot up the goddamned car she was in!"

Levi's eyes glittered dangerously. "You know, for a silent partner, you really never seem to shut the fuck up."

I took a step toward him, itching for a fight. "Maybe that's because you're so fucking *dumb*, you couldn't understand me the first time—I have to keep repeating myself!"

"You should stick to what you know: your special hybrid Porsche, your infinity pool, and your ergonomically correct standing desk." He laughed, taunting me. "Christ, you can't even keep Lauren in line!"

I grabbed his shirt and pushed him against the wall. "Shut your mouth."

"There he is." Levi grinned at me, perfectly at ease underneath my death grip. "That's the Gabe I know and love. The one I remember, who liked to rip people apart for sport. Dad never saw it, but I did."

I shoved him one last time and then stepped back. "Then you should have let me stay in Boston. I could have been an asset to your team."

Levi looked at me smugly. "You seem happy playing the pretty-boy CEO. Maybe Dad was right—maybe you *are* too good for the rest of us."

"Fuck you." I gave him one last murderous look as I stormed out of the kitchen and headed into the backyard, toward the pool. I had to get away from him before I gave in to my instincts and broke his nose…again.

Apparently, Levi hadn't learned his lesson.

Maybe I hadn't either.

I took several deep breaths, trying to calm myself. This had been one of the shittiest days on record, and no one pushed my buttons like Levi. I would love to fight him right now—hell, I'd love to fight *anyone* right now—but it wouldn't help. I had to keep it together, to keep Lauren safe and get Hannah back.

I looked up and saw Lauren stalking toward me past the helipad, her expression sour.

"Did you talk to Bethany?"

"Yes—she's going to dive in and keep drafting tonight. What's the matter with *you*?"

"Levi's driving me to drink."

"Oh."

She went quiet for a minute, probably thinking I shouldn't complain—that I was lucky my brother was here, unlike Hannah.

I sighed. "It's just some longstanding family stuff. Plus the fact that he almost got you killed today."

"Gabe, it wasn't his fault." She sounded weary. "And as for the family stuff—I'm listening."

"It's nothing you need to worry about—especially after the day you've had."

"I'd like to know what's going on."

I headed over to the hot tub and sat down, sticking my feet in. "Just stuff that should be water under the bridge, but isn't."

Lauren followed me, looking lost. She must be. For the majority of her twenty-five years, all she'd done was work and spend time with her sister. Both of those things had been taken from her—roughly, wrongly—and she seemed completely off-kilter.

"Tell me more," she said. "Just talk—please. After what happened with Hannah…I literally can't stand to think anymore. I might go crazy."

I could still feel the raw adrenaline coursing through me from earlier in the day, and now, from the encounter with Levi. I needed to calm down. She needed me, and I was no use to her like this. "Fine. But I'm still pissed."

She sighed. "I know."

"We'll get your sister back, but not at the expense of losing you. Do you understand that, once and for all?"

She sat down next to me, taking off her shoes and tentatively sticking her feet into the tub. "I didn't have a choice about the way things happened today. I wasn't trying to be a hero. I just wanted to get Hannah in the car and get her out of there. And then everything fell apart. Okay?" She slumped, exhausted, and I could tell she was near tears again.

"Come here." I pulled her against me, my anger ebbing away. I wasn't going to forget what had happened, but she was here and she was safe.

And I wasn't letting her out of my sight again.

"Please talk. Please tell me about your family," she whispered. "If I think about Li Na anymore, or Hannah, I'll end up in a psych ward."

I kissed the top of her head. "Okay, okay. So the thing with Levi, our baggage… Ugh." I scrubbed my hands across my face. "Ugh" was the only accurate word I possessed for talking about family stuff. "Levi and I have issues about his business. I don't know if I've told you this, but I own part of his firm, and he and Ash own part of Dynamica. We did a cross-purchase thing a few years ago to fund their start-up."

"So—you're fighting about money?"

"Not at all. I wish it was that simple." I laughed, but it came out flat. "It's a long story."

"Even better. Please, go on."

I sighed. "My father was in security too. It's a Betts-family thing. Everyone's in the business except for me."

"Did your dad run his own firm?"

"Yes, and I always wanted to be like him when I grew up. I knew he protected people, and I wanted to do that, especially when I was little."

She leaned her head against my chest, relaxing a fraction. "I bet you were cute." It was the most normal she'd sounded in a long time.

"Of course I was cute. And I was a bright kid—exceptional, my teachers said. They tested me, and I was off the charts for everything. My dad clung to that. He'd been blue collar all his life, never went to college. He told me before he died that he wanted me to go to Harvard—that was his big dream for me. He insisted that I pursue some sort of business career, preferably one that included a nice, safe, ornately carved desk."

"Your dad sounds like he was nice."

"He was a great guy." I smiled, thinking about my dad.

Lauren slid her arm around my waist and waited for me to continue.

"You know my father died when I was ten. That fueled my fire—I wanted to follow in his footsteps. My mom humored me when I was younger, but when I was in high school, my whole family ganged up on me. They insisted on Harvard, which I unfortunately had the grades for. Levi started Betts Security a few years later, after I'd already come out here and started Dynamica. He took my money in exchange for a minority stake in his firm, but that was all he would accept from me."

"Because he was honoring your father's wishes?" she asked.

I shrugged. "Because he was protecting me, I guess. He probably thought I'd go after the people who killed my dad if I went back to Boston and got into the business."

Lauren pulled back, her eyes searching my face. "I didn't know your father was *killed*."

I looked down at the water. "That's because I didn't tell you. It's not something I talk about."

"Who…who did it?"

"We don't know." I shrugged again, trying to appear calm even as I felt my throat tighten. It had been over twenty years, but I missed my dad every day. His death still had me reeling. "He was shot on assignment, investigating organized crime."

Lauren hugged me hard. "I'm so sorry. Why didn't you tell me?"

I splashed my feet in the water. "I didn't say anything because I…couldn't. I don't like to talk about it."

"Gabe." She rubbed my back. "I want to know about your family. It's important to me."

I stiffened. "What was I supposed to say? That my father did dangerous work so that he could support his family in a nice lifestyle? So that my brothers and I could go to camps, play travel hockey, and go on ski trips? That he died doing a job that paid for my Ivy League education, but that I dropped out because I was so angry all the time?" My voice came out sharper than I wanted.

Lauren held me close, undeterred. "I thought you dropped out because you wanted to come out here and start your company."

"That's true. I did. But it wasn't the only reason."

Neither of us said anything for a moment. Levi's words rang in my ears. "*…happy playing the pretty-boy CEO…too good for the rest of us…*"

"I moved out here to start something of my own. I wasn't chasing this." I motioned toward my massive house.

"Gabe. No one thinks that," Lauren said. "What you have, the things you own, are just a by-product of your hard work. Your work helps people. And your father knew you were special—that you were capable of great things. He wanted you to have every opportunity, and he probably wanted to protect you. Your whole family wanted that for you."

"I want to believe that. All of that." I just wasn't sure if I did.

I should be the person Lauren thought—she deserved that and more—but I had my doubts. "Sometimes I think my father was wrong about me, and that Clive Warren was right. I *am* a thug, hiding behind the CEO package. Yes, I went into biotech because I thought I could help people. But I've done some things… things you wouldn't approve of."

"Like what?" She pressed her head against my chest. "You can tell me."

I blew out a deep, resigned breath. "I've done some things with my business dealings that you don't know about. Things I haven't shared."

I felt Lauren tense ever so slightly. "Like what?"

Fuck. It's now or never. I'd been dreading this moment. "Like when people have hacked me in the past, I've had them beaten. When people have stolen from me, I've threatened them."

"Can you explain the term 'threaten' in this context? Do you mean *threaten* threaten?"

"Yes, I mean *threaten* threaten. As in, you steal the underlying technology from my patent application, I have my guys break your face." I grimaced.

Her eyes widened. "You've done that?"

"I've *had* to do that, in order to keep people from ripping me off. You know what it's like—it's *rough* out here. There's a lot of growth and opportunity, but with that come the lowlifes, the copycats, and the hackers. People who want to shortcut their way to a payout—although I haven't run into anyone quite as flagrantly criminal as Li Na before."

"She's special, all right."

"You know firsthand that there's a lot at stake—and in *this* game, your proprietary technology is all you've got. I haven't held back when I've protected what's mine. I'm sorry if that's a shock."

She was quiet for a minute, looking up at the sky.

I put my hand on her thigh and squeezed. "I guess I should have told you all this. Before I moved you in here and asked you to make me all sorts of promises."

"You don't owe me an apology. I know who you are. And it doesn't change how I feel, not at all." She shook her head, some of her former spark lighting up her blue eyes. "Underneath the jeans and T-shirt—and that hybrid car—you might very well be a thug. But you're *my* thug."

She pulled me in for a brief, tender kiss. "I love you for who you are, and for the things you've done. Even the bad things. Because they're a part of you, and I love *all* of you."

"I love you too." I rested my forehead against hers, relief washing through me. Now that we'd had this conversation, I didn't have to hide the truth from her. I no longer had to wonder how she'd feel if she found out.

"When we get Hannah back, when this is all over…" she started.

"What?"

"I just want us to be safe. I want your inner thug to take a sabbatical—or maybe a permanent vacation. I don't want to have to go after hackers, or kidnappers, or deal with any corporate espionage."

"In our industry, the hackers and the espionage are part of the package. The kidnapping is a new low, though. Hopefully it's a one-off."

She buried her face in my chest. "I don't know if I have a future in high-tech. I don't know if I'm cut out for it."

"Of course you are. And we need to keep the good guys on the playing field. You can't quit."

She sighed and stood up, drying her feet carefully. "Speaking of not quitting…I need to get back to work. Poor Bethany can't be the only one pulling another all-nighter."

"Have her come here for the next few days, okay? I'm worried about security more than ever."

"Okay." She leaned over and kissed me. "Thank you for everything."

"Thank you for not running away from me, even though I've given you plenty of reasons."

"You'd catch me anyway."

I smiled at her, trying to lighten the heavy mood. "I might enjoy that. Maybe when things get back to normal and we get everybody out of the house, that's a fun game we can try."

"Remind me—and I'll get you a leopard hide to wear and a club to wield." She managed a smile. "For the record, I'd put money on you in a fight with Levi."

"Babe, I appreciate that. A lot."

"I know. That's why I said it." Sadness radiated off her, visible from the slump in her shoulders and the shell-shocked look in her eyes. Still, she was trying to comfort me.

She doesn't deserve this pain. She deserves so much better...

"I love you," I called as she headed toward the house.

"Well, I love you too, little brother," Levi said, sauntering out of the house.

I groaned. "We really need to get Hannah back so you can move the fuck back to Boston."

I could see the outline of his grin in the semidarkness. "Please, tell me how you really feel."

I accepted the bourbon he offered me: Levi's version of an olive branch.

I made sure Lauren was out of earshot before I spoke. "This is how I really feel—we didn't get Hannah back today, and Lauren almost got shot. And now Li Na knows that we've been working against her this whole time with the help of the FBI. We're worse off than we were this morning, which is pretty bad. And you're being an asshole," I reminded him.

I'd been trying to distract Lauren, but I still felt sick about the events of the day and where we stood. What if they killed Hannah? What if Li Na decided that this was all too much trouble, she was cutting it too close, and it was finally time to walk away?

Levi sat down and stuck his feet in the water, which I noticed he did at every opportunity. This was most likely a by-product of living in crappy weather in Boston for most of his life. "I understand. And I'm sorry I got angry with you earlier."

"Sorry I threw you against the wall. And called you dumb."

"No, you're not."

I shrugged. "Remorse isn't really my strong suit."

"Today was terrible," Levi admitted. "And you're right, Hannah's in greater danger now than she already was. It's on my conscience. You aren't responsible—it's on me."

"But I *do* feel responsible. Hannah's like my sister, and I need to make this better for Lauren. This is tearing her apart. Sitting by, not being able to do anything—that's tearing *me* apart."

"I get it." Levi looked out at the pool. "It's interesting to finally see you with someone, you know. An equal… I never thought it would happen, honestly."

"*You*, the eternal bachelor, are saying this to me?" Levi had been engaged once, but we never brought it up. Not unless we wanted to land in the emergency room.

My brother visibly stiffened. "Let's get back to what's important. We have an opportunity now to search locally for Hannah. Li Na's most likely keeping her nearby, unless she's decided to bail on the plan."

"What do you think? It's getting riskier for her to keep this up."

"She doesn't seem too worried." Levi shrugged. "I think she's been coming at Lauren hard for so long, she's not going to give up—not when she's so close to getting what she wants. We need to make searching the area our number-one priority. Ash has a team, but I'm going to bring our whole staff out here. It's going to be a manhunt."

The fact that he was throwing every asset available at the task made me feel better—his firm was one of the best in the country for a reason. Due to circumstances beyond his control we'd fucked up today, but I still had every confidence in him. "Can I help?"

"About that. I've been thinking," Levi said, but he didn't say anything for a minute. "I know you want to help. But we all have our special gifts, okay? You isolated the stolen plate number using an equation—that's something I couldn't have done. In fact, I'm going to hire a new tech guy who can do shit like that all the time, because it really came in handy..."

"Were you about to make a point?"

"Yes. About your ability to contribute. You can help, but you should stay out of the line of fire and behind a computer, where you belong—and please don't punch me for saying that. I mean it as a compliment."

"Right." All the fight had drained out of me, though, so I waited to hear what he had to say.

"I've done some research, but I'm wondering, what do you actually know about Zhao?"

I shrugged. "Probably not a lot more than you. She's in her early forties, she graduated at the top of her high school, undergraduate, and graduate classes, she's divorced with no kids, and she started Jiàn Innovations a few years ago. They've been successful in the Chinese market, but she's made it clear that she wants a bigger piece of the global economy. Other than that, I know she considers herself above the law in China. She's said repeatedly that she is helping to rebuild Shenzhen, and that her government has no interest in having her extradited."

"And those seem to be the only details available," Levi agreed. "But I'd like to know more. I'd like to know about her background, her ex-husband, and how her company got to where it is today."

"So you want me to do your research, like some unpaid intern?"

Levi shrugged. "I want you do some more digging, and then use your superior intellect to help piece together more about her character. She must have some sort of weakness—but we've been letting her run us in circles, and we haven't been able to find it. You and Lauren have been so busy playing defense, you haven't had the opportunity to consider an offense."

"Like what?"

"You'll think of something." Levi patted me on the shoulder. "Dad always said you were the smart one. Let's see if he was right."

CHAPTER 17

LAUREN

Bethany met me at the house that morning. There were dark circles blooming like bruises beneath her eyes. "You look how I feel," I told her.

Bethany gave me a tired smile. "You look worse than I feel."

"I'm not surprised."

"Have you heard anything?"

"Nothing after Li Na texted me and basically told me that she'd kill Hannah if I messed up again."

"I'm so sorry." Bethany squeezed my shoulder.

I nodded. "Let's get to work so I don't go crazy thinking about it."

"I didn't get as far as I wanted last night, so we really need to buckle down. Can we set up in Gabe's office?"

"Of course." I motioned for her to follow me down the hall. "He wants us to stay here for security purposes, anyway. It's fine for today, but I need to get to Paragon later this week and hold an employee meeting."

"Does everyone know what's happening?"

"Everyone knows I'm working on some sort of deal with Li Na. And the board knows what the details are, of course." I grimaced, remembering what Gabe had told me. "Which reminds me—someone on the board leaked the news to our international distributors, trying to throw the sale. With everything else going on, I forgot to mention it."

"Someone on the *board*?" Bethany looked shocked. "Who?"

"I don't know yet."

"What're you going to do?"

"Gabe offered to handle the issue, to get to the bottom of it. With everything else going on, I accepted."

Bethany set her laptop down and started pulling documents from her bag. "Wow. This is big for you. You don't delegate easily—I should know."

I nodded. "It actually feels good. Instead of feeling weakened or threatened, I feel…stronger. Because I know he has my back."

Bethany grinned. "I never thought I'd see the day."

"Stop." Blushing, I opened my own laptop and clicked on one of Paragon's financial statements, which I needed to review. "Back to business—about the staff. I haven't made a company-wide announcement yet, but Gabe's offered all my employees positions with Dynamica."

Bethany's eyes sparkled. "He's good, huh? He's even starting to grow on *me*."

"He's very good. But please don't start up about the prenup again," I said. "We aren't there yet."

"You will be. And when you are, I'll be ready with my laptop."

I groaned and set my attention to the numbers in front of me. Whatever else was going on, I could always count on Bethany to be a pain in my ass.

I was grateful for the piles of work—it took my mind off yesterday. I hadn't slept, worrying what might've happened to Hannah. The guard who'd been watching her had been rough, and she'd clearly aggravated him. I didn't want to think about what he could've done to her when they got back to wherever they were going…

I checked my watch. The house had been quiet all morning. "I'm going to go check in with Gabe, okay?"

He wasn't in the kitchen. I found a note from him on the counter:

Babe.

Meeting with your board and catching up at work. Levi and Ash are doing surveillance. If they find anything, they'll call us right away. I'll be home tonight. Love you.

I decided not to call him. I'd accepted his offer to help with the board. I didn't need to micromanage him. And with all the drama, he must be falling behind at Dynamica. I should let him work.

I let hope well up in my chest that maybe, by the time everyone got back tonight, there would be some good news.

But as I headed back to review accounts payable and receivable aging reports, an image of Hannah flashed in my mind: my beautiful sister in a filthy shirt, kneeling before Li Na's henchman, saying she didn't want to be a liability anymore.

And the hope died a quick, although not painless, death.

***

GABE

Ryan had taken the step of contacting each of Lauren's board members directly, calling an emergency meeting regarding Dynamica. They didn't know the specifics, and they didn't know Lauren wouldn't be present at the meeting.

No Lauren meant no nice cop. They were going to have to adjust accordingly.

It felt awkward going through the doors of Paragon, signing the visitor log, and hustling past the curious employees to the boardroom. I'd been at Paragon without Lauren before, of course. When she'd gone to Menlo Park to work remotely for Li Na, I'd been smuggled into the building to help secretly launch the patch. This time felt different because the items on my agenda included tracking down an internal traitor and opening a can of whoop-ass on them.

"Gabe," Allen Trade said, looking surprised. "It's just you? No Lauren?"

I nodded at the board members as they assembled. "She asked me to handle this matter for her."

They looked at each other, concerned, but no one said a word. Things had been so crazy at Paragon for the past year, they probably didn't know what to expect next.

"Do you have an update on Hannah?" asked Mimi White, another longtime board member.

"Unfortunately, I don't have good news. We tried to get her back yesterday, but things didn't go the way we'd hoped. We're working on it." I wanted to reassure them. Between what had happened to the security guards and Hannah, everyone was already on edge.

"Is Li Na still expecting Lauren to hand over the company? Even though she's criminally liable for kidnapping?" Mimi sounded outraged.

"Li Na has not backed down *at all.* That's part of the reason why I'm here. It's crucial that we follow her instructions from here on out. Our failed attempt to get Hannah back has put us in a worse position—we've lost what little trust we had."

A worried murmur broke out in the group.

"The fact is, I'm worried that she'll do something terrible if there's another misstep. That's why I'm here, actually."

Mimi arched her eyebrow. "Please explain."

"I had a conversation with one of my overseas partners. They claimed someone on this board has been attempting to upset the sale to Jiàn Innovations by preemptively leaking news of the takeover."

Everyone started talking at once.

"Are you accusing *us* of corporate sabotage?" Allen Trade asked, his voice rising above the din.

"I *am* accusing someone on this board of trying to throw the sale. And I need to know who it was, and I need them to stop—before this has dire consequences for Lauren and her family."

I stood up. "We need to handle this *today.* I'd like to speak to each one of you privately in Lauren's office. Come down in whatever order you like, when you're ready."

I doubted that any one of them would confess to me early this sunny morning, but I hoped to at least glean more information from this process. I'd reviewed the contracts between Paragon, Dynamica, and our international distribution partners. I'd also asked Kami to do the same. She'd called me this morning to confirm what I'd suspected: our third-party distributors couldn't unilaterally withdraw from the contracts if Paragon was sold. They could, however, refuse to renew their contracts after a year-long trial period with the new partner.

I paced back and forth in Lauren's office, waiting for someone to come down. The person who leaked the information had most likely known this as well. They were attempting to start rumblings within the network. If our United Kingdom, Australian, and Belgian distributors decided that a partnership with the Chinese was undesirable, they could scare the other distributors, creating mass panic. Collectively, they could agree to boycott Jiàn Innovations in the future, ultimately sabotaging the sale and forcing our hand. If Li Na became aware of this situation before the closing, Paragon would seem a less lucrative venture, one which she might choose to let go.

Which would be fine, if she wasn't holding Hannah hostage.

Whoever had leaked the information had breached the board's confidentiality and violated their relationship with Lauren, with potentially devastating implications. It was a reckless move, one they were going to have to pay for.

Stephanie buzzed in a minute later. "Allen Trade is ready for you."

Allen, a former NASA advisor, looked seriously pissed beneath his immaculate white hair. "That was quite a spectacle you just put on, in a long line of recent spectacles."

"I didn't do it for the entertainment value."

"You have a lot of nerve riling us all up like this at such a crucial time. People are *upset*, Gabe. We all love Hannah, and we love Lauren too. No one wants to see their family hurting like this. And the fact that we're about to lose the company? It's terrible. Disgusting. But you have no right to come in here and treat us like a bunch of criminals."

"Are you finished?"

After a moment, Allen nodded. "Yes."

"Then sit down. Please." I started pacing again, channeling Lauren. "One of my partners called to tell me they knew a Chinese buyer was about to take over Paragon. They already wanted out of their contract, and several other distributors have followed suit. When I pressed her, she told me that a board member was the source of the information. How do you think that made me feel?"

Allen looked beside himself. "Who cares about you? How did *Lauren* feel? On top of everything else, she has to worry about…"

"Lauren is upset, but Lauren has bigger things to deal with. *Lauren* had to watch her sister get dragged away at gunpoint yesterday, so I figured I'd spare her this debacle." I ran my hands through my hair, feeling a headache coming on. "Jesus. The last thing she needs right now is to have someone she trusts working against her. She's dealing with too much already."

"If it's any comfort, it wasn't me. But I will get to the bottom of this, I swear. We don't want to lose the patch, but nothing is more important than family."

"Why should I trust you?"

Allen shrugged. "You don't have to trust me. You just have to let me find out who did this. You can trust me afterwards."

My phone buzzed, and I quickly read the text that came in—a text that made my heart drop. *No no no.*

"What's the matter?"

"It's my friend the neurosurgeon—about Wesley, the security guard who was shot. He's not doing well." I looked up at Allen. "Can we get back to this later?"

"Of course. I'll get you some answers. Please tell Lauren that we're all rooting for her. And poor Wesley too. Jesus," he muttered as he left the room. "That Zhao woman has a lot to answer for."

CHAPTER 18

LAUREN

As soon as Gabe called, Timmy and I rushed to the hospital. "Did Mr. Betts tell you what was going on?" he asked, his voice tight.

"Just that the doctor texted him and told him to come in right away. He said Wes had taken a turn for the worse, but he didn't get specific. At least, Gabe didn't tell me anything else." I stared out the window of the car, not seeing anything as we flew down the freeway. Wesley couldn't die. If that happened, I didn't know how I'd bear it...

Gabe was waiting for us in the lobby, his face pale and strained. "I just talked to Dr. Kim," he said. "He said that Wesley's heartbeat had become erratic... He's worried something's going on. He wanted us to come in right away."

The floor spun beneath me. "To say good-bye?"

Gabe's eyes darkened. "He didn't say that."

"Can we see him? Do you any idea what's causing it? Have you seen the doctor since you've been here?"

"Dr. Kim's with him now. The nurse said he'd be out in a minute."

We paced the lobby, and thoughts swirled through my mind. I wished Hannah could be here. I truly believed that if she could just hold Wesley's hand, he would get better. The thought that his condition could be worsening sent me into a spiral as I paced. I couldn't lose my sister, and I couldn't lose her boyfriend. They were in mortal danger because of *me.*

The ugly truth crushed me. I collapsed into a seat.

"Babe? Are you okay?"

"No." My voice came out in a hoarse whisper.

Dr. Kim came out just then, looking like he hadn't slept in a few days. "I'm glad you're here. We've stabilized his heart rate, but I'm not sure what caused the arrhythmia. We're going to be monitoring him closely, and he'll be moved back down to the ICU."

I jumped up. "Can we see him?"

"Only for a minute," the doctor said.

"Is this common for people in his condition?" I asked.

The doctor shook his head. "Induced comas are used rarely, and only for the most extreme cases. His body is supposed to be resting—that's the point. The fact that his heart is struggling under these conditions… It isn't a good indicator."

"Can you be more specific?" Gabe asked. "We need to be prepared."

"It means his heart is working too hard. Which could mean his body is being taxed too much by his injuries, even though we took the extraordinary step of putting him into a coma."

"Do you think he's going to make it?"

Dr. Kim gave me a tired smile. "He's young and he's strong. He was in excellent health before he was shot, and that's wonderful. I'm hoping we can keep him stabilized. I know that's a non-answer, but it's the only answer I have at the moment."

Tears threatened, but I nodded. "Thank you."

The doctor squeezed Gabe's shoulder. "I'll text you immediately if anything changes. You can go see him now, before they move him."

Gabe and I headed to the room, followed closely by Timmy.

My security guard looked grim. "His brother's on assignment on the other side of the world—he's special ops. We've been communicating with him daily via email. He'd planned to take leave and fly home next week, but I'm wondering if we should tell him he needs to come now."

"Do it," Gabe said immediately. "Just in case. I'm sure it would help Wes to have his brother here."

The three of us went into the room, and I was shocked to see how much worse Wes looked. His skin was blanched, his lips a whitish color. I went immediately to the bed and reached for his hand.

"Hey, big guy. You scared us just now." I squeezed his hand, listening to the hum of the machines and his heart rate monitor. "Please get better, and *please* come back to us. Hannah's coming home soon. She can't wait to see you. I need you to be okay for her, for me, for your brother...and for you. Okay?"

There was no answer, but I squeezed his hand again.

Gabe and Timmy each took turns speaking to Wes in low tones, each of them taking his hand for a moment. Tears welled up in my eyes, blurring my vision as I considered the past twenty-four hours. They were some of the worst in my life. I hadn't ached like this since I'd gotten the call from the police about my parents' accident years ago.

I wiped my eyes roughly as we headed back to the lobby. "Timmy, do you mind staying here? I don't want to just leave him..."

"I was going to ask if that's okay, ma'am. And I'll try to get in touch with his brother again while I'm here."

I patted Timmy's arm. He was close to Wesley; this had to be hard on him. "Thank you."

Gabe turned to me. "Are you heading back home to work?"

I nodded, swallowing over the lump in my throat. "We're getting a lot done, but we need to finish this."

Gabe tapped me on the chin, his gaze locked on mine. "It's going to be okay, babe. I promise."

I nodded. But my heart felt heavy as I turned to go, and I realized I didn't believe him.

***

A few days later, as I crossed through the sleek doors into the sunny lobby of Paragon, I wondered: how much time did I have left?

Not enough. I didn't know how long, but it would never be enough.

I headed to my office. "Stephanie, can you do me a favor?"

"Anything," she said.

"Call a staff meeting in the cafeteria in ten minutes. I need everyone."

"Of course."

I was nervous as my staff assembled. I smiled at Eva, my chief lab technician, and Dave and Leo, but they only nodded in response. They looked as anxious as I felt.

"Thank you for taking a break and coming down on such short notice." My voice carried through the large room, which felt oddly quiet. "I wanted to update you all about Wesley and Hannah, and what's happening with Paragon."

I swallowed hard. "Wesley has been moved back to the ICU unit at El Camino—*but* he's stable, and he's receiving amazing care at a cutting-edge facility, and his doctor is one of the top neurosurgeons in the country. I'm praying for him, praying he pulls through. It would mean a lot to me if you would too."

There were worried murmurs throughout the room. One woman started visibly crying.

"As you know, Wesley was injured on duty while he was protecting my sister. Hannah was taken captive. She's alive—I've seen her and spoken to her."

Everyone started talking at once.

"I'm negotiating to get her back. I'm sorry, I can't discuss the details because I don't want to complicate the matter any further. Trust me, it's complicated enough—and most importantly, I don't want to do *anything* to hurt Hannah or put any of you at risk. I will tell you more when I can, but for now, just know that we're doing everything in our power."

I sighed. "Which brings me to my last point. And *please*, for Hannah's sake, all of this must remain confidential. Anything I tell you can't leave these walls."

The room went quiet again, the silence ominous.

"Every one of you has made these last six years a true joy." I turned and looked at each of their faces, acknowledging them individually. "Your contributions and sacrifices have made my company great. That's why what I'm about to tell you is so hard."

I took a deep breath, trying to steady myself. "Paragon is being sold to Jiàn Innovations. Our company will cease operations as soon as we close the deal, which could be as early as next week."

No one looked surprised. They were too busy being appalled.

Tears threatened, so I took another deep breath and tried to get the rest of the words out before I fell apart. "The good news is that our partner, Dynamica, has plans to open a large research and development division, and they've asked every single one of you to come work at their San Jose headquarters. They've asked me to come too, as the Vice President of R&D. As soon as Paragon winds up, you'll have a new home in Silicon Valley, if you want one. And I hope you do—each of you has proven your loyalty, professionalism, and intelligence to me over the years. I don't want to lose *any* of you."

Everyone started talking at once. It took a few minutes for them to calm down. Then Alexandra, one of my longtime lab technicians, stood up. "I'd follow you anywhere, Lauren. Of course I'll go. Thank you for the opportunity."

There was clapping and cheering.

Then, one by one, each of my employees stood up and accepted the offer.

And I didn't even bother trying to stop the tears.

***

GABE

At my office, I reviewed reports and sales data. Then I had a long telephone conference with Kami. I'd asked her to work on several new agreements recently, and we needed to review them, to make sure the details were in place. After we hung up, I knew I could move forward with my plan—the part involving Lauren's second act. I didn't see a way to stop the sale of Paragon, but that *didn't* mean the game was over.

I wanted to take Li Na down. I couldn't do it alone, but I could help Lauren do it.

Now I just had to convince her that she should.

The week had dragged—I felt sick, almost hungover. My brothers had been gone on surveillance, tracking down leads, and there'd been no further contact from Li Na. She was letting Lauren sweat it out. Seeing Wesley had been a punch in the gut; I winced every time I thought about him, how pale and shrunken he'd looked. Dr. Kim said he'd stabilized, but I wondered how much more Wes's body could take.

Allen Trade was right: that Zhao woman *did* have a lot to answer for.

But how could I make her answer? Even though she'd hurt people I loved, she was no more real to me than a smooth voice on the other end of a line, a sender of curt texts. I thought about what Levi had asked me: *what made Li Na Zhao tick?*

I did a Google search and pulled up the most recent pictures of her. I considered the woman who'd ripped my world apart: long dark hair, bright lipstick, an immaculate, slim-fitting suit. Li Na projected style and confidence in her press photos. But who was she, really?

And why was she so certain that she could get away with murder, kidnapping, and intellectual property theft on such a grand scale?

I did a little more digging. She'd gotten married when she was twenty-five and divorced ten years later. Her ex-husband was a doctor. He'd gone on to remarry, have a child, and was still practicing medicine, as far as I could tell. Chinese social media was different from the American version, so I got a little lost as I looked online. Dave had had the foresight to install beta translation software on my laptop; he'd written the code himself, and I hoped to Christ it worked right.

I texted Dave and Leo. *Please do a social media analysis on LNZ and her ex-husband. Send it to me soon.* If anyone could piece together something useful, it'd be our IT experts.

I read up on Jiàn Innovations. The company had enjoyed robust growth since its formation. However, its sales were primarily Chinese. I'd known from the beginning that Li Na wanted to increase her global market share. There was no better person to steal from than Lauren, who'd had overnight international success.

Overnight international success seven years in the making.

I read some more, looking at the practice of IP theft in China—it was big business. Everyone who worked in Silicon Valley was aware of the ongoing security threat, but now that I was dealing with it personally, I saw how real the damage was. We were about to lose a billion-dollar technology because of Chinese government-sanctioned hacking. From all accounts, the government was aware of, and even participated in, the hacking of North American technology. From what Levi had told me, they'd been completely uncooperative with the NSA and the FBI—Li Na was free to proceed as she wished.

But although Li Na had successfully hacked Lauren, she still couldn't make the patch work. Even with a legitimate sale on the horizon, Li Na was worried she couldn't re-create the patch's success, and keep it up and running, without the help of Paragon's most valuable asset—Lauren herself.

That was why Li Na had resorted to kidnapping. She needed to have personal leverage in addition to all the material she could steal. She knew even when she owned the company outright, and had all the correct specs, the patch's technology was so sophisticated, so advanced, she would still need Lauren to hold her hand through the process of getting production and distribution started. Taking Hannah had been the best way to ensure Lauren's performance.

Li Na was biting—hard—the hand about to feed her a feast.

She must have run out of options to be this desperate. But what, exactly, was she desperate for?

My phone buzzed with a text from Dave. *LNZ has no social media—she's completely off the grid. Her ex looks dull. He's a GP, remarried, and all he does is post pictures of his daughter, who is admittedly pretty cute. He works at a foreign-run hospital in Shenzhen. Do you want me to dig into him further?*

No, I wrote back. My instincts, which always served me well, told me that the ex-husband remained of little interest to Li Na. She seemed completely focused on her company and her ambition.

This troubled me. If she didn't love anyone, there was no one we could kidnap to hurt her—not that we would do that, but still. She seemed impenetrable. Levi said that we needed to play offense, but what sort of run did you take at a person without any personal connections?

An economic one, stupid.

I turned the idea over in my mind. To me, greed was a weak motivating factor. I didn't believe that Li Na was taking these extraordinary measures because she loved money. She was smart enough to know that you couldn't take it with you.

I scrolled through Jiàn's website, looking at their press releases. They were frequent, mostly boring financial posts. But in the past year, there were several, more colorful entries about the new technology Jiàn was working on acquiring. These reports included projections that Jiàn Innovations would become an "international leader in cutting-edge technology" and would "help establish Shenzhen as the world's biotech economic and innovation epicenter."

Li Na was bragging about what stealing the patch would do for her company and her city.

International leader…establish Shenzhen… Something clicked with me.

One of the things I'd learned from dealing with distribution partners all over the world was that every country had a different culture, a different set of values, and a different way of doing business. When I'd started Dynamica, I had to study the business practices of each country we dealt with. China was enormous, so there were cultural fluctuations within the country itself. Getting familiar with the ins and outs of each region made doing business there easier.

Still, there were unifying themes throughout the vast country, like the importance of showing respect to your business partners and associates. Respect was a recurring theme in China's business landscape. A concept tied to the importance of respect was "face"—somewhat similar to the Americanized "saving face." In Chinese business culture, face meant that you were respected. The way I understood it, it was like your social currency, your standing in the opinion of your peers.

In China, face was extremely important, especially to someone who cared only about their business.

I stood and paced, working through my thoughts.

Li Na had made pubic proclamations about her company's impending market advancement and its ultimate dominance. She had also promised to advance Shenzhen's overall standing in the global marketplace. If she failed to deliver at a grand level, she would lose face.

We were on the verge of selling Paragon to Li Na, and Lauren had agreed to help her with the transition. I went back to my desk and scrolled to Li Na's picture again. If I'd known nothing about her, I would find her attractive. But Li Na didn't care about *that* kind of face—she wanted more than recognition for just that, much more.

I needed to make sure people—*her* people—saw behind her mask. If she was exposed as someone who bragged, but couldn't deliver on her promises, she would lose face. The stigma could be potentially devastating.

Potentially devastating sounded...promising. After all, Li Na *did* have a lot to answer for.

I shot off a quick email to Kami, asking her to have all my international agreements with my patch distributors updated immediately. Then I spent the rest of the day getting ready, finally feeling like I had the foundation of a plan.

CHAPTER 19

LAUREN

After another emotional day, I was happy to be home in sweats, nursing a glass of wine with Gabe.

He put his arm around me. "Dr. Kim called this afternoon from the hospital—Wes is the same. Still stable, but still in ICU."

"Thank God. At least he hasn't had another arrhythmia. Did Timmy get in touch with the brother's unit?"

Gabe nodded. "His brother—Ellis—is taking leave and coming home."

I sighed. "That's good. I hope it helps Wes."

"It will." Gabe sounded confident, as though he were trying to stay upbeat. "Getting Hannah back will help too. I'm sure Wes will be able to sense their presence. Dr. Kim said continued visits and support are extremely important."

I nodded. "I'll go see him again tomorrow. So…what have you been up to since I last saw you this morning?"

Gabe shrugged, looking nonchalant. "Just some research. You?"

"I held a staff meeting, to talk about the future."

"And?"

"*And* everyone single one of my employees agreed to transition to Dynamica. They're thrilled. I can't thank you enough." I kissed his cheek. "Really…you made an impossible situation bearable."

He smiled, playing with my hair. "And what about you, huh? Have you decided about what you're going to do? I'm not trying to push, I swear. I'm just...curious."

"I know." I leaned against him, trying to gather the energy to tell him how I felt.

"So?"

"In theory, I would love to come work at Dynamica. We already have an existing business relationship, we work well together, and I'd be free to develop new technology—I know you'd give me all the space and support I need to build something great."

"But? Because I can tell that there's a 'but.'"

"*But...* I don't—I don't want to work for anyone else!" I put down my wine, got up, and started pacing. "I don't want to say no to you. I *want* to keep things on as even a keel as possible—to follow my staff, to start working again as soon as we get through this. I can't stand being idle, just reacting all the time to different stressful situations. It's making me crazy."

"I can see that."

I looked at him, feeling helpless. "I want to say yes, but I can't."

Gabe watched me patiently. "And that's because... Can you explain the 'because' part again, babe?"

"Because I'm a *CEO*. I like running my own company and being my own boss. I could never work for someone else, not even you."

I started pacing with renewed fervor. "I built Paragon from nothing except my dreams, but I made it work. It was a big deal for me to take on Dynamica even as a partner. I've never trusted anyone enough to do that—but even though I trust you, I still want to call the shots. I can't give up control and just be a vice president. Even if it's for *your* company—because it's yours and you built it. I want something that's mine, that *I* built. Do you understand?"

His dimple flashed. "Yes, I know Your Grace doesn't play well with others."

I put my hands on my hips. "Don't make fun of me."

"I'm not—and quite frankly, I'm happy to hear you say it. I was wondering if Li Na had taken all the fight out of you."

"I do feel a bit like a deflated balloon," I admitted.

"Don't. And don't be worried about my feelings—wait a minute, you aren't worried about my feelings, are you?"

I couldn't help it—I laughed. It sounded foreign coming from my mouth. "Your self-esteem seems pretty intact to me."

"You got me there." He chuckled. "So, what do you want to do? Screw Li Na? Rescue your sister, keep Paragon and the patch? Stay on as CEO?"

"In a perfect world, yes. But that's not reality. I need this to be over with Li Na. I don't want to live looking over my shoulder—or worse—for the rest of my life. Clive Warren warned me. He said she wouldn't stop, and I should've listened to him. When I screwed her over and launched the patch, I made an enemy for life. And now look what's happened. Hannah, Wesley..."

Gabe held me close. "It's not your fault."

"I appreciate you saying that, but this is my cross to bear. I need to make this right—I *need* to get Hannah back, to have Wesley be okay, and to never go through this again. If Li Na gets Paragon in exchange, it's worth it. Without my company, my life might not look how I always envisioned it, but that's a price I'm willing to pay. All I want is to be able to walk away with my family intact."

Gabe nodded, holding me close. "In order to move on...I think you need to let Paragon go. I hate to say that, but I think you're right, babe."

"That's exactly how I feel. Now that my employees are settled, I just want this to be over. And then I'll start all over again."

Gabe nodded, then went quiet for a minute. I thought the conversation might be over until he looked up at me.

His eyes glittered. "Maybe there's a way we can win."

"*Win?* That's not even a word I'm considering right now. I don't see a situation where we can walk away with both my sister and my company. And Hannah is the only thing I *really* care about."

"Of course she is, and I would never do anything to jeopardize getting her back. But if we can find her before the closing...maybe there's a chance we can get her out."

My heart raced. "Do you know something I don't? Has Ash called you?" Ash and Levi were out with two teams running surveillance in Oakland, trying to find where they were hiding Hannah.

Gabe held up his hand. "No, and I don't mean for you to get your hopes up. I've just been thinking...about Li Na."

"What about her?"

"I've been thinking maybe she should go fuck herself. Because why should the bad guys win?"

"They shouldn't. But I need to get her out of my life. That's what I want, once and for all."

Gabe nodded. "I get it."

"She's never going to leave me alone—I can see that now. It breaks my heart to lose the patch, but my family's more important to me."

"That's why you can't go to Shenzhen."

I sighed. "I don't want to fight about that right now, okay?"

"Fine." He didn't look like he meant it.

"Back to Paragon—once the sale goes through—yeah, Li Na wins, the bad guys win. It isn't fair, but who said life was fair?"

"No one. But you don't have to leave everything to fate." Gabe's gaze held mine. "I think Li Na can get Paragon and still lose."

I shook my head, confused. "Can you elaborate? Because I'm not seeing this."

"I'm still thinking it through. But let's say that you *do* sell Paragon and start over. I agree that you can't come to Dynamica—you can't work for someone else. You're too stubborn and set in your ways."

"Ha-ha."

"So I've asked Kami to draw up a sales agreement—I'm going to spin off my subsidiary biotech division and sell it to you. We can close this week. You won't be a vice president; no sense in going backwards. You'll be the CEO of your own company. Of course, the building *is* in the same office park as Dynamica, so you might not be as far away from me as you'd like. Your employees will continue to work for you and only you, Your Highness."

"But…but…with everything that's going on, I can't get all the financing together right now—"

He grinned at me. "I know. That's why I'm selling it to you for a dollar."

Shocked, I said, "Don't be ridiculous."

"I'm not. All the elements of a valid contract are there: offer, acceptance—as soon as you accept—and consideration. A dollar counts as valid consideration. Kami assured me it was legitimate."

"I don't know what to say."

"You could start with 'yes.' And then maybe move on to something more interesting, like 'thank you,' or 'I love you and your big muscles.' That'd be nice."

"Gabe…" I stroked his face, overwhelmed by his generosity. "I'll pay you back, someday."

"Of course you will." Gabe laughed. "Knowing you, you'll outearn me within the year."

For the first time in a long time, I smiled and it wasn't forced. "Not that this is a competition, but…I'm sure as hell going to try."

"Good. Then you can keep me in the lifestyle I've become accustomed to." He pulled me onto his lap again. "Back to Li Na. The thing with her is, we need to keep our eye on the ball. This is a long game—so even if she gets what she wants right now, it doesn't mean she's ultimately going to emerge victorious."

This sounded suspiciously like sports talk, which didn't compute. "Honey? I don't really understand what you're saying…"

"What I'm *saying* is, maybe we should set her up. Lull her into a false sense of security, and then, when she thinks she's done with us, we crush her."

"And *how* are we going to do this, exactly? I'm not comfortable with the idea of sending an assassin to Shenzhen to take her out. It would probably be cathartic, but I'm not a murderer." It sort of felt like a personality defect in light of the circumstances.

"Neither am I, and that's not what I'm talking about." Gabe's eyes shone with excitement. "Li Na cares very much about her reputation and her standing within her country and with the government. If she gets Paragon and begins to dominate the market, her standing and position will increase exponentially. That's what she wants—to be important. To have face."

"*Huh?*"

"It's a Chinese sociological concept. In Chinese business, the idea of having face is very important, maybe even more so than money. Face means your social standing—your importance with your peers. Li Na's made it very clear that what matters to her is Jiàn's market dominance, and making sure Shenzhen is on the map as a leader in global commerce. That's what she cares about—that's what makes her tick."

"I'm still waiting for the part where we crush her."

"*You* have what it takes to beat her. Do you see that?"

"I'm still not following you."

Gabe reached out and stroked my face. "You can make something better than the patch. So let her have it. And then you can take the market back from her and publicly crush her black little soul."

"I can't make something better than the patch."

"Of course you can."

I gaped at him. "No, I *can't*. That innovation is one-of-a-kind, and I can't make something better than it and I can't improve upon it. I was perfecting the technology for years. It's completely unique."

"And so are you," Gabe said. "You are capable of great things, great things like the technology behind the patch. If you put your mind to it, I know you'll be able to find something that will improve upon the technology—something that will take the market back when you launch it."

I stared at him, incredulous. "You want me to go *after* her, when this is all over? Seriously?"

"All I'm saying is, I don't want you to give up. You worked for years to realize your dream. None of that's in vain, babe, *whatever* happens next. My brothers are out here now, and they're staying, God help me. She's never going to sneak up on us again. We can circle the wagons, make our company—er, *companies*," he corrected himself, "safe and secure. And we can go after her once and for all. We can show the world her real face—which is the face of a criminal, of a *hack*, someone who's cheated her way to the top. You're the one with the real promise. That's why she stooped so low and did such terrible things. *That's* what she is capable of. You can beat her because you're smarter than her and you're better than her. Then, the good guys still win."

"I'll think about it," I said, my mind whirling, "as soon as we get Hannah home."

The phone rang—my heart sank when I saw the number. "It's Li Na."

"What the hell does she want now?" Gabe's voice was ice. "Our first-born child?"

I motioned for him to be quiet and then answered the phone with shaking hands. "Hello? Is my sister okay?"

"That's not why I'm calling," Li Na said. "I spoke to my attorney this afternoon—she confirmed most of the documents are in order. We're ready to proceed. She's run the numbers, and she'll send the final ones to you tomorrow. I'd like to schedule the closing for the end of the week, and I want to talk to you about your role in the final transaction, which I want to remind you *is critical*."

I felt Gabe's eyes boring into me, but I didn't look at him. "Go on."

"The closing will take place at my attorney's firm in San Francisco. I'll have your sister nearby. She will be returned as soon as the documents are completed and the wire transfer is made. However," she took a deep breath, as if she were preparing to be annoyed with me, "you *must* come in her place. You will be flying to Shenzhen directly after the closing. Your laboratory equipment will be shipped as soon as we close—I want to get everything assembled, and I want your help making sure my people are trained efficiently enough so that we can get production moving as soon as possible. We have contracts to fulfill, after all."

I grimaced. Those were *my* contracts. "I understand."

"Is that a yes?"

She would never accept a no, but Gabe was about to freak out, and I had to try. "It's a non-answer, Li Na. I understand that's what you want, but we *could* accomplish this remotely. I'm sure you can understand that after everything, I'm not exactly eager to be in Shenzhen, vulnerable and alone."

"This is nonnegotiable—I need you here to ensure a smooth transition. I need the patch up and running as soon as possible in order to recoup my considerable investment. If you want your sister, this is what I'm asking for. I called to tell you this, CEO to CEO. You'll be released and returned safely just as soon as everything's settled. I'm giving you this opportunity even though you've crossed me. Twice. I have continued to keep my word, even as you've broken yours."

I shut my eyes tight so I couldn't see the menacing look on Gabe's face. "Then my answer is yes—I'll do it."

I kept my eyes closed after I hung up. Even though I couldn't see him, I could feel the rage-spiral from where I stood.

***

GABE

"Babe, we've had this conversation before. Do you *want* to get locked in the house?"

She looked at me pleadingly. "What am I going to say to her? 'No, thanks, I don't want to go to China? And since I didn't manage to rescue Hannah before, and you still have her—please feel free to have her raped, beaten, and then *killed*?'"

She got up and stared out the windows at the stars. "Li Na's not going to kill me. Too many people know about what she's done already. I'm more famous than

Clive Warren, and I have you all looking out for me. She'll let me live, and she'll let me come back. If it comes down to it, I *have* to go."

"Over my dead body."

"With everything that's happened, can you *please* not say that?"

I clenched my hand into a fist, on the verge of losing it. I couldn't stay here and fight with her about this again. She seemed determined, but so was I. I could think of only one way to get out of this, and that was to get Hannah before the closing, so Li Na's hold over Lauren would be broken.

"I'm going to go see my brothers—to see what the status is."

Lauren looked at me hopefully. "Can I come with you? Please?"

"I'll have to check and see if that's all right with them." Of course, then they'd know I was coming, and they wouldn't be thrilled.

Lauren's phone buzzed again, and she read the text, her brow furrowed. "It's Bethany. She just got off the phone with the lawyer. We need to get everything finalized now. I guess I can't tag along."

My jaw tightened—I didn't want to fight with her, but I didn't I want to leave her alone either. "Timmy's in the guesthouse. I'll have him come over. Okay?"

"Okay."

I kissed the top of her head. There was so much I wanted to say, but I could feel it getting backed up, lost in my anger—anger born from fear. I had to do something. I couldn't let Li Na get her hands on Lauren. The best course of action was to *take* some action, so I grabbed my jacket, shrugged into it, and slammed the door to the house before I slammed my fist into something.

I roared out of the driveway and flew toward Oakland. Levi and Ash were running two different crews, combing through the residential neighborhoods near the airport. I texted Ash as I pulled into the city; he sent me an address. My GPS led me to an abandoned parking lot in a rough-looking neighborhood.

I locked my car and hopped into his. "Any luck?"

Ash nodded. "We're narrowing it down."

"What does that mean, exactly?"

He sighed. "It means we believe she's in this neighborhood. A lot of these condos are owned in blocks by foreign corporations and trusts. The FBI already had this neighborhood on a watch list because of so much foreign investment and activity. When they lost me on the way back from the Oakland airport, we were close to here. We're just trying to find the unit." He pulled out and headed slowly down another residential street, followed by another car filled with agents from Betts Security. I was pretty sure there were so many of their agents on the West Coast now, I'd never keep track of them all.

Ash handed me a list of cars. "We're looking for these makes and models, and also these license plates. Or some combination thereof—I'll take anything I can get. These are vehicles recently rented or recently stolen in the area. Some are both. Keep your eyes open."

I scanned the information on the sheet, then looked out the window at the nondescript neighborhood. "Li Na just called Lauren. The closing is going to happen soon, probably by the end of the week. Li Na said she absolutely needs Lauren to come to Shenzhen to help her set up—otherwise the deal is off."

Ash didn't say anything for a minute. "I know what *you* have to say about that, but what about Lauren?"

"She says she has to go—and that she'll come back."

"She might have a point."

"Don't be ridiculous." I stared out the window, fuming. "So you think I should just let her go—and take her sister's place in Li Na's noose?"

"I'm not saying that. But Lauren's a public figure. Li Na's not going to bring her to China just to kill her. It doesn't make any sense."

"Does it make any sense that Li Na killed one of Paragon's board members, or that she's kept Lauren's sister captive and beat her senseless over the past few weeks?"

"It's not the same," Ash said. "I know you don't want to consider doing this, but if we can't find her before the end of the week, it may be the only way we get Hannah back."

"Then we're going to find Hannah first. Or there's going to be hell to pay."

We canvassed the neighborhood for hours, driving up and down side streets, passing an endless line of cookie-cutter, boxy, beige condominiums. Before I knew it, the sun had come up, and residents were starting to leave for work.

My phone rang as we pulled down another side street. "Who's this?"

"It's Allen Trade. I need to talk to you."

"I'm listening."

"I had meetings with some of the members of the board that I thought might be…inclined…to share the information we talked about. And I've isolated the problem."

"Well, that's good, at least *someone's* made some progress—"

"Wait a minute," Ash said. "Shut up."

"What's going on?" Allen asked.

I turned to my brother. "What is it?"

Ash gripped the steering wheel. "I *said*, shut up. Hang up the goddamn phone and pay attention."

"Allen, I've got to go. Is the situation under control?"

"Yes, call me when you can." He hung up without asking anything further. I might like him better than I thought.

I peered out the window at one of the condominiums. "What are we looking at?"

Ash slowed the car to a crawl, staring at one of the condominium's garages. "That door was closing as we just pulled down here. Something about the car… I'm not sure, but I think it's worth checking out."

"Did you get the plate number?"

"Only the last couple of digits." He grabbed the list he'd given me and scrolled through it. "Bingo. I think we have a match."

"A *partial* match."

"I told you, I'll take anything I can get. That's all I need."

We turned around, heading back to the same parking lot, Ash on his cell phone. "Brian, send some guys back now to get the equipment, and tell Levi we need to set up a space for surveillance. And I need you to do a real estate search on this address." He rattled off the street address for the condominium.

"You're setting up a surveillance space based on a partial match?" I asked once he'd hung up.

"A partial match in the perfect neighborhood." He turned to me. "This is it, and I *know* it."

"A gut instinct isn't good enough for me right now."

"It's not a gut instinct, asshole. It's *a partial plate in the perfect neighborhood where I lost these bastards once before.*"

I shook my head. "You better be right."

"I look forward to proving that I am. For the record, you don't have to thank me now. I will thoroughly enjoy you thanking me later."

Chapter 20

LAUREN

I woke up with my stomach feeling like lead. I rolled over to find the bed empty; Gabe had never come home last night. I grabbed my phone and was greeted by a text from Li Na. It must've come while I slept.

The closing is officially scheduled for the end of the week, it read. *Are you ready to go?*

No, I thought. I pictured Gabe and winced. *Never.*

Yes, I wrote back immediately. *But I want to see Hannah and talk to her this morning.*

While waiting to hear back from Li Na, I called Gabe. It went straight to voice mail, so I fired off a text. *Where are you? Is everything okay?* My phone remained frustratingly silent for a few minutes, so I headed out to get some coffee and found Timmy in the living room.

"Is everything okay?"

Timmy nodded, but he looked haggard.

"I can read your face," I croaked, fearing the worst. There were a lot of things on that list. "Just tell me."

"It's Wesley, ma'am. He had a minor heart attack last night."

The world tilted underneath my feet. I grabbed on to the island so I didn't fall over. "Oh Jesus. Is his brother on his way?"

"He got in late last night. He's with Wesley now—I spoke to him this morning. He said the doctor was worried that Wesley…might have suffered some brain damage. His heart's working too hard… He's worried that the oxygen supply might've been cut off."

I was still gripping the island when my phone buzzed. I lunged for it.

Your sister will be live in five minutes. My attorney will send the closing agenda later today. Please be prepared with everything we discussed—let's finish this.

I opened my laptop while Timmy shot me a worried look. "Hannah's going to Skype me," I explained. My nerves were jittering, my stomach roiling. "Did you hear from Gabe? They never came back last night."

Timmy nodded, his big, beefy neck straining underneath his button-down shirt. "Mr. Betts said they were doing some surveillance in Oakland. They might have a lead."

My heart froze. "Really?"

"That's what he said—but I don't know anything more than that. I'll be over here, out of sight." Timmy went to the other end of the room just as the application opened.

The screen came to life with an image of Hannah sitting, staring at the floor listlessly. Another large bruise ran down her chin to the top of her neck—the size of a large palm.

"Oh my God, *Hannah*!" My voice cracked. "What did they do to you?"

She looked up at the computer, but her eyes didn't seem to focus. "I told you they were assholes—and I told them that too. I guess they didn't want to hear it." Her voice came out funny and thick. She pointed to her face. "That's how I got this."

I felt like I might pass out, but I gripped the island and put on my game face. "Listen to me, you are out of there. *Just a few more days.* Don't say another word to them. You are coming home, and this is going to be okay. I need you—Wesley needs you."

A flicker lit up Hannah's eyes. "How is he?"

"He's okay," I lied. "His brother got back from deployment to come and see him. But he needs you. He's been asking for you." God would probably strike me down for lying like this, but I needed to motivate her, to make her feel needed.

Hannah nodded and managed a weak smile. I noticed that her lips were dry, chapped, and cracking. "Good. That's really good." Her words were slightly slurred.

"Hannah—are you on something? Did they make you take something?"

"They gave me a sedative. They said it was for my own good—so I wouldn't mouth off so much that they wanted to shoot me."

The floor swerved underneath me again, making me woozy. "Oh my God."

She shook her head. "Don't worry. It's almost better that I'm out of it, because I can't yell at them or even yell at you. But I remember everything that's happened, and I'm going to say it again: *I will never forgive myself if something happens to you.*"

"Nothing bad's going to happen. Don't worry about it—Li Na and I have everything worked out. I will be here for you, and everything's going to be okay." More lies, but hopefully someday, this would be true. I just had to find a way to come back to her.

"Okay," said a male voice in the background. "Tea time's officially over. We'll see you soon." And with that, the screen went black.

I put my face into my hands. "Timmy, can you call Ash for me? They need to know about this, and I need to find out where they are."

"Of course, ma'am."

I hustled to my bedroom and got dressed, ignoring my dizziness and the roaring in my ears. Seeing Hannah look injured and disoriented hit me like a mortal blow, but I didn't have time to fall apart right now.

I brushed my teeth, dragged a brush through my hair, and raced back out to the kitchen. "Let's get to the hospital, okay?" I didn't even wait to hear Timmy's answer. He looked as worried as I felt. I knew he'd want to see Wesley as soon as possible.

The waiting room at El Camino was busy, but we immediately spotted Ellis Eden—there was no mistaking Wesley's older brother. The family resemblance was striking. Ellis was six-foot-four and built like a linebacker, his hair closely cropped.

He stood as we approached and offered his hand for a firm handshake. "Ms. Taylor, it's a pleasure."

I must've looked surprised, because he said, "I recognize you from the articles I've read. I wanted to know who my brother worked for."

"I'm so sorry about Wes. He's an amazing employee, an asset to our team, and he was protecting my sister when he got hurt. He sacrificed himself for her," I said, and promptly burst into tears. "I just hope he's going to be okay. He means so much to all of us."

Both Ellis and Timmy chivalrously averted their eyes, simultaneously offering words of comfort.

"No need to apologize, ma'am," Ellis said. "Wesley loves his job, and he's aware of the risk involved."

"How's he doing?" Timmy asked as I wiped my eyes and tried to stop bawling.

"Okay. The doctor said the tests they ran earlier don't show any negative impact, but they can't be sure...not until he wakes up. He can't have any visitors this morning."

"Of course." I pulled myself together enough to talk. "*Did* he have a heart attack?"

"A minor one." The muscle in Ellis's jaw popped. "The doctor said his heart's been working too hard, pumping blood to repair the damage..."

"What's the next step?"

"They said they'll run some more tests while he's resting. They may consider waking him up, but they don't want him to experience any more trauma right now."

My phone buzzed with a call from Gabe. "I'm at the hospital with Wes's brother—can I call you right back?"

I hung up and looked at Ellis. "You should stay with us while you're here."

"I'm fine. I checked into the hotel down the street—I need to be at the hospital while I can."

"How long will you stay?"

"As long as it takes, until he's stabilized," Ellis said. "Eddie told me a little bit about what's happening out here. I'm sorry about your sister."

"Thank you." I blew out a deep breath. "We're working on getting her back. I'll bring her to see Wes once we do. I think it'll help." I gave him my cell phone number, and he promised to call as soon as there was an update.

I called Gabe as Timmy and I headed back to the car. I felt lost—it was a weekday morning, and I should be at work, but everything was coming unraveled.

"Babe—how's Wes?"

"Not good. He had a minor heart attack. The doctor's worried that his heart's working too hard, trying to repair his body. He's concerned there may have been brain damage. But they don't know anything yet."

"Oh *fuck*. That's fucking terrible." I could feel his pain through the phone.

"His brother's here—Ellis. He said he'd text us any updates."

"I'll call Dr. Kim too, and see if he can give us any details."

"Listen, I talked to Hannah this morning. She looked terrible. She had a huge bruise on her face and neck. Her eyes couldn't focus—she said they'd given her a sedative."

"How were you allowed to speak with her?"

"Because I asked to." I swallowed hard and prepared myself—lying wasn't an option this close to the closing. "Li Na texted me last night. They've scheduled the closing for Friday. She wanted to make sure that I was on board with all of her demands. I said that in order for us to go forward, I needed to speak with Hannah again."

Dead silence radiated from Gabe's end of the line.

I licked my lips nervously, desperate to change the subject. "So why didn't you come home last night? Timmy mentioned they might have found a lead?" With all the bad news this morning, I hadn't been able to focus on the glimmer of hope Timmy had mentioned earlier.

"Ash thinks he found something. We've been watching this one condominium."

"Watching for what? What did he see?"

"Just part of a plate, one that could be on our watch list—don't get your hopes up yet."

"Don't worry." I laughed, but it sounded bitter. "Getting my hopes up isn't really my thing right now."

He cursed under his breath. "I hope Ash's right, because you are *not* getting on a plane to go to motherfucking Shenzhen! Do you understand?"

"Do *you* understand that I can't handle fighting with you right now, on top of everything else?"

Gabe exhaled in a hiss. "Yes. I don't want to fight." But he was fighting to keep his voice even. "What are you doing this morning?"

I bit my lip, staring out the car window. "I guess I'm going to work. I need to…wrap things up."

"Is Timmy with you?"

"Yes. Are you staying in Oakland?"

"Yes—at least until we figure out if this is actually a lead. I'll call you in a little while, okay?"

"Okay," I said. But as the driver headed toward Paragon, I had never felt less okay in my life.

***

GABE

The scalding coffee burned my throat, but I drank it anyway. The burn was better than feeling out of control. I could barely process the morning's events.

Wesley—young, strapping Wesley—had suffered a heart attack.

Hannah had been drugged.

And Lauren was threatening to do what Li Na wanted. I understood, but Lauren *couldn't* get on that plane. It would be over my dead body—even if she didn't care for my word choice. It was accurate.

Levi and I sat in the back of the surveillance van, waiting and drinking our respective coffees. We'd parked a few streets over from the house Ash was checking out.

"Why're you here, again?" Levi asked.

"Because I'm not your silent partner on this case anymore. This is *my* family, and I'm done sitting around, doing nothing."

"What did you find out about Zhao?"

"I found out that she's scheduled the closing for Friday, and she's still expecting Lauren to get on a plane afterwards."

Levi waited for me to continue.

"Li Na called last night, to ask Lauren, CEO to CEO, if she would honor the agreement."

"And?"

"And Lauren said she would. And when she just called, she said that she's spoken to Hannah this morning via Skype, and that Hannah was beat up, drugged and semi-catatonic."

Levi leaned his head back against the interior of the van. "And Wes had a heart attack. Jesus. This could not be going more wrong."

"That's why I'm here—we need to find Hannah before the closing."

"And you think you can help?"

"No," I admitted, "but at least I won't have to sit at home and wait to find out what's happening."

"What else did you find out about Zhao? Anything useful?"

"I think so." I frowned. "She doesn't seem to have hung on to any personal relationships after her divorce. But it made me think about what she *is* after."

"You mean aside from Lauren's multibillion-dollar technology?"

I nodded. "I don't think it's just the money."

Levi looked interested. "Well, then, she's deeper than I thought. Tell me."

"I think it's about her standing, her reputation. I think she's someone who has big dreams and is used to accomplishing them. She also has an important business standing in Shenzhen, and she's been boasting about the technology her company's about to acquire. But she hasn't been able to create something as technologically sophisticated as the patch, which is what's necessary to be a star in a rapidly changing healthcare market. In order to deliver, she's taking the alternate route to success."

"Okay...so? What're you going to do about it?"

"I've got some ideas. The most important thing is getting Hannah back. Then it's getting Li Na out of our lives."

"Without Lauren going to Jiàn Innovations."

"Of course. That's the whole point."

My brother inspected his coffee. "When's the closing scheduled for, again?"

"Friday."

His gaze rose to meet mine. "So Ash had better be right—this needs to be it."

"That's what *I* said."

The door burst open and Ash came in, breathing hard. "Guys." He grinned at us, then leaned over to catch his breath, as if he'd literally sprinted back to the van. "Be prepared to shower me with gifts, compliments, and food—you both owe me."

CHAPTER 21

LAUREN

I settled into my desk and went through my backlog of emails. This would be one of the last times I sat here like this...but I refused to think about it, just like I refused to think about how terrible Hannah had looked this morning, and how Wesley was in danger.

I allowed myself to focus on my work for a few hours. I had to do something, and it was the only thing I'd ever been any good at.

When I finally looked up, my gaze automatically went to the windows and at the grounds below. This was one of my favorite views in the world, the acres of neatly manicured lawns glistening in the early morning dew. Soon, the property would be on the market. Another CEO with another vision would buy it and make it their home.

I didn't know who I'd be without Paragon. It'd been my life's dream for so long, I wasn't sure where I ended and my company began.

Don't think about it. Find a new dream to dream.

But this wasn't the time to dream—I had to be laser-focused, to see this through to the end. I'd been excited when Gabe had offered to sell me his subsidiary company, but what was happening with Li Na, Hannah, and Wesley had me reeling, eclipsing all hope.

How could I focus on the future when I wasn't sure if I, or the people I loved, even had one?

I pushed the thoughts from my mind. The image of my sister haunted me, but selfishly, it was Gabe I couldn't extricate from my thoughts. *What if I have to leave him? What if this week brings...the end of us?*

My gaze wandered over my desk, coming to rest on the picture of my parents. I was glad they weren't here to witness Hannah's kidnapping. Still, my heart hurt looking at it—I missed them. When they died tragically, too young, my heart had broken. My parents were why I never wanted to fall in love in the first place. Who could bear another loss like that, when people you loved were taken from you?

But even though my heart ached with missing them, I knew they were still with me. Because that was what love did—it changed you forever. It marked you on the inside, making you grow stronger even as it made you vulnerable. Because loving somebody was brave. It was if once you took the leap to care about someone else, your heart muscles got stronger.

They had to—it was an evolve-or-die situation—because when you loved someone, your heart was walking around outside your body.

Or it was being held captive.

Or it was in a medically induced coma.

Or it was on the other side of the world, cursing you, because you'd left it to fulfill an unbearable duty.

I put my face in my hands, and Stephanie buzzed in, jolting me from my reverie. "Mimi White is here to see you."

This surprised me. Mimi rarely dropped in. "Okay?"

Mimi nodded curtly as she came in, then sat across from me. She looked pulled together as usual, in a plum-colored blazer, her silver bob a sleek helmet. "I came to apologize."

"For what?"

She shot me a look. "For calling Olivia, our United Kingdom distributor."

I opened my mouth and then closed it. Mimi White had been the one to sell us out.

Mimi crossed and uncrossed her legs, looking as nervous as I'd ever seen her. "Before you say anything, let me explain myself. Paragon is important to me. My time on the board has been an honor."

"Thank you for that." I took a deep breath. "But you had no right to share the news—I told you it was confidential."

"You did, and I went against your direct order." Mimi pursed her lips. "I was trying to sabotage the sale."

I felt like I'd been punched in the gut. I'd known Mimi for years. I couldn't believe she'd betrayed me like this, in my hour of need. "It's not your sale to sabotage."

"I understand, but this technology isn't Li Na Zhao's to steal either."

"That's true, but it's not the most important thing. *Hannah's* safety is the most important thing."

"I know what I did was wrong—and I admit, it's not like me to be this reckless." Mimi nodded tightly, her face turning red. "But the injustice of all this... I couldn't tolerate it."

I waited for her to collect herself and go on.

"Olivia's a friend of my daughter's from prep school. I thought if I could tell anyone, to try to do something about this, it should be her. But then she didn't follow through, so I contacted some of the others."

I put my face in my hands. If our partners were alerted about Paragon's impending sale, there could be a backlash. I knew from reviewing the international contracts recently with Bethany that they were assignable; but I also knew that our distributors could opt out after a twelve-month period. No one was supposed to know about the sale yet. That might've made me a poor business partner, but I didn't want to give any of them notice—any time to prepare to jump ship.

"I don't understand why you did this—you know it could've compromised the sale. If Zhao hears that our partners are nervous about the transition, it could make her hesitate. I can't afford that right now."

"You have to understand that I would *never* do anything to hurt Hannah. I wasn't thinking about that aspect." She winced. "I was trying to stir up an international coalition to stop the sale. I don't believe in negotiating with terrorists, Lauren. I'm sick about what's happened to Clive Warren, your sister, to the security guards."

"So am I—"

"*I* think giving in to Zhao is encouraging tactics like this—and I don't want to do that. We can't let the healthcare landscape be transformed into a war zone. If she's allowed to get away with trade secret theft, kidnapping, and *murder*, what's to stop others from doing the same? People will be too afraid to compete in this market. It will deter innovation."

"I understand what you're saying—"

"The older I get, the more I understand that it's about the greater good." Mimi clasped her hands tightly together in her lap. "We're better than this—*you're* better than this, and you deserve more than to see your company stolen out from underneath you. People *need* this innovation, Lauren. Your invention is going to help millions of people. We can't just let it go."

I couldn't be angry with her, because I understood exactly how she felt. Still, I felt sick. Any compromises right now could put Hannah in even more danger.

"Mimi...I've always admired your principles and your strength. But you have to understand, this is my *family*. I agree with everything you're saying—I am the last person who wants to see Paragon go out like this. But it's my *sister*. It's *Hannah*. And no other kind of loss compares to that. Do you understand?"

Her face softened. "Of course I do. I called Olivia and the others when I was too angry to consider the consequences. I had second thoughts as soon as I did—which is why I admitted to Allen that I was responsible. It's also why I'm here. *I'm so sorry.*"

I nodded. “I know.”

“I believe you can bring civil charges against me for breach of my fiduciary duty to the board and to the company.” She jutted her chin. “It would probably make us both feel better if I was punished for what I did.”

“Mimi, I’m not going to do that.” Still, my stomach churned with nerves. Everything was stacked against Hannah right now. Any more false moves on our part, and she would be doomed.

“I hope you understand—I was trying to save what you’ve worked for. I’ve always believed that the patch would make the world a better place. I don’t want to see this happen…”

“No one does. We’re just doing the best we can with a terrible situation.”

Mimi nodded and stood to go. “Any news on Hannah or the security guard?”

“Nothing good.” I bit my lip.

“I’m sorry it’s come to this.”

“Me too. But we’re not done yet.” I forced myself to sound slightly upbeat, to give us both some hope. “I’m not giving up.”

Mimi nodded. “Good. The world needs you.”

As the silence settled back over my office, I wondered if that were true…and what, if anything, I could do about it.

***

GABE

“Look at this.” Ash fired up his laptop and opened a file in Dropbox. He played a short video, showing the white SUV pulling out of the garage. The driver’s face was visible for only a split second as he turned, backing the car out of the driveway. Ash paused the video.

“I’m feeling underwhelmed,” I said, but Levi motioned for me to shut up.

“Just wait.” Ash opened another file, the surveillance film from Lauren’s house on the night of the attack. He stopped when it showed the invaders leaving the house with Hannah in tow. He focused in on one of the men and opened a facial-recognition program. He placed the markers over the man's face in the surveillance feed, then he did the same thing with the driver's face.

The program beeped: it was a match.

"Told you!" Ash continued to manipulate the files, looking excited. "We use the same program the NSA uses."

That beep wasn't good enough for me. "Is this *conclusive*?"

"No," Levi said immediately. "But it's enough for us to set up full surveillance on the property. We need to find a place nearby to set up shop."

Ash nodded. "I'll get on it." He pulled up the Airbnb website and immediately started scrolling through the Oakland listings.

Levi watched the screen. "The closing is soon—we have to confirm that this is where Hannah's being kept. Ash, is there any update on the car rental?"

"Whoever rented it used one of those 'special government liaison' passports that you can get from Dominica for five hundred thousand dollars." Ash didn't look up from the screen. "Which just makes me feel more certain it's them."

"Let's not get ahead of ourselves," Levi cautioned.

"There's nothing that would work on Airbnb—on to Craigslist," Ash said, opening the other site.

Levi scowled. "Ew."

"What're you looking for?" I asked.

"A rental property nearby, one that we can take possession of immediately. There aren't any hotels close enough—" Ash stopped and clapped his hands together. "Bingo—here's a lovely, boxy condominium for rent, right in the same neighborhood."

"Make sure you use a fake name to rent it, and pay cash." Levi peered at the screen. "A lot of foreign investment companies own real estate around here—no one knows who the hell they actually are. I don't want to give Li Na a heads-up that we're moving into the neighborhood."

I stood to go. "I need to let Lauren know what's going on."

"Of course," Levi said. "We'll brief her too. But tell her not to get her hopes up—not yet."

Ash grinned at me as I climbed out of the van. "She can get her hopes up. I know what I'm doing."

I heard Levi and him arguing about that, but I closed the door, shutting out the noise, anxious to get home. I couldn't wait to tell Lauren that we *finally* had what appeared to be a viable lead.

***

She came home from Paragon, Timmy in tow, a few hours later.

"Babe." I wrapped her in my arms and kissed the top of her head. "It's so good to see you."

Timmy cleared his throat. "I'll just...leave you to it." He hustled to the guesthouse.

Lauren poured us each a glass of wine and took a long sip. "Mimi White came to my office today. She's the one who leaked the news of the sale to your distributors."

"I know. Allen Trade called me earlier." I studied her face, which was pale and tense. "How did it go?"

"She said she couldn't bear to see us give in to terrorist tactics. She wanted to fight back."

I rubbed her arm. "She has an activist streak, huh?"

"She's probably right. I'm not helping with the big picture. I'm giving in to violence, which means I'm resetting the new normal to a *very* low place to conduct business."

"I'll say it again: it's not your fault. What're you going to do about Mimi?"

"She said I could bring a civil suit against her, but I declined. The only taste for revenge I have is the one I'm itching for with Li Na." She raised her gaze to meet mine. "Is everything okay with the distributors? I can't handle this deal blowing up right now. We're so close."

"I've got them all in line. It's going to be okay."

"Good." She blew out a deep breath. "Thank you."

"I have other news. My brothers found a lead." I silently prayed that they were right—we needed this break. I reached out and took her hand. "They found a house in Oakland. They think it might be the guards who have Hannah."

"How…?"

"Ash videotaped one of the guys, and he matched it to the surveillance feed from the night they broke into your house."

"When you say matched—"

"I mean he used facial-recognition software. It was a match."

Lauren opened her mouth, but no words came out for a moment.

"So she…she could be in Oakland?"

"Yes. But they're not sure, not a hundred percent." I wanted her to have hope, but I needed to keep her feet on the ground.

"So, what are we going to do? Have they contacted the FBI? Are we just going *in* there?"

"They need to be certain that these are the right people, and we need to be smart about the timing, for your sister's sake. They're going to rent a house in the neighborhood and set up surveillance. We're working on it. They only have a couple of days, so they're moving quickly—I promise."

My phone buzzed with a text from Levi. *Coming back to the house for a team meeting before we set up.* "Okay. Everyone's coming here to get ready."

Lauren nodded, lost in her own thoughts. "I'll have Bethany come too—just to keep her in the loop. We need to act like everything is going forward as planned."

"Okay…and Lauren?"

She looked up.

There was no way in hell I'd let her go to Shenzhen, but every second we had together seemed precious. "I love you, babe."

She leaned up on her tiptoes and kissed my forehead. "I love you too."

While we waited for everyone to arrive, Lauren and I checked our respective emails and paced. I called Dr. Kim to check in.

"Hey, Gabe." He sounded out of breath.

"Did I get you at a bad time?"

"No," he puffed, "I'm taking my break on the treadmill. I'm glad you called."

"How is Wes?"

"Stable, but I'm still concerned. The tests show normal brain function, but this isn't the type of thing you can ever call before the patient wakes up. I'm starting to worry about atrophy too. I need to make the call soon—I'd like to bring him out. I just hope this is the right time."

"Does his heart seem better?"

"It's tough to tell. It's been functioning properly since the attack. There's just a lot of things we don't know the answer to right now."

"Is his brother still there?" I asked.

"Ellis, yes—he hasn't left Wesley's side. I really think that helps. If you and Lauren can come back soon, please do. Wesley is tough, but he needs all the encouragement he can get."

"Thanks, Dr. Kim. I'll talk to you soon."

"Any changes?" Lauren asked when I hung up.

"No. He seems to be stable—the doctor said they're thinking about waking him up."

"We need to get Hannah back—Wesley needs her."

I went and wrapped my arms around her. "I know. Hopefully, it'll be soon." *For everyone's sake.*

Levi, Ash, and eight of their men showed up, followed shortly thereafter by Bethany. I called Timmy and had him join us too—he should know what was going on.

In case I asked him to lock Lauren in her room.

"What's going on?" Bethany asked Lauren.

Lauren looked pale but excited as she sank down on the couch, waiting for Levi to start talking. "They might've found where Hannah's being kept."

"Okay," Levi started. "Ash did some great work this week, tracking down a rental vehicle we suspected was being used by Zhao's team. Ash followed it to a residential neighborhood in Oakland, only a few miles away from Langham Place—where the exchange 'event' occurred. The person who rented the SUV has a very expensive passport, the kind you buy when you need to stay anonymous. That's not all. Ash was able to film the driver's face, and he matched it to the face of one of the guards who abducted Hannah."

"Matched *how*?" As usual, Bethany sounded skeptical.

"With the same facial-recognition software the NSA uses." Levi bristled. "Is that okay with *you*?"

"Wow—yeah, that's okay with me—it's great." Bethany smiled at him in approval. "Finally, some good news."

Levi didn't smile back, but he looked less annoyed. "We were able to locate a condo for rent in the neighborhood. One of our men is dealing with the transaction now. As soon as we can take possession, probably tonight, we'll move our surveillance equipment in and start watching the house."

"What's the plan after that?" Lauren asked.

"If we can confirm Hannah is on the premises, we'll go in. If not…we may wait until Friday to see if they bring her out. If they do, we'll intercept them."

"What if she's not there?" Lauren asked. "What if this isn't the same people?"

"Right now, it makes sense for us to concentrate our efforts on this location. We don't have any other leads. If it turns out we're wrong, we'll deal with it at the closing."

"Which means *what*, exactly?" Bethany was back to sounding unimpressed.

"It means if we have to, we'll get Hannah at the law firm, and then we'll intercept Lauren before she gets on a plane. We'll come up with a more detailed plan for that later. Right now, we need to stay focused."

I didn't like the sound of that *at all*, but I kept my mouth shut. For the moment.

"Does anyone have any other questions?"

"Can I come with you to the site?" Lauren asked hopefully.

"Not right now," Levi said. "You need to get Paragon ready. Zhao can't have any idea that we've found a lead—we need the element of surprise."

I stood up. "I'd like to go with you. I need to do something. If I sit around here and wait, I'll go crazy."

"That's fine," Levi said. "But please stay in the background, and let us do our job. If there's something you can help with, I'll tell you. I promise."

"But nothing dangerous, right?" Lauren asked him. "Please?"

"Of course not," Levi assured her.

I leaned down and kissed the top of Lauren's head. "You don't have to worry."

"I need you to mean that."

I stroked her cheek. "Of course I do. I love you. And you have enough to worry about—I'm a big boy. I can take care of myself."

"Okay," she said, but it sounded like a lie.

CHAPTER 22

LAUREN

Sunlight streamed into the room when I woke the next morning. I stretched, feeling the bed empty next to me, and then remembered—Gabe had gone to the surveillance house. I hoped Ash was right—they'd found where Hannah was being kept. Just the thought of Gabe and his brothers being close to her made me feel a little better.

Maybe this can work. Maybe we can get her out.

I threw on some sweats and went out to the kitchen, where I made myself a coffee and tried to collect my thoughts.

What *would* I do about Paragon if we could rescue Hannah before the closing? I supposed I could refuse to sell. I could tell Li Na, once and for all, to bugger off.

But I didn't know if we'd get Hannah first. There was only one way to find out, and I had to wait too long for the answer. My already frayed nerves were close to snapping as I showered and dressed quickly, anxious to get back to the office and meet with Bethany. We planned to finish the documents. I felt impatient to do anything that would pass the interminable time.

Being back at Paragon offered no relief. "Ms. Taylor," Stephanie said, following me into the office, "do you want some help packing up?"

I looked around my office, which I hadn't touched. "I think I'm going to…wait."

Eddie was overseeing the company-wide packing, getting ready for the move to San Jose. Gabe and I hadn't even signed a contract yet, but I wasn't worried about it. In fact, I wasn't even thinking about the future at all, even though I had to imminently deal with a move and starting a new company. I could only focus on the next seventy-two hours, during which I might or might not be reunited with Hannah.

Stephanie reached out and tentatively rubbed my arm. "Is there anything I can do?"

"No, but I appreciate it. Just continue acting normal—I appreciate you keeping things on an even keel around here. I'm not capable of it at the moment."

"Everybody understands," she said. "In fact, we're all in awe that you're able to be so calm and to keep things moving forward. But we're used to that—being in awe of you."

"I hope I can figure out something for us all to do, now that we're…saying good-bye to the patch." I could barely bring myself to say the words out loud.

"You will. Everything's going to be fine once we get your sister back."

I nodded at her, touched by her kindness.

After she left, I went and stood by the windows, looking out at the grounds. I put my hand on the glass, as if I could touch the view.

And then I went back to my desk to finish winding up my company.

***

Gabe texted me intermittently throughout the day. They hadn't seen any activity at the house they were watching, but the surveillance site was set up and the men had settled in.

There was nothing to do but wait.

I texted Ellis Eden, who reported that Wesley was still in stable condition. They were running more tests on him today, before they decided how to proceed.

The morning dragged. Bethany sat perfectly still, plowing through a pile of equipment-description documents. I paced some more, returning to the window occasionally, watching the sun as it made an excruciatingly slow path across the sky. We barely spoke.

Halfway through the day, Bethany went out and grabbed lunch. She pushed a container filled with peanut noodles, stir-fried vegetables, and crispy tofu toward me. "Any news?"

"Not yet. They have the house set up and the surveillance equipment's assembled, so now they're just waiting. As far as I know, they haven't seen anyone else coming or going." I pushed the food around in its container.

"Please eat that—it's from Okayama. They make the best bento box in San Jose."

"Thank you." I took a bite and chewed listlessly, Bethany watching me.

"So...what's the plan? If Levi actually pulls this off, I mean?"

I groaned. "I know you like to vet the people around me, but honestly, you don't need to give Levi such a hard time."

Bethany shrugged, her platinum hair swishing over her shoulder. "I have a feeling he'll rise to the occasion. I know men like Levi—they don't appreciate being challenged. But if someone calls them out, they like to make a big show of being right."

"So that's why you've been so hard on him—trying to shame him into being a hero?"

She rolled her eyes. "Enough about Mr. Musclebound and Brooding. Let's get back to the point: if they rescue Hannah before the closing, are we still going through with it?"

"I don't want to sell if we don't have to, but I can't let myself think that far ahead. I don't want to get my hopes up, and worrying about what's going to happen with Paragon seems wrong because I should only be thinking about my sister." I didn't want to put the cart before the horse, and I didn't want to jinx Hannah—I had to keep my eye on the more important prize.

She nodded. "I get it. This waiting thing sure sucks."

I took a bite of bitter-tasting broccoli. "Tell me about it."

"But if we *don't* get Hannah, what happens then?"

"Then we close the deal and get her back as soon as everything's signed. Hopefully, Levi can manage to intercept me before they put me on a plane."

"I don't want to deal in 'hopefullys.' That's not good enough."

"*Hopefully*, we won't have to."

"Ha-ha." Bethany didn't sound amused. "So, then what happens? We have you and we have Hannah, but Li Na gets Paragon? That's the end? She just…wins?"

I shook my head. "No. Then I invent something better with my new company, and I steal the market back from her."

Bethany held up her hand for a high five. "I like it."

"Let's just hope I can pull it off once this is all over."

"You will." Bethany sounded confident. "That's why every single one of your employees is following you to the new company—you've got the goods. We all believe in you."

I pierced some crispy tofu with my fork. "I just hope you're right."

"I'm always right," Bethany reminded me, "which is why my hourly fee's so outrageous."

***

GABE

"You can take a shift watching the surveillance feed," Ash offered. He and the rest of the guys were spread out around the stale-smelling condo. Empty coffee cups littered every available space.

"Thanks." I jumped up, stretched, and headed for the chairs in front of the monitors. "Better than sitting here, reading emails."

I'd been reviewing documents that Kami had sent over. She'd finalized the paperwork for the sale to Lauren. I would be excited about it if I could focus on anything other than anxiety-fueled waiting. We had to get Hannah back. Today. I couldn't risk Lauren trying to save her sister—and we'd officially run out of time.

I sat down and checked the various video feeds set up around the house: there was nothing to see except a normal, sunny, endless day in Northern California.

And then a crack appeared at the bottom of the garage door.

And it kept getting bigger.

"Ash." I pointed at the screen. "There's movement—I think they're coming out."

Ash cursed and got on the phone, barking orders at Brian or one of the other guys who were out near the house. I kept my eyes glued to the screen. The garage door opened fully, and a white SUV backed out.

"Get a picture—but stay the hell out of his sight line!" Ash yelled into the phone.

No one in the room took a breath as we watched the car back out and drive down the street. "Are they following them?" I asked. "Are we going to intercept them?"

"We have another car down the street—they'll pull out and tail them. But we won't go after them, not unless Hannah's in the car."

The room crackled with tension.

Ash got a call. "Are you sure? Okay. Just follow him."

He turned to us. "Only the driver's in the car—Brian got a clean picture." He hustled to his laptop and opened a file in Dropbox, his knee bouncing up and down as the pictures populated the screen. He opened the facial-recognition software.

I watched as he used the arrows to target the new picture. The program beeped.

"*Yeah*, motherfucker!" Ash jumped up and did a fist pump. "It's the same guy—I knew it, I knew it!"

I frowned at my brother. "But you *already* knew it. That's why we're here."

"I know—I just really enjoy being right."

I shook my head at him, exasperated.

"Don't act like you're above it," Ash said, "and remember: you owe me. I'm thinking I'd like a Porsche Spyder like yours. One with those fancy doors..."

I scoffed. "Let's not get ahead of ourselves."

"Now you sound like Levi."

"Don't ever say that again."

Ash shrugged. "If the Italian loafer fits…"

"I might break *your* nose next," I said under my breath.

***

I called Lauren a little later. "We've positively identified one of the guards—he went out to get gas and go to the store. We're one hundred percent certain this is the right place."

She sucked in a deep breath. "Okay…so what's next?"

"Right now, we're watching them. Levi said that it might be easier to wait until the day of the closing to get Hannah."

"*Wait?* Why would we wait—"

"Because it might be safer to get her from the car than the building. We don't know who's in there, or what the setup is," I interrupted her gently. "We can intercept them on the way to San Francisco."

She was quiet for a moment. "Okay…I guess I need to rely on your brothers' judgment."

"They know what they're doing. They have a plan."

"I want to be there. I won't be able to stand it."

"Let me talk to Levi about that. For now, you need to go through the motions. You need to be seen at work, getting everything ready."

"Time's moving too slowly." Lauren groaned in frustration. "What about you? Are you coming home?"

"I'm going to stay here. They have a lot going on, and at least I feel like I'm doing something."

"Must be nice," she said.

"You're playing the most important part—keeping Li Na on track. Have you heard anything else from her?"

"No. She's probably getting ready to bask in the patch's glory."

"Just remember: this too shall pass."

She groaned again. "Not fast enough."

***

LAUREN

The next two days were excruciatingly slow. Most of the documents were finalized; we were just going back and forth on minor details. I instructed Bethany to work from home because Stephanie had convinced me to finally start packing my office. I did so listlessly, stopping every so often to examine old notes, trial results, and early sketches of the patch.

The only thing I left on my desk was Hannah's graduation picture. It was the motivation I needed to keep going.

I didn't accomplish enough, but I still went home early, anxious and eager for the next day. Even with a security team guarding the premises, the house seemed silent, lifeless, without Gabe and his brothers. I picked at Chinese takeout, then went to bed impossibly early. I just wanted it to be tomorrow. I just wanted Hannah.

I tossed and turned all night, then woke up at dawn, showered, and dressed in a black pantsuit. I got a text from Li Na as I finished my coffee. *Looking forward to seeing you in person.*

Wish I could say the same, I mentally typed back, but I kept myself from replying. I truly hoped I got the opportunity to tell Li Na to fuck off—if not today, then someday. She seriously needed to hear it.

I called Gabe. "I'm packed and ready for the closing. I'd like to come to the site now."

"I don't want you here."

Tell me how you really feel. "You can protect me better if I'm in arm's reach."

"Nice try, but absolutely not. Timmy's got you—I already talked to him this morning."

"Gabe—"

He sighed, cutting me off. "Levi said we can Skype you in, but that's all. No arguing, Lauren. I'm sure Li Na has you under surveillance, and the last thing we need is for you to accidentally show our hand. You need to sit tight until the closing—for Hannah's sake."

I simmered with absolute fury, but Gabe had played the Hannah card, and I couldn't deny the truth of his words. "I'm not happy about this."

"I didn't expect you to be. But you're safe, and that's good enough for me. Love you." Before I could object further, Gabe said good-bye.

I stalked around the kitchen, feeling sour. But still, a bright bubble of hope rose in my chest. *We might get her back today. Maybe there was a chance.*

The closing was scheduled for later that afternoon. I called Bethany as I set up my computer. "I'm working from home this morning—they won't let me come to the site."

"I'm sure you're pissed, but that's the right call."

I rolled my eyes—of course my overprotective attorney would agree with my overprotective boyfriend. "I'll see you this afternoon. I'll text you on my way to the law firm—let's go in together."

"Is everything…on track?"

"As much as it was yesterday. Cross your fingers."

I kept my own fingers crossed, and said several silent prayers, as Timmy joined me in the kitchen. I handed him a cup of coffee. "Gabe won't let me go to the site."

"Of course not, ma'am."

I crossed my arms. "Don't bother telling me it's for the best."

"I wouldn't dare."

Timmy really deserved another raise.

I Skyped into the site in Oakland. Gabe nodded at me as he set up on his end. "I'll try to show you what it looks like here." He lifted his laptop and gave me a "tour" of the room, which consisted of nondescript beige walls, empty takeout containers everywhere, and security team members sprawled out on folding chairs. They were watching several different video surveillance feeds.

I peered past Gabe to Ash.

"Have you seen her?" I asked him immediately.

He shook his head. "Not yet. We're waiting for the drivers to bring her out to drive her to San Francisco."

I looked at the clock: we had six hours until the closing.

My head was pounding. "So what are we going to do? Will there still be shooting? How can we keep Hannah safe?"

Ash's face softened. "There will definitely still be shooting. I'm sure Li Na's men aren't just going to hand your sister over. But we can get her out. I let her get away once before, and I'm so sorry."

I shook my head, unable to speak, overcome with emotion.

"I won't let that happen again, Lauren."

I nodded, fighting back tears. "I believe you."

"Let me show you what we're doing." Ash brought the screen over so I could clearly see the surveillance feed. "We have several drones in the area, and some other cameras positioned close to the house where she's being held. We're watching with everything we've got. We also have another team waiting in San Francisco, just in case, along with more men out in the neighborhood. We've got them covered."

I watched the screens. They showed the same images of a nondescript condominium, a driveway, a roof, and a side door over and over. "Are you *sure* she's in there?"

Ash nodded. "This is Li Na's team. The FBI confirmed it from our pictures—these men are mercenaries. They often take international clients and sometimes do contract work for organized crime."

"Okay." If his words were meant to calm me, they didn't. I could only think about my sister and watch for her on the screens.

"Whatever happens this morning, the other team will be waiting for you in San Francisco. Levi will be there too, to personally attend the closing with you. No matter what, you need to be in that office in San Francisco at two o'clock. We want Li Na to think everything's on track. If we can intercept Hannah on the way to the closing, it's incredibly important to get her back to Gabe's right away. She needs to be someplace secure in case they decide to come after us and attack. Do you understand?"

I licked lips suddenly gone dry with fear. "Yes."

"I'll meet you at the law firm—if we get all the guards when they come out, Li Na might not be clued in on what's happening. At least, not right away."

I knew Ash probably meant "shoot" when he said "get" the guards—it made me feel dizzy.

I could hear Gabe even though I couldn't see him. "I'm coming to San Francisco too."

"No," Ash and I said in unison. Ash jutted his chin at his brother. "You're on point with the team we've assigned to Hannah. You'll need to get her back to the house quickly. Let Levi and me handle the closing—let's circle the wagons and finish this the right way. We'll leave the rest of the crew behind to coordinate with the FBI, deal with the fallout at the scene and also with the local authorities."

Ash turned back to me. "Do you have someone you can call to arrange medical care for Hannah at the house?"

Having allowed myself a small spark of hope, I'd already thought of that. "I just texted Gabe the name and number of the general practitioner Hannah and I both see. She promised to make a house call this afternoon, if we're...lucky enough to need her."

Dr. Lourdes Fisher had been our doctor since relocating to California. She was thorough, kind, and compassionate. After I filled her in on Hannah's situation, she said she'd come prepared with an IV and antibiotics.

"Gabe." His face appeared on the screen. "You need to get in touch with Dr. Fisher as soon as you're on your way home—she'll be expecting the call. I just texted you her number."

"Got it. I'll take care of Hannah, I promise."

No one spoke after that. Even via Skype, I could feel the tense silence that descended upon the group. I couldn't focus on anything but the clock and the screens. Gabe positioned his computer perfectly so I could keep monitoring the security videos. Nothing changed on the screens. No one left the building where Hannah was being kept, and no one entered. I started to pace. An hour passed.

I kept pacing. I kept watching the screens.

Every minute passed like an hour. My heart thudded as though I was struggling to finish a marathon. I wondered where Hannah was *exactly*, what she was doing right now, and if she was okay. I wondered if the guards had done anything to her since the botched exchange...worse than drugging her, and the bruise I'd seen on her face.

As the morning stretched on, Ash and the rest of the team continued to calmly monitor the situation, intermittently tapping out texts. Timmy stood in my kitchen, his weapon at the ready, and frequently checked the perimeter of the house. Everyone was tense, but everyone was keeping busy.

I kept busy pacing.

I took a few calls from Bethany, who'd pulled together all the final details for our meeting that afternoon. I went through a backlog of emails and cleaned out my inbox. But the phone calls and busy work weren't enough to occupy me, so I reorganized the items in the refrigerator, and then re-arranged all of Gabe's glassware by height.

Then I paced some more. Finally, we were getting closer to the afternoon, my anxiety ratcheting up to a fever pitch.

"We need to get out there. They'll be leaving soon if they're going to make it in time," Ash suddenly announced. He looked at the screen. "Lauren, watch the clock. You need to leave for the closing shortly. Remember, the timing's crucial."

I nodded, my heart pounding. "Got it. Good luck." I double-checked to make sure my bag and paperwork were ready to go.

I turned back to the screen, watching as several of the men checked their weapons. "Gabe, you're with me," I heard Ash say. "William, you take the team that's out there. Tell them to get ready."

"Got it." I heard Gabe, but I couldn't see him.

That stopped my pacing dead in its tracks. "Gabe? Gabe!" I shouted, until he put his face near the screen. "You're not going *with* them—"

"Babe." Gabe's voice was firm. "This is not your call. They need the help because they're running more than one team, and I'm happy to do it. I'm here to help protect my family."

The floor spun beneath my feet. "I think your family's good. They have years of experience and automatic weapons, for Christ's sake."

His eyes flashed. "I meant Hannah."

Before I could fully comprehend what he was doing—and yell at him, beg him to stay, anything—he hustled from view. That left me with only Timmy, the Skype feed of the remaining surveillance crew...and what felt like an ice pick in my heart. Gabe had just blindsided me.

Now the two people I loved most in the world were in danger. I swallowed hard, gripping the marble island. I looked over at Timmy, who was watching me warily. "We should go there. I need to make sure they're okay."

Timmy shook his head. "We can't, and you know it." He motioned for me to sit. He came to the screen and cleared his throat. "Excuse me?"

The two men in front of the surveillance feed turned around.

"Can you make sure we can see the screens? Ms. Taylor's very worried about her sister, and Mr. Betts too."

Nodding, they arranged the laptop so I had a perfect view of the feed. I hoped I wouldn't see anything terrible. My head was pounding, I felt sick, and my hands were coated in a sheen of sweat. *Gabe, what are you doing?* Gabe wanted to save

Hannah, and he wanted to prove something. I wasn't sure if it was to me, his brothers, his father, or himself. I clenched my hands into fists.

I was going to kill him...if he ever came back to me.

I held my breath and watched the feed. Nothing appeared except for the driveway, the door, and the roof, on an endless, mind-numbing loop.

After what seemed like forever, something happened in the video feed. The garage door opened. A white SUV began backing out.

"We've got movement," one of the guards said into his mouthpiece. He appeared to listen intently. "Copy that, Team A. Proceed."

But nothing happened. The car kept backing out. *Is Hannah inside?* I waited, biting the inside of my cheek in order to keep from screaming. *Is Gabe out there, somewhere?* I watched as the car started to ease out onto the road.

And then it stopped.

There was no sound attached to the screens. "What's happening?" I asked the remaining guards, no longer caring if I was interfering or being a pain in the ass. That was Hannah out there. And *Gabe*, damn him.

The man shook his head and motioned for me to wait, not turning around. He listened for another beat, his brow furrowed. "Fuck," he said to the other guard.

"Fuck *what*?" I asked. I felt as if I were going to jump out of my skin.

And then, suddenly, I knew what the "fuck" was for. In the video feed, Gabe stormed across the tiny lawn of the house, holding a gun and shooting at the driver's side of the car. I watched as he pulled the driver out through the broken window and threw him to the ground. I couldn't tell if the man was alive or not. Gabe didn't seem to care—he crouched down and aimed his gun at whoever was in the passenger seat.

I gripped Timmy's arm. "Oh my God."

Ash and several other men swarmed the car. I saw them pull Hannah out of the back. All I caught was a flash of her long hair before she was yanked out of the frame.

Then I saw Gabe shooting at someone else.

And then the screen went blank. "Surveillance is down," one of the men called.

I shut my eyes tightly as the image of Gabe in the middle of that chaos, shooting people, seared itself permanently onto my brain.

A minute went by with the guards murmuring to themselves and checking the equipment. "Wait, I've got Ash on the line," one of them said.

My heart pounded painfully as he listened. "Good news," he said, finally looking back at me through the screen. "That was clean. Even if it didn't go according to plan."

The guards in the room started clapping, but I couldn't even catch my breath.

"Right. Let's get going. We need to pack up and clear out." The guard smiled at me. "Ms. Taylor, Gabriel's okay. And they got your sister out. Ash said she's fine—she didn't get hurt just now."

My hands were clenched into fists, my nails digging into my palms. "Are you sure Gabe didn't get shot?"

"Not yet," the guard said. "But Levi might shoot him for pulling that back there."

"Ms. Taylor," Timmy said, clicking off his phone. "They're leaving the scene, but we need to move. Ash is already headed to San Francisco."

"O-okay." I licked my lips, which had gone dry. "Is Hannah really okay?"

Timmy nodded, smiling for the first time in what seemed like months. "She is, and so is Mr. Betts."

"I'll call them from the car." I gathered all my paperwork together and my computer, feeling disoriented. *Hannah is okay. They have Hannah, and she's coming home.*

I needed to ask a lot of questions and formulate a plan, but my mind went blank as I staggered out to the car. Timmy climbed in, and my driver pulled out immediately, making sure that I would be at the closing in the Financial District of San Francisco on time. Up to the last moment, we had to try to keep Li Na in the dark about what had happened.

But I couldn't think about Li Na now. I could only think of Hannah.

Desperate to see her, I pulled out my phone, FaceTiming Gabe—I needed to see my sister with my own eyes.

"Hey," Gabe answered, his tone clearly pleading for forgiveness.

"Let me talk to her."

He twisted the phone around so I could see Hannah, but she was turned away from me—all I could see was her hair, which was dirty and matted almost beyond recognition. "Is she okay?"

"I can hear you, you know." Hannah's voice came out weak and gravelly. "And I'm fine."

She turned her head toward me and grabbed the phone. I saw bruises on her face and neck, a thin film of dirt covering her skin. In perpetual great shape, she now looked frail, as if she'd lost about fifteen pounds since I'd last seen her.

She raised an eyebrow. "*You* look like shit, though."

I burst into tears. "Oh my God. Oh my God...I'm so glad you're back..."

"Stop crying, you'll smear your mascara." Hannah smiled at me weakly. "I'll see you at the house?"

"Yes," I said immediately. I had no plans to tell Hannah what I was about to do. "Get some rest. I'll see you soon." I hung up before I lied to her more, and before Gabe could try to talk to me—I was *not* speaking to him. I did, however, plan to scream at him—in private, as soon as I made sure both he and my sister were okay.

I knew I was about to face Li Na, but I couldn't seem to focus. All the way to San Francisco, I prayed Hannah would make it safely to the house.

If that happened, I could face anything.

CHAPTER 23

GABE

After Lauren hung up, I called Dr. Fisher. She promised to meet us at the house. Then I motioned to Brian, the driver, who'd become one of my favorite members of the team over the past few weeks. "We need to get going. Ash said it had to be fast."

My gaze flicked to the seat next to me, where Hannah leaned back against the leather interior, looking frail and exhausted. I didn't want to mention that Li Na might be coming after us with guns, fighting to get her prize back.

Brian nodded. "Ash briefed me. I have three vehicles backing us up—we're ready for anything." He put the big SUV into Reverse, backing out slowly.

"Good." I turned to Hannah and hugged her gently but enthusiastically. "I'm so glad you're back."

"How's Wes?" she croaked.

I handed her some bottled water. "He's better," I lied. Brian's eyes met mine in the rearview mirror, and I shook my head. "We'll catch you up on everything just as soon as we get back."

"Gabe, wait—what's in San Francisco? I heard your brother say something about joining Lauren there. What's she doing?"

"Just going to a meeting." I kept my tone noncommittal.

"I know she wouldn't leave me with you and your SWAT team—after you literally *just* rescued me—to go to some random meeting." Hannah turned in her seat and grimaced as if in pain. "It's Li Na, isn't it?"

I nodded.

"Is Lauren actually selling that bitch our *company*? I'll—"

"Hannah. One thing at a time. Let's get you home, cleaned up, and checked out. Then you can kick some more ass."

"Fine," she said, but it didn't sound as though she meant it.

Brian pulled out of the Oakland neighborhood flanked by three other cars. I kept watch as we drove slowly out of the condominium complex, waiting to see if Li Na had more men nearby, at the ready.

I waited until Hannah seemed to drift off, then I called Levi. "How does it look over there?" I kept my voice down, trying to let her rest.

"I'm surprised you had the nerve to call me," he said by way of an answer, "after the crap you just pulled back at the scene. I know you think you might be better than me at my job, but you *don't* have the right to put my mission and my men's lives at risk. Do you understand?"

I swallowed hard, biting back the urge to argue. "Yes." Admitting I was wrong had never been my strong suit.

"You're not cleared for that sort of activity, and Agent Marks from the FBI's going to be livid." Levi paused, letting that sink in.

"I'm…I'm sorry." I *was* sorry. I could've been killed, or worse—I could've gotten one of the crew killed. My cheeks burned with remorse, and I was glad my brother couldn't see me. "I shouldn't have gone ahead of orders. But I had a clean shot—I felt like I had to take it."

"I'd dig into you, but I'll save your hide for Lauren to deal with. If I were you, I'd think about moving into the guesthouse tonight."

"Ha-ha," I said, but he was right, and I knew it. "We're on our way back to the house now."

"Is Brian driving? Is everything clear so far?"

"Yeah, and there's no sign of trouble. The security team's following us, and the doctor's meeting us at home to check Hannah out."

"How is she?"

"She seems okay—she's asleep. She's too skinny and she's bruised, but her spirits seemed good."

"I'm so glad."

"So am I. But I'll feel better when we get her home."

"The team has strict instructions. They're going to secure the premises as soon as you're through the gate. No one gets in except for the doctor, and they already have shifts to guard the perimeter."

"Good. One more thing." I swallowed hard. "Promise me...promise me you'll bring Lauren home. *Please.*"

My brother sighed. "I'm here with seven armed men—some in cars, some in the building already, some on rooftops nearby. Ash is already on his way here too. I've *got* her. I promise to bring her home safe and sound. Text us as soon as you're secure at the house, and keep an eye out. Li Na's going to be on the warpath."

"Will do," I said. "I'll see you soon."

"Yes, you will."

***

LAUREN

Hannah's alive. Hannah's on her way home. I repeated the information over and over to myself for a few minutes after we hung up. I had to let it seep in; I had to calm myself before I dealt with the next part of this day.

I refused to think about what Gabe had done—it made my head and heart pound with a dull fury. I'd deal with him later. I practiced yoga breathing to try to calm down on our way into the city. I didn't get an angry text or a phone call from Li Na, which I hoped was promising.

Ash texted me the address for a parking garage downtown, and we pulled in. I hugged him as soon as I saw him, waiting for us by the exit. "Thank you for saving Hannah."

He smiled tightly. "Don't thank me yet. I want to hear from Gabe that she's home safe, locked up like Fort Knox. Have you heard anything from Li Na?"

We headed down the steps to the street below. "She hasn't called. I hope that's a good sign."

"She might not know what happened, still," Ash explained. "We took them by surprise, and I personally confiscated all three guards' electronic devices first thing. Now the authorities have them. I doubt they've been given the opportunity to reach out to her."

"But I'm sure she knows something's up. She would have been in constant contact with them—she knows something's gone wrong."

"We'll see what happens," Ash said. "Also, Agent Marks said you owe him a phone call, and he needs to interview Hannah."

"I'll have Bethany call him—he's going to have to wait until we're both up to it."

"Fine." As we walked, Ash pointed at the rooftops of the nearby buildings in the Financial District. "We've got eyes all over the place, so you'll be safe. We're going to get you out of here, no matter what happens."

"Thank you." I didn't quite have it in me to feel completely at ease.

We quickly arrived at Sullivan & Wheelock, the upscale law firm where Li Na's attorney was a senior partner. Bethany was waiting on the sidewalk. "Everything okay?" she asked.

I reached out and hugged her. "Yes. I don't want to say anything more right now, but *yes.*"

Bethany's eyes sparkled. "Does this change things?"

"Maybe." *Maybe, if the car that's fleeing Oakland with Hannah and Gabe inside isn't intercepted before it gets back to the house.*

"Any instructions?" Bethany looked eager.

I shrugged. "Maybe just to drag this out a little, until I say so."

She nodded, looking happier than she had in weeks. "I love it when you have a plan."

Levi appeared on the sidewalk, seemingly from out of nowhere. "Are you ready?"

I nodded. "I think so. I haven't heard from her—Li Na—so I'm not sure how to proceed. I don't know how much her lawyer knows about what's been going on, and what's expected of me today." *Now that we just shot up Li Na's guards and rescued my sister.*

"We'll follow her lead, then. But listen," he said to me and Bethany, "if it seems like this is going south, you need to do what I say. Even *you*." He gave Bethany a warning look.

She rolled her eyes. "Okay. Geez."

"We might have to move fast," Levi said. "I hope not, but we're about to find out—so be ready, and stay alert."

My nerves thrummed as we went through the revolving doors. Bethany let out a low whistle as we entered the opulent lobby. "Can you imagine this firm's overhead? Yikes. You think *I* charge a lot. Imagine what Li Na's paying—oh wait, that's right. We don't care!"

Bethany checked in with the black-clad, immaculate receptionist. "We're on the sixth floor," she said, coming back and eyeing the group. "*All* of us."

There *were* a lot of us, I noticed as we filed into the elevator. In addition to Timmy, Levi, and Ash, there were three other Betts Security employees attending the closing. I wondered if Li Na's attorney, Petra Hickman, would be surprised by my entourage, or if she'd expect it.

Another sleek receptionist ushered us into a vast, modern conference room on the sixth floor. Levi took a seat at the table, close to me, while Ash and the others spread out around the room. Bethany started setting up her paperwork. "Petra texted me early this morning—she said she'd received the signed documents from Li Na via Federal Express."

I swallowed hard. "Then we should be good to go."

I looked nervously at the men. "Have you heard anything from Brian yet?"

Ash nodded. "They're on their way. No signs of trouble yet."

Yet. My heart pounded as I focused on the *yet.*

Attorney Petra Hickman sashayed through the doors in a stylish suit a few minutes later, a nervous-looking paralegal at her heels. Petra didn't even glance at the men I'd brought—Li Na must've prepared her well. Her tawny hair hung in perfect panes around her heart-shaped face; she would have been very attractive, but she had a nasty scowl on her face as she sized up me and Bethany.

"Let's get this over with, shall we?"

Bethany didn't look up from her files as she said, "It's a pleasure as always, Petra. Could we get some water, please?"

Petra rolled her eyes and got on the phone with an assistant, asking for water. She glared at Bethany when she hung up. "Anything else?"

Bethany smiled widely. "Just some coffee, with extra cream. And crackers, if you have them."

If Petra were a cartoon character, she would've had steam billowing out of her ears as she got back on the phone. When the water, coffee, and crackers arrived, she put a hand on her hip and glared at Bethany again. "Are you finally satisfied?"

"For now." Bethany jauntily tossed a bite of cracker in her mouth.

I cleared my throat, interrupting before Petra launched herself across the conference table at my attorney. "Let's get started."

The paralegal practically tripped over herself as she set up stacks of paperwork, casting nervous glances at her boss. Petra, clearly a joy to work with, ignored her and the rest of us. She tapped out nonstop texts and emails. I held my breath, praying that my sister was about to make it home.

The paralegal gingerly slid a stack of paperwork my way. I tapped out a text of my own before I started signing the documents. *Any word yet? Is Hannah safe?*

Gabe texted back right away. *No sign of trouble. Ten minutes from home.*

I blew out a deep breath and began signing. A few minutes later, I sent a text to Ash and Levi, even though they were in the room. *Things are about to get ugly.*

Levi replied immediately. *Goody. Are the two lawyers about to have a catfight?*

Choosing to ignore him, I went back to reviewing the patent transfer agreement in front of me. My nerves thrummed as the words swam in front of my eyes.

Bethany worked slowly through her stack of documents. It seemed to take longer than usual.

"Is there a problem?" Petra sniffed as Bethany checked and rechecked some numbers.

"I think it's important to be thorough," Bethany said. "You can't trust anyone these days."

Petra rolled her eyes. In response, Bethany reached for the document she'd just finished with and pretended to reread it.

I finished with the patent documents and moved on to the next pile. Halfway through the distribution agreement I was reading, my phone buzzed with a text from Gabe. *Home safe and sound. Locked up like Fort Knox. No sign of anyone tailing us. Your sister really seems okay, and Dr. Fisher's going to examine her.*

I fired off a response immediately. *Thank God.*

You can thank me for saving her later, he wrote. *Even better, you can thank me naked.*

You don't want to go there, I wrote back.

So...is this an appropriate time for me to beg for your forgiveness?

I looked at the pile of papers in front of me, my mind racing. *Later. I have some important shit to deal with right now.*

Important, revenge-like shit?

I suppressed a smile—it wasn't time for that. Not yet. *Something like that.*

Go get 'em, Your Highness. And come back to me, even if you aren't speaking to me. Yet.

"Hold on," I told Petra, putting the phone down. "Get Li Na on Skype. There's a problem. I need to talk to her, face-to-face."

Petra went pale. "What sort of problem?"

I could only image what Li Na would do to her attorney if she'd screwed something up. "Nothing you did. Just get her online. *Now.*"

Petra's nerves were clearly frayed as she barked at her paralegal, who went scampering for the laptop. Petra grabbed her phone and fired off a quick text, probably to Li Na. Her paralegal hustled back and set up the Skype site quickly, not looking at her boss.

"What the hell is this?" Li Na asked when she appeared on the screen. She wore one of her signature dark suits, her bright lipstick perfect as always. She glared at her attorney. "I'm waiting for an explanation."

Petra nodded stiffly. "L-Lauren wanted to talk to you. She said there's some sort of problem." She quickly turned the screen toward me, the coward.

"Li Na."

She narrowed her eyes. "What."

"You don't deserve my company."

"Not this again." Li Na rolled her eyes. "The concept of 'deserving' is so American, and so irrelevant. That sort of emotional thinking doesn't interest me. A seamless transaction for this deal *does*. I'm out of patience, Lauren—I never had much to begin with."

"I don't need you or your patience. *I have Hannah back.*"

If I'd surprised her, it didn't show—she didn't hesitate. "Events outside of this closing have no bearing on our agreement."

I leaned forward. "That's not how I see it."

"It doesn't matter how you see it. We have a contract, one that *I'm* prepared to honor. Today."

"It's not going to happen—not today and not ever."

She sighed, suddenly and dramatically. "I was hoping we could avoid any more…tactics."

"Do you know what *I* was hoping?"

Li Na blinked. "I'm sure you know I don't care."

"*I* was hoping that I'd have the opportunity to do this!" I grabbed the Purchase and Sales Agreement I'd signed and gleefully ripped it in half. I kept ripping until tiny pieces of paper fluttered all over the conference table.

Li Na arched an eyebrow as if she found my antics ridiculous.

Good. Let her. "Even more than that? I was really, *really* hoping I could tell you to fuck off today. That's what I've been hoping for. And now that my sister's safe, I can!"

I hopped up, smiling at the screen. "So, *fuck off, Li Na*! Paragon's still mine, and I'm taking it with me. If you try to come after me or my family again, I'll make you pay." I leaned toward her image on the screen. "No one messes with my family and my company and gets away with it. You want the patch? Figure out how biotechnological science works and make one of your own—oh, that's right, you *can't*, because you'll never be as smart as me, you murdering, kidnapping, conniving *bitch*!"

I slammed the laptop closed and proceeded to fan myself to calm down. I looked from Bethany to the others. Bethany was clapping, Petra had her fingers pressed against her temples, the paralegal looked like she might burst into tears, Levi was taking a video, and Ash and the other men looked thoroughly entertained.

"Let's go," I said. "I need to see my sister."

CHAPTER 24

GABE

It killed me not to go to the closing, but I'd promised to get Hannah home safe.

I paced while Hannah was being examined, waiting to hear from Lauren. If she'd done something to Li Na, I wanted to know what it was. More important, I wanted to know she was safe.

The minutes crawled by like hours. Finally, Levi texted me. *Lauren just told Li Na to fuck off and it was AWESOME. Got a video for you. We probably need to quadruple security. See you soon.*

He sent me the video, and I watched, speechless and incredibly turned on, as Lauren ripped up her contract and told Li Na to fuck off. *Finally.*

I immediately fired off a text to Charlotte, my UK distributor. She was waiting to hear from me. *Paragon isn't being sold to the Chinese. Please let the others know.*

Bloody brilliant, she wrote back at once.

Lauren is bloody brilliant, indeed, I texted back. As a backup plan, in case we'd been forced to close, I'd had Kami update all of Dynamica's agreements with our international distributors. Instead of a one-year waiting period, they'd had the instantaneous right to withdraw from their contracts upon the sale of Paragon Laboratories. And Charlotte had been about to get them all riled up for a mass exodus, just like I'd asked her to.

The revised documents had been approved by Li Na's attorney, but the revisions were buried in the thirty-fourth amendment of each agreement, located roughly on page nineteen. I'd done this so if Li Na bought Paragon, she'd get the company without its international distribution channels, a hobbled version of its former powerhouse self.

But it didn't matter anymore. Lauren had rescued the company, and Hannah was safe.

I smiled as I paced the hallway, waiting for my badass girlfriend to come home to me.

***

We'd set up one of the guest suites for Hannah. An hour after Levi had texted me, Lauren rushed inside, making a beeline for her sister. I followed close behind. Dr. Fisher was sitting on the far side of the room, talking quietly on her phone. Hannah was propped up on the bed, glowering at the IV tube connected to her forearm. It looked as though she'd showered; she was wearing an old T-shirt and leggings.

Lauren climbed onto the bed, gently wrapping her arms around her sister's bony shoulders. "You're too skinny, oh my God! I'm so sorry this happened to you."

Hannah patted her back. "It's okay. I'm okay."

They held each other and cried for a minute. I looked away.

Dr. Fisher ended her call and came closer. "Lauren, I'm sorry, but I need to get back to the hospital."

"Of course." Lauren pulled back and wiped her eyes. "And thank you so much for coming here—it means a lot."

"I'm happy to do it." The doctor took a step in, smiling at the sisters. "I did a thorough examination, and Hannah is mostly fine." Dr. Fisher and Hannah locked gazes briefly. "But I'll need to see her for a follow-up in my office."

"What can we do for her here?" Lauren asked.

"As I explained to Hannah, she *is* a bit dehydrated, so we took the precaution of starting an IV. You need to make sure she's drinking lots of fluids. I *also* explained to your sister that it's very normal to experience post-traumatic stress after something like what she's been through. She might need therapy, an antidepressant, or an antianxiety treatment—"

"And I told *you* that I'm fine." Hannah scowled at the doctor. "But I forgot to say thank you. I know you're super busy and that you made a special house call for me." She tried to sound conciliatory.

"It's my pleasure. I'm thrilled that you're home safe and okay," Dr. Fisher said. "I'll send one of my staff to check the levels later and change the IV."

"Thank you again," Lauren said. The doctor left, and she turned back to Hannah. "If Dr. Fisher says you need an antidepressant, you're taking an antidepressant."

"I don't *need* an antidepressant, and I don't need you bossing me around either!"

"Okay, okay. Easy." Lauren wrapped her arms back around her sister. "Let's not fight—let's hug."

"I'm glad to see you, even if you are bossy." The aggressive tone leached out of Hannah's voice, and she sounded gravelly with exhaustion. "Why did you guys have to go to San Francisco—is it what I think?"

Lauren pursed her lips. "You don't need to worry about anything right now—just rest."

Hannah sat up a little. "Don't tell me to rest—not when you just sold your multibillion-dollar company and the technology you've been working on for your entire adult life!" Hannah arched an eyebrow, a flash of her old self shining through.

"Okay." Lauren smiled. "I won't."

"Because…?" Hannah looked too afraid to be hopeful.

"*Because* I didn't sell Paragon. Not to that overdressed, unscrupulous hack known as Li Na Zhao, and not to any other bully either."

I held my phone out to Hannah, grinning. "I have a video of your sister telling Li Na to shove it. It's *awesome*."

Lauren blushed while Hannah watched the video, her hand clasped over her mouth. "Wow. I mean…*yeah*. Hell yeah." She looked up at me. "What've you been doing to my sister? I mean, don't answer that—"

"*You* inspired me," Lauren interrupted. "You fought this whole time, and you weren't afraid of anything. All I had to deal with was Li Na's sour face on a screen—you dealt with a lot worse than that. I figured it was the least I could do." She tucked a lock of Hannah's hair behind her ear. "Paragon is *ours*. We built it, and we're keeping it. We have to continue our work to help the greater good."

Hannah's eyes were wide. "You don't have to convince me."

"Your shares have gone up in value, by the way."

"Great. When I'm feeling better, I can go shoe shopping," Hannah joked.

"When you're feeling better, you can buy an entire shoe-manufacturing plant," Lauren corrected her.

Hannah looked stunned, but only for a moment. "How is Wes? Gabe swore he's fine, but I didn't believe him."

"He's still in El Camino." Lauren shot me a look. "He's doing better."

Hannah sat up straight. "I think you're lying too—why did you just look at Gabe like that?"

"I don't know what you're talking about," Lauren lied. "Just rest—*please*. And don't worry about Wesley right now. You've been through a lot, and you don't need to think about anything but recuperating." Lauren paused for a moment, her lips pursed as she inspected her sister. "Is there anything you want to tell me? Did they…do anything to you?"

"They didn't touch me—aside from the occasional chokehold or punch—if that's what you're worried about."

Lauren blew out a deep breath and put her face in her hands. "Okay."

"Can I go see Wes?" Hannah looked from Lauren to me. "Please?"

"Of course," Lauren assured her, "just as soon as you're feeling better."

Hannah sat up. Without flinching, she pulled her IV out. "I'm feeling better."

"Jesus, Hannah—"

I put my hand on Lauren's shoulder. "Let's bring her over. It'll be good for both of them."

Timmy had brought some clothes from the house. Hannah tore through the duffel bag, threw on a Stanford sweatshirt, and pulled on some UGG boots over her leggings. "Let's go."

Lauren looked tense, but to her credit, she didn't argue. She just followed her sister out the door.

Hannah was mostly silent on the drive to El Camino. "Tell me how Wesley is—how he *really* is. Tell me everything that happened. I told you—I thought he was dead. He was shot right in front of me, and he hit the island *hard*. The guards dragged me out of there right when it happened. I never even got to check him."

Lauren sighed and reached for her sister's hand. "When he got shot, the bullet nicked his heart. He passed out and hit his head when he fell—there was swelling from that, so the doctors decided to put him into a medically induced coma."

"Oh...oh God..." Hannah started crying.

"They wanted his body to have time to heal itself without more trauma. Everything was fine for the first few weeks."

"*But?*"

"But then he had an arrhythmia, and he had a mild heart attack. They're worried that his heart's been working too hard."

Hannah clenched her hands into tight fists. "Do they think he's going to be okay?"

"They *do*—"

"But they won't be one hundred percent sure until he's awake," I interrupted. Hannah needed to know what we were dealing with; we couldn't protect her from the truth forever.

"The doctors who are taking care of him are amazing," Lauren said. "They're the best. I'm sorry I didn't tell you everything."

"I understand." Hannah blew her nose, crying for another minute. It was hard news to deal with, not what she'd been expecting.

Finally, she calmed down. "I'm scared, and I'm worried, but I can't wait to see him. What's his brother like?"

"His name's Ellis," Lauren said. "He's special ops and he *looks* like he's special ops. I think he's bigger than Wes, and I didn't even know that was possible."

Hannah looked out the window. "Is he nice?"

"Yeah—I mean, he's quiet, but this is also hard on him, I'm sure."

"He's going to hate me."

Lauren looked sharply at her sister. "What are you *talking* about?"

"I'm the reason Wesley's in a coma and almost died. If there's something wrong with him when he wakes up—*if* he wakes up—it's my fault."

"Hannah." Lauren reached out and gently touched her sister, but she flinched. "No one blames you for what happened to Wesley. It was his job—"

"I was *distracting* him—"

"If this is anyone's fault, it's mine." Lauren's voice was sharp, but it was also shaking.

"I'm pretty sure this is my cross to bear." Hannah glared at her. "So *enough* of that."

"That goes for you too."

"Fine," Hannah said, turning back to the window.

"Fine," Lauren said.

We drove the rest of the way in tense silence. Ellis jumped up when we got to the lobby. "You must be Hannah." He approached her, and she stiffened as if she were expecting him to attack.

But instead, he hugged her hard.

She burst into tears. "I'm so sorry. I feel terrible about everything. Poor Wes!"

"You don't have to be sorry—it's his job, and I know he loved protecting you." Ellis rocked her back and forth, rubbing her back. "He's going to be so happy you're here. I'm so glad you're okay."

"Thank you. I...hope...he's going to be...happy I'm here." The words came out choked, in between racking sobs.

"Shh, it's okay." Ellis led her to a chair and handed her a tissue. "Take your time calming down, and then we can go see him."

I texted Dr. Kim, letting him know we were here and asking for any updates. *Most recent tests indicate normal brain activity,* he wrote back. *We will probably take him off medications to bring him out in the next few days.*

Hannah calmed down, wiping her eyes and straightening her shoulders. She nodded at Ellis. "I'm ready."

He motioned for us to follow, and we headed down the hall to Wesley's room. I sucked in a breath when I saw him—even though it'd only been a few days, it looked as though he'd shrunk in size. His skin and lips were pale and lifeless. I suddenly understood Dr. Kim's concern about atrophy. Wesley needed to be woken up so he could start moving around and regaining some strength.

At least, that was the *hope.*

Hannah didn't wince or hesitate—she rushed to Wes's side and laced her fingers through his. "Hey…it's Hannah. I'm back. I'm back, and I'm so, so sorry about what happened…" Her shoulders shook for few minutes as she cried.

She forced herself to recover quickly, taking a deep breath. "I met your brother. Kind of not the circumstances I was picturing, but he's still really nice…" She looked over and smiled at Ellis through her tears, then she turned back to Wes. "Oooh, and Gabe *rescued* me. Like, with a *gun*. Lauren hasn't forgiven him yet, but I bet *that's* going to be interesting—"

Lauren scowled. "*Hannah.*"

Hannah shrugged defensively. "Just catching him up." She turned back to Wes. "The point is, I'm home now, and I *need* you. Lauren was about to sell Paragon to You-Know-Who, but she ripped up the agreement. It was *badass.* I have it on video. We're ready to get back to work, but I need you with me…" She continued talking and crying, squeezing Wes's arm.

I motioned for Lauren to come into the hall.

I pulled her against me. "Do you want to leave them alone for a little while?"

She pressed her face against my chest. "For a few minutes."

"Do you want me to have Timmy take you home? You look exhausted. I can stay with Hannah for a little while longer, until she's ready to go."

"I don't think we should let her stay much longer. I haven't even mentally dealt with the fact that she disconnected her IV. We're going to have to call the doctor…" She leaned up and kissed my cheek. "I'm going back in. I'm worried she's running on adrenaline and she's going to collapse."

My phone buzzed with a call from Levi. "I'll be right there."

"Gabe—are you at the hospital?" Levi sounded tense.

"What's the matter?"

"It's Mom—she's fine, it's nothing serious. Well, it's sort of serious…"

"Can you please tell me what the hell is going on?" I roared, my nerves shot from the long, fraught day.

Levi sighed. "She wants to know if she should move back the wedding because of everything that's going on."

My body sagged in relief. "Oh."

"That doesn't sound like an answer."

"It's not up to me!"

"Mom thinks it is." Clearly, he thought this was a mistake.

I couldn't believe *this* was the newest crisis. "When's the wedding again?"

Levi *tsked.* "Next weekend."

"Tell her it's fine. Lauren and I will be there."

"Good—she'll be happy to hear it. I'll make sure that I have my best team covering Hannah and Wes."

"Great."

"It *is* great," Levi agreed, "especially because you're paying for all this coverage."

I pinched the bridge of my nose. "I'll see you at home."

"I'll be the one with the bourbon. See you soon."

CHAPTER 25

LAUREN

"The nurse is coming back over. They're going to reconnect your IV."

Hannah put her hands on her hips. "Call them and tell them to forget it—I don't need an IV. I need to be mobile; I'm going back in to see Wes first thing in the morning."

I sat on the bed and scooted over next to her so our shoulders were touching. "You've been through a lot, and you need to get better. You're no good to Wesley if you're not healing."

Hannah rolled her eyes. "I'm *fine*."

"Listen, I appreciate that you want to be there for him. I knew you would, and I think it's awesome. But you *have* to take care of yourself. Promise me."

"I promise." Hannah picked at her T-shirt for a minute. "But Lauren?"

"What?"

"What if...what if he's not okay when he wakes up? Or...what if he *doesn't* wake up?" Her voice cracked.

I hugged her to me. "Then we'll deal with it."

"Okay," she said, even as she wept against my chest. "Okay."

***

Later, after my poor sister had finally gone to sleep, Gabe and I went to bed. Gabe propped himself up a little, the sheet falling away from his broad chest. I looked away and then closed my eyes so I could think straight. "It's been a hell of a day."

"I know." He brushed the hair off my face and stroked my cheek. "I gotta tell you, I really wanted to go after Li Na myself. I was ready to fight her, and if I couldn't do that, I at least wanted to take out more of her guards. If I couldn't do *that,* I was looking forward to having all our international partners bail out and leave her in the dust. I would've enjoyed the hell out of that. But do you know what's so much better?"

"Um, no?"

He traced his thumb along my jawline. "Watching you rip up that contract and telling Li Na to fuck off. That was awesome. That was *hot*, babe."

"Thanks for the, er, compliment, but I'm still *very* upset about what you did. I thought I was going to lose you..." Even all these hours later, I shivered at how close he'd come to being killed.

"You couldn't lose me if you tried." He flashed his dimple.

"Don't try to use your dimple on me right now. I'm still angry at you. About the...shooting." I could barely get the word out. I shifted away, my wrath resurfacing. "It was terrible seeing you like that—I was so worried you were going to get killed. You don't have to prove anything to me, you know."

"I wasn't trying to prove anything to you."

"You don't need to prove anything to your brothers either."

He moved closer. "It didn't have anything to do with them."

"Then *why*? Why would you put yourself in harm's way like that?"

The muscle in Gabe's jaw jumped. "If things were different, I would say that the reason I did it was to prove something to *myself*. Because I wanted to know if I could be brave...if my father might've misjudged me. But I understand that my father didn't think I was weak—he just wanted to protect me. A very special person showed me that." He leaned down and kissed the top of my head. "So that's *not* why I went out there."

"I'm glad that's settled. But I'd like to know the real reason you risked your life."

"Because I love you. You're my *family* now, babe. I wanted to save your sister more than anything..." He looked over and gave me a tentative smile. "And I got to the car first. Okay?"

I could only pretend to be mad at him after that—he *did* save Hannah. "It's only okay because you're not dead."

"I appreciate that." He kissed me, our tongues connecting lazily at first. I started to get excited, to get wet with need as my heart rate picked up, my breath coming faster. My hands roamed over his chest, tracing the planes of his muscles greedily as he stripped off my clothes.

I wanted to stop, but I couldn't help myself. I wanted him, despite my exhaustion and my anger from earlier in the day. I *always* wanted him. My body reacted even as my mind told me to stop—that he should be punished for what he'd done, risking his life like that.

Still, as if they had a mind of their own, my hands ran down his back to his firm ass. I pulled him closer.

My body was such a traitor.

"I told you I'd enjoy having you thank me when you were naked."

"I didn't say thank you."

His eyes flashed. "You will."

"You really don't ever stop, do you?"

"You'd get bored if I did, babe."

Gabe nudged my legs apart with his knee and brushed his fingers along the inside of my thigh. I shivered in pleasure. His hand inched its way up to my soft folds, which he expertly parted. I moved eagerly against his hand, and he chuckled darkly. "You're still angry—I can tell—but you're also wet for me. I can *also* tell that."

He circled my clit, and I felt a sharp need radiate from deep inside me. My body ached for him, for him to fill me the way only he could.

Gabe spread my legs farther apart and put his face between my thighs, sighing happily. "I can't wait to get back in here. But I'm going to make you come like *this* first." His tongue lashed at me, causing my body to instantly spasm in response.

I cried out in spite of myself, and he laughed between my legs, his breath hot on my sex.

He toyed with my clit, lapping at it until I dug my fingers into his hair. He stopped for a moment and blew on my swollen nub, making me shiver. And then he put his mouth over me again, slowly and expertly.

I panted as he nipped me with his teeth. The combination of sensations was too much, and also exactly enough—I screamed as he overwhelmed me with sensations, pleasure ripping through me. And then I came, *hard*.

He kissed me gently and fingered my swollen clit. "I think you need more. You don't seem grateful enough." He gently pulled up my shaking body and rolled me over onto all fours. "So now I'm going to make you come like *this*."

I was woozy, breathing hard, still not recovered from the depth of my orgasm. But I still shivered in anticipation as he notched the top of his cock into me. He slid in an inch, and I cried out, my body quaking around him, wanting more.

Gabe filled me with his cock and started to thrust.

"Oh, *fuck* yeah!" I cried.

"That's my girl. I'll give you what you want, babe." He circled my asshole with his thumb and then slid it in gently so that every part of me was filled with him. He pressed down as he thrust, increasing the pressure and sensation. The edges of my vision blurred as another orgasm built inside me.

Gabe's thrusts grew more intense as he pounded the tension and frustration of the day into me. I took it greedily. His thumb slid in and out of my ass, fucking me, and I felt my body spasm and tremble, out of my control.

"Oh," I said, my voice quaking as I started to come again. "*Oh!*"

Gabe's hips thrust against me, and he cursed as he came in a hot torrent. I started to cry in joy and relief as my body crumpled around his, sucking his seed greedily out of him, overcome with pleasure, relief, and exhaustion.

All thought ceased. All anger ceased. There was nothing but me and Gabe, and for a brief, precious time, the rest of the world fell away.

"Babe?" he said later, when I'd thought he was asleep.

"Yes?"

"You're welcome."

And even though I could barely move and my brain was mush, I laughed.

***

GABE

"Are you sure you're going to be okay without us?" I asked Hannah as I followed her into the laundry room. She'd accepted our offer to stay and had settled in at the house. She'd been busy visiting Wes for hours every day, and she seemed to be getting back to normal—doing her laundry, catching up on email and texts from her friends and coworkers, stocking the refrigerator with sushi and foul-smelling green drinks from Whole Foods. Packages were being delivered every day from her online shopping efforts; she'd bought Wesley at least ten new pairs of very stylish pajamas.

"Yes, I told you. Go and have *fun*. Ellis and I will be with Wesley. Everything will be fine," she insisted. "Dr. Kim said he wants to run some more tests before they try to wake him up, so there's still nothing new with his condition. It's just a waiting game. Trust me, I can hold down the fort around here."

"You aren't afraid to be alone?"

She unleashed an eye roll on me. "I'm hardly alone—Levi has ten guys watching me."

"Well, then, good." I shrugged.

Hannah watched me from where she was standing, neatly folding her clothes. "Why are you still standing there?"

"No reason."

Her eyes sparkled. "Something's going on."

I shrugged. "Maybe."

"Is Lauren *pregnant*?" she shrieked.

"Shh—*no*."

Hannah jumped up and down. "Then what is it? Tell me."

"I wanted to ask your permission for something—"

Hannah launched herself at me, enveloping me in a hug. "You have it. And I *knew* it—I knew it!"

I hugged her back. "Please, don't say anything."

"Oh, I won't." She released me and started pacing, gleefully rubbing her hands together, a manic gleam in her eye. "We'll have to book the Ritz—no, that's too obvious—The Palisades. That'll be perfect! And I always wanted to see Lauren in a lace gown. I saw the perfect one in Ralph Lauren's bridal collection last spring… strapless…she'll have a fit, but tough luck. We'll have to have vegetarian-friendly catering, of course, but that shouldn't be a problem…"

"Hannah?"

She didn't seem to hear me—she just kept pacing and talking to herself. I backed out of the room, wondering if Lauren would ever forgive me for unleashing her sister, the ultimate event planner, on her impending nuptials.

That she didn't even know about.

And that she hasn't even said yes to, I reminded myself.

I swallowed over a sudden lump in my throat, then went to collect Lauren and my brothers to head back home to Boston.

CHAPTER 26

LAUREN

I got a text from Li Na as soon as we landed in Boston. *I'm not even close to done with you.*

Well, I'm sorry to hear that, because I'm certainly done with you, I texted back. *I know rejection's hard to handle, but you really need to stop embarrassing yourself like this. Take a hint and back off. Create some technology of your own, if you think you're so great.*

I smiled, then muted my cell phone.

Li Na had threatened to bring a lawsuit for breach of contract, violation of covenant not to compete, and to enforce the material terms of our now-defunct contract on the basis of constructive assent. Bethany assured me these were baseless claims. Frankly, the idea of Li Na having *us* prosecuted was laughable—I imagined if she acted as a witness and had to swear an oath, she'd burst into flames.

I tried not to worry about what Li Na might do. Hannah and Wes had a large, experienced security team watching them. Gabe and I had Timmy, Levi, Ash, and a whole unit assigned to us in Boston. Another full Betts Security unit was assigned to the grounds at Paragon. My employees were happily back to work, everything unpacked and back in order.

The patch's numbers continued to soar through the roof. I wondered how that made Li Na feel.

I laced my fingers through Gabe's, deciding to stop thinking about her, for the first time in what felt like forever. Instead, I looked at the charming lights of downtown Boston as we pulled up to the Four Seasons.

"It's nice having you right next to me," Gabe mused. "I'm sort of sad you're not going to be in the same office park."

"It's probably for the best." I winked at him. "This way, you and your big muscles won't distract me while I'm trying to work."

He flashed his dimple. "Babe, stop." He threw his arm around me. "Just kidding. Please go on about my big muscles."

A few minutes later, we were ushered to our room. "This is…opulent," I said as Gabe tipped the bellman. I turned in a circle, looking around our suite. There were overstuffed chairs, dozens of carefully selected throw pillows, crystal chandeliers, and vases filled with flowers. A fire roared in the fireplace, completing the enticing, luxurious atmosphere.

"My mother insisted we stay here." Gabe closed the door and swept me into his arms. "She wanted everything to be absolutely perfect for the wedding. The reception's here, and she didn't want us traveling anywhere else. She doesn't want to let us out of her sight."

My stomach twisted with nerves. "But she's never even *met* me."

"My brothers have met you—and they both like you. Even Levi, and he never likes anybody." Gabe grinned. "My mom's going to *love* you. She'll probably love you so much, you'll have to wipe yourself down with a sanitizing wipe once I peel her off you. And you already know my soon-to-be-stepfather—he's a big fan of yours. So stop worrying."

Cynthia Betts's fiancé was an old professor of mine from MIT, Alexander Viejo. I hadn't seen him in years, but I could never forget him. He was a famous biochemist and also a brilliant professor. I'd audited one of his senior-level classes my sophomore year and found him fascinating. It would be wonderful to have another scientist around, someone to brainstorm with.

Gabe's phone buzzed. He looked at it, a deep V forming in his brow. "Here we go," he said, right before he answered it. "Hi, Mom." He rolled his eyes at me as she jabbered away on the other end of the line.

I got up and headed into the bedroom to give him some privacy. I marveled at the enormous, ornately carved four-poster bed. At least the bed, and what we could do in it, would make Gabe happy. He seemed genuinely stressed out about spending time with his family, which was funny. The big, bad alpha CEO's mother gave him a headache.

I went to the walk-in closet and examined my clothes. Since she'd been feeling better and had too much time on her hands, Hannah had insisted on buying me an entire new wardrobe for this trip. "You're meeting his *mother*, Lauren. This is it," she'd said, packing dress after dress into my garment bag.

"This is *what*?" I'd asked.

Hannah looked pained, as if I were about to leave the house wearing white after Labor Day. "Never mind."

I touched the different clothes she'd chosen for me. The outfits were beautiful and stylish, more formfitting than anything I was used to wearing. They'd also cost the equivalent of a year's tuition at a trendy boarding school, but Hannah wouldn't listen to my protests.

Gabe poked his head in, looking wary. "We have an hour, then they're on their way up."

"Who?"

"All of them." He sighed and looked at the bed, then looked back at me. "Do you think we have time to…take the edge off a little?"

I arched an eyebrow. "Whatever do you mean?"

Gabe closed the space between us, pressing his lips to my neck. He rubbed his thickening cock against me, making me swoon.

"I mean something like this." He grabbed me, hoisting me up until my legs were wrapped around him. "Hmmm…now, what should I do with you, babe? So many positions, so little time…"

"Whatever you want. You know I'll like it."

He laughed, setting me back on the ground. He kissed me deeply, making me woozy. "You *will* like it. Now, walk over to the bed and just stand there. Don't turn around."

I did as I was told, listening to him as best I could over my own breathing, which had turned ragged. He unzipped his suitcase and, after rustling around for a bit, came back, still behind me where I stood at the foot of the bed. "Put your hands up over your head."

I did, and I watched him twine one of his ties around my wrists to the bedpost. He pulled it tight.

Gabe was tying me up.

"Um…honey?"

"What, babe?" He feigned innocence.

"Should we really be doing this right before I meet your mother?"

"Can you maybe not talk right now?" He tied the tie carefully in a knot, then tested it, making sure it wouldn't give. Then he grinned, his dimple on full display. "Babe, I am *going* to fuck you like this. From behind. While I bend you over. Hard. Deep. And you aren't going to be able to get away from me."

My body shook in anticipation. I licked my lips again. "I don't ever want to get away from you."

"You might in a minute." His grin turned wicked. "When you're begging to come, and I won't let you until I say it's time."

I groaned—not this again.

"Just relax, babe. I love you. You can trust me."

"I know—so can you hurry up?"

He chuckled, then undid my bra and freed my breasts, which felt heavy and full as he took them in his hands. He caressed my sensitive nipples and rubbed his cock against my ass—my panties were already drenched. He grabbed the thin material of the bikini strap and ripped them off me.

He held up the flimsy scraps of material. "Too bad. These were nice." He pulled my hair back and kissed my neck as I relished the feel of his naked, hard body against mine.

All that was left were the heels. And his tie, tight around my wrists.

"One more thing. I'm going to blindfold you."

My heart rate quickened as he placed another tie gently over my eyes and fastened it at the back of my head. "I just want you to feel." He kissed my neck. "I want you to forget everything else." With my sight gone, the painful rush of desire between my legs seemed that much sharper and in focus. I noticed again how hard I was breathing. He had me now. I couldn't see, and I couldn't use my hands. I was naked and defenseless against him, and all I wanted was his dick.

He sure knew what he was doing.

I backed up against his cock. He grunted, then laughed a little. "This is why I had to tie you up. Otherwise, you'd just get your way. Now lean over as far as you can. I want to see you."

With my hands tied to the bedpost, I could only bend over enough to expose my sex. I heard Gabe kneel behind me, then he exhaled hotly against my slit. "This is fucking perfect," he said as he dove in. He licked me from back to front. By the time he reached my clit and pulled it between his teeth, I was quivering, already close to coming.

So of course, he stopped. *Dammit.* He took the tender bud in between his teeth again, making me cry out. He stuck two fingers inside me, fucking me insistently, until I was about to explode. Then he pulled them out and took his mouth off me, leaving me on the edge. My body shook, desperately wanting the release Gabe was keeping from me.

I heard him stand up and finally felt his cock between my legs. He trailed it up and down my slit, getting it slick with wetness, and allowed me to grind my clit against it for a few glorious moments. Then he grabbed my hips and positioned himself against me. "Lean back toward me. We don't have much time." His voice was thick and urgent.

I used my wrist restraints to hold me up as I leaned back. Gabe's hands were on me, pulling me down onto the head of his glorious erection. He proceeded to thrust into me, entering me swiftly, all the way. *Holy fuck.* He went so deep, I saw stars underneath my blindfold. He held on to my hips and bounced me up and down on his hard length, grunting, finding his own fast, hard pace.

I groaned and bucked against him, wanting to feel him explode deep inside me, needing my own release. He continued to thrust, and I continued to take it—he was in deep, thrusting hard, unyielding, just the way I liked it. Gabe held me tight, grunting. I could feel the power of his orgasm building as he flexed his hips and cursed—and then poured his hot release into me. My body clenched and shook around him. His fingers went to my clit and circled it, pushing me over the edge, my whole world going white as I almost blacked out from the intensity of my orgasm.

My body rocked against him. Then eventually, utterly depleted, I went limp. He carefully pulled out and, without letting go of me, undid the tie around my hands. I weakly pulled off the blindfold as we collapsed onto the bed. My legs felt like jelly.

Gabe opened one eye and looked at me, a satisfied smile on his face.

"What?" I could only manage the one syllable.

"I love you." He kept his eye open. He clearly had something else to say.

"And what else?"

He closed his eye, still grinning. "And you better get cleaned up—you have to meet my mother in fifteen minutes."

"Ugh—*stop*!"

He held up the tie he'd blindfolded me with. "How about I wear this tonight?"

"Shut *up*."

And then, even though we had a million things we needed to do, we both collapsed in giggles.

***

The giggles came to an abrupt halt when Gabe's phone buzzed a little while later. "Oh boy. My mother says she can't wait any longer—they'll be here in a few minutes."

I yelped and headed directly to the shower.

After the fastest shower in human history, I threw on some Hannah-approved clothes. I did my makeup in three minutes—I didn't need much; I had a post-sex-with-Gabe glow.

Gabe kept talking as he showered. "She's so excited, she's mortifying. Be prepared for lots of hugging and excitement."

"About the wedding?"

"No—she's excited about me and you. Mostly just you. She's a little…exuberant, is all. You'll see."

A few minutes later, there was a knock at the door, and Gabe briefly put his face in his hands. "Get ready for the firing squad."

"Gabriel!" Cynthia Betts whooped as soon as she came through the door, followed by Levi, Ash, and Alexander Viejo.

Cynthia was petite, with an elegant blonde chignon. Still, she locked her much larger son in a bear hug, rocking him back and forth. "My baby."

I could see his back stiffen. "Mother, I'm not a *baby*."

She pulled back and swatted him. "You'll *always* be my baby."

Then, as if she had a homing device, she turned toward me. "You must be Lauren." She swept me into her arms, and now it was my turn to be rocked back and forth.

"Mom, you're probably cutting off her circulation." Gabe sounded mortified.

She ignored him, pulling back to inspect me. "Well, I can see why Gabe's wild about you—you're stunning. And a *natural* blonde. I didn't even know God made those anymore. You look like an angel."

Gabe groaned while I smiled at his mother. "Thank you. I'm honored to meet you—you raised a wonderful man."

Cynthia's eyes filled with tears, and she started fanning her face, trying to protect her makeup. "Thank you. I'm just so glad you can appreciate him. He can be *so* difficult, and he's controlling, I was starting to wonder if he'd ever—"

"Mom!"

"Oh honey, sorry." But she didn't look sorry. She clapped her hands, and her face broke into another wide smile, revealing her perfect teeth. "This is the best day ever. All my boys are here, I finally get to meet Lauren, and I'm getting married tomorrow!"

Gabe and Alexander were catching up, so Cynthia took the opportunity to pull me over to the couch. "You know, dear, none of my boys have ever been in a serious relationship that lasted. Levi was engaged once, but we don't speak about that, not ever. *Tara.* If I even say her name, he goes ballistic." Her eyes were wide. "But I'm excited, and I'm babbling. I'm *so* happy to hear that you got your sister back—but I'm sorry for all the trouble you've been through."

"Thank you. She's home now, and she's safe. We're still waiting to see how her boyfriend's doing, but I'm trying to stay positive."

She nodded, and I could tell that she was listening to me intently, filing away each detail. She kept smiling, reaching out, and holding my hands. She asked me more about how I'd met Gabe, then questions about Hannah, my company, and my parents. Five minutes into the conversation, we were both sniffling into our respective Kleenexes. There was just something about the Betts family... The last thing I ever wanted to do was talk about my personal life or the loss of my parents, but they had this way of extracting things from me.

"I'm so sorry about your mom and dad." She blew her nose with one hand and patted my knee with the other. "Gabe was just in third grade when Lou died. It broke my heart to watch him cry like that."

I don't know if Gabe heard his name or finally noticed both of us were crying, but he extricated himself from the men and came over. "What's wrong?"

Cynthia blew her nose again. "Nothing, dear. Lauren and I were just talking about her parents, and I was just telling her about Lou. It's terrible to lose the people you love."

She reached over and held my hand. "But *we're* family now. You won't ever be alone again."

"You just might wish you were," Gabe said under his breath.

His mother swatted him again. "That's enough out of you. Now, tell Alexander to come over. He's been looking forward to seeing Lauren again."

He must've heard us, because he ambled over immediately. Just as I remembered from my time at MIT, Alexander was a dapper dresser, wearing an impeccable shirt and tie.

I shook his hand. "So nice to see you, Professor."

He smiled, his eyes crinkling at the corners as he pulled me in for a brief hug. "I consider it an honor to see you again. I'm thrilled that our paths have reconnected. You left school too early, you know."

"Alexander. Do not badger her!" Cynthia called good-naturedly.

"All right, all right," the professor said easily. "But I can't wait to catch up with you and hear about all the wonderful things you've done. Thank goodness we'll all be a lot closer soon and have more time."

"Closer?" I asked, confused.

He just winked and patted my arm.

Ash and Levi came over, both already wielding bourbon. Ash leaned over to hug me. "We missed you this afternoon. I'm getting used to being your roommate."

"Don't get too used to it," Gabe said under his breath.

I had a feeling there was going to be a lot of that—the talking under his breath—this weekend. Gabe was regressing into a petulant teenager before my eyes.

Of course, being madly in love with him, I found it adorable.

"Lauren, I feel like I need a hug too," Levi said, reaching in. "All we've done is work since I met you—we haven't had any fun."

Gabe moved next to me and protectively wrapped his arm around my shoulders. "You can stop touching her now."

Levi laughed and released me. "Do you believe this guy? He can't even stand to share you for a second. Ever since I took little Evie Brittain to the prom, you just can't let it go—"

"You knew I was going to ask her," Gabe said heatedly. "You could've asked anybody else."

Levi smiled wickedly. "Yeah, but Evie was nice. Classy." He got a dreamy look in his eyes, and Gabe's grip tightened around me.

Levi took a sip of his bourbon, and I realized that he'd started drinking on our flight, hours ago. "You know who else is nice?" He leaned toward me conspiratorially. "Your lawyer."

I sat up straight. "*Bethany*?"

Next to me, Gabe cursed while Ash did a double fist pump, celebrating as though he'd just scored a winning touchdown. "Yes! I *called* it. Pay up." He held out his hand to Gabe, who was fishing in his wallet.

Gabe handed him a hundred-dollar bill, cursing some more.

Levi watched the exchange, scowling. "You guys were betting on me?"

Ash shrugged good-naturedly. "I knew you thought she was hot—she's got all that swishy blonde hair, and she keeps bossing you around."

"Which is totally your type," Gabe said.

Levi puffed his chest out. "Is not."

Gabe puffed *his* chest out. "Is too."

"Aw, come on—knock it off." Ash held up the money. "The drinks are on me. Let's get this wedding party started!"

Both Gabe and Levi deflated and amiably accepted Ash's offer for drinks. I learned, over the next few hours, that with Gabe's family in celebration mode, there were drinks followed by more drinks. I lost track of how many bourbons they drank after we headed downstairs to the lounge, drinking, laughing, and eating until the place closed. Once Gabe loosened up, he and his brothers told story after story about growing up in Boston, and how wild they were after their father had passed away. Cynthia rolled her eyes at many of their stories. Others made her threaten to retroactively ground them.

They talked about Lou. "He was tough, but he was a good man," Cynthia said, dabbing her eyes.

She patted Alexander lovingly on the arm, making sure his feelings weren't hurt because she was speaking of her late husband. He nodded at her kindly, encouraging her to continue.

"He would be so proud of you boys today," Cynthia said. "You've become great men, just like him. I even think he would approve of me marrying Alexander. He told me on his deathbed that he wanted me to move on. To live my life to the fullest."

She took another sip of her wine and motioned to her boys. "But all I wanted when you kids were growing up was to be there for you. To be a good mother. Even though you boys ran a little wild, you always came home. You were always my good boys."

The brothers all looked touched. Gabe raised his glass in a toast. "To Mom. I'm so glad that you've finally found someone extraordinary to share your life with. You deserve it. Alexander, as you are a biochemist, a genius, and a tenured professor, I expect that you will be very civilized and take excellent care of my mother. Not that she needs it—we all know she can take care of herself. And the rest of us." Gabe secured his arm around my waist, pulling me closely against him, making me feel included, safe, and loved. Making me feel like I was part of the family.

"To Mom," Levi said, raising his glass.

"Mom," Asher said.

I clinked my glass too, feeling warm and happy inside.

Cynthia dabbed her eyes again. "I'm so glad we're all going to be close again," she said, sniffling. "I missed my Gabey. And now, especially with Lauren in the picture, being in California's going to be so much fun."

I felt Gabe stiffen. "Huh?"

"Alexander's accepted a faculty position at Stanford, sweetheart," Cynthia said. "So we're moving out in the spring. And your brothers are too. Levi's decided to expand his West Coast operations."

Gabe turned to Levi. "Why didn't you tell me you'd made it official?"

"Don't sound so excited," Levi said. "Besides, the way you're burning through my agents, you should be relieved that we'll be closer. I'll be able to ship an endless amount of men over, and I won't have to charge you airfare for a change." He grinned at Gabe.

"I'm coming too," Asher said. "I'm sick of the winters out here. Besides, I wouldn't want Mom to miss me too much…since I'm her favorite."

There were more drinks, discussions about the upcoming move, then we all stumbled off to our respective hotel rooms. By the time we climbed into bed, I needed a fire hose, or quite possibly a gamma ray, to blast Gabe's booze breath away from me.

He crawled toward me on the bed with droopy eyes and a happy, slightly dazed look on his face. "Lauren, I'm coming for you…"

I rolled out of his way as he collapsed onto my pillow. "Babe." His voice came out muffled. "Where'd you go?"

I couldn't help laughing. "Away from your dragon-like breath, *babe*. Go to sleep. I think you and your brothers finished almost all the alcohol in the bar."

"Babe. Come back." His voice was still muffled against the pillow.

"I'm not going anywhere." I sank back down beside him on the bed and ran my fingers lightly through his coarse hair. "I will not be kissing you until that breath has abated—hopefully by tomorrow—but I promise, I'm not going anywhere."

Ever. Because, after being lonely my whole life, I'd finally found a home.

***

GABE

The wedding was scheduled for four o'clock at the Parish of St. Paul in Cambridge, affiliated with Harvard University—Alexander was a proud graduate, and I was an equally proud dropout. After the ceremony, we'd head back to the Four Seasons for the formal, proper reception Cynthia had planned. More than two hundred guests would attend the black-tie affair.

I adjusted my tuxedo while Lauren finished with her makeup. "I don't know why my mother's insisting on having a big, formal wedding. It's her second marriage, and quite frankly, they're *old.*"

"Stop." Lauren frowned at me. "She seems happy—I think she wants to celebrate. Plus, she said they have a lot of friends coming. It's sort of a going-away party for them too."

I popped an ibuprofen—my mother's impending move, my persistent hangover, and my nerves about *other things* were giving me a headache. "I can't believe they're all moving out to California. I have a feeling they're going to try to cramp our lifestyle."

"You should be excited." Lauren hustled out to the bedroom to get dressed. "You're lucky that they're going to be close by. I think it's wonderful."

I followed her, looking for my other cufflink, and saw Lauren zipping up her dress.

My heart stopped as I looked her up and down. "Holy *shit*, babe."

"What—is this not the right kind of dress?" She looked panic-stricken as she smoothed it. "Hannah picked it. Oh no."

"Stop right there. Turn and look at me, so I can see the whole thing."

She stopped and turned. The black-sequined gown was floor length, strapless, and fit snugly, embracing her curves. I put my hand over my heart, making sure it was beating again. "I take back what I said about my mother insisting on a formal wedding. I'm thrilled about it."

"Okay...?" She sounded confused.

"You look absofuckinglutely gorgeous in that dress."

"Oh. Huh. Thanks." Her shoulders relaxed. "You look very handsome. I've never seen you in a tux before."

"That's because I can't breathe in them."

She grinned at me. "I can't breathe in this either."

"We're quite the pair, aren't we?"

I closed the distance between us and pulled her against me, wrapping my arms carefully around her waist. "I want to kiss you—actually, I'd like to push you back on the bed and utterly defile you—but that dress looks delicate, and I know you just finished your makeup. I can't wait to show you off to everyone. Now I'm glad my mom and Alexander invited everyone they know in Boston. All the more people I can parade my beautiful, brilliant girlfriend in front of."

Lauren blushed, but she looked pleased. "Stop."

"Not ever, babe."

CHAPTER 27

LAUREN

The Catholic ceremony seemed to go on forever. My agnostic parents had never taken us to church, and I was baffled by all the sitting, standing, and kneeling—but it *did* help me figure out how to maneuver my dress without ripping it. Good thing Gabe was one of the attendants. He would've laughed if he'd seen me struggling to keep up with the priest's nebulous instructions.

When the priest announced Alexander and Cynthia as husband and wife, the crowd cheered. The couple grinned at each other and sealed their vows with the traditional kiss. When they turned to face the pews, they both looked exuberant.

Gabe turned from his mother and stared at me, an intense look on his face. I smiled, and he flashed his dimple, but his eyes were fiery...almost as if he were seeing me for the first time.

***

Back at the Four Seasons, enormous floral arrangements dominated each table. A giant crystal chandelier and hundreds of flickering candles washed the room in a warm, elegant glow.

Even with the gorgeous backdrop, Gabe's mother stole the show. She couldn't stop smiling, and her enthusiasm as she held on to Alexander while hugging her family and friends was infectious.

She greeted me warmly, pulling me in for a hug. "You're so beautiful, Lauren."

She turned to Gabe, giving him a long, admonishing look—almost as if she was about to ground him—then leaned over and whispered something in his ear.

She winked at me when she pulled back.

A faint blush crept up Gabe's cheek—something I'd never seen before. He glowered at her. "See you on the dance floor, Mother."

Gabe pulled me away and hustled me through the reception, grabbing two flutes of champagne as we went. "Please don't let her scare you away."

I shook my head. "I *love* your mother." She had many of the same good qualities as Gabe. She was open, confident, and loving. Gabe had all those traits, but they were wrapped in an aggressive, relentless package; his mother wore them more softly.

He had a long sip of champagne—more like a slug. "She's obviously crazy about you. In an absolutely mortifying way."

"What did she just say?" I didn't mean to pry, but he seemed rattled.

He scrubbed a hand over his face. "She wanted to talk logistics."

"Logistics of what?"

Gabe suddenly held my pocketbook—which he'd been carrying for me—up to his ear. "I think that's your phone. You should check it in case it's Hannah."

It *was* Hannah's number on the screen. I answered immediately. "Are you okay?"

"I'm fine," she sobbed.

My heart pounded in my ears. "Then why are you *crying*?"

"Wes is awake." She erupted into fresh sobs. "He's awake and he's *okay*."

"Gabe, Wes is okay—"

Gabe squeezed my hand. "I can hear her."

"Is he lucid?" I asked.

"Yes. That's what I was worried most about—and he *was* a little disoriented at first—but he's okay! Everything is normal. He doesn't remember getting shot, but that's probably a good thing..."

"What did Dr. Kim say?"

Hannah blew her nose. "He said he's going to make a full recovery, but the rehabilitation process could take a long time. He needs to be careful about his heart, and the atrophy is pretty bad, so he'll have to do an aggressive course of physical therapy. *But* he's stable enough to be moved out of ICU, probably tomorrow."

"That's amazing." I clutched Gabe's hand. "Please tell him Gabe and I send our love—we'll be home tomorrow afternoon. I can't wait to see him."

"Tell him I'm thrilled," Gabe said, joy and relief evident on his face.

Hannah sniffled. "I will."

"Okay. I love you."

"I love you too—but wait, don't hang up!"

"What's the matter?"

"Nothing." Hannah blew her nose again. "I just wanted to see...what's new with you."

"Um, nothing? Except I'm at a wedding on the other side of the country, and I met Gabe's mother for the first time. But you already knew that."

"But what's...*going on*?"

I looked around hopelessly, wondering what she meant. "We're in Boston at Gabe's mother's reception. The wedding was beautiful. I'm wearing the dress you picked out, and I can't breathe in it."

"She looks totally hot," Gabe called, "so I owe you one."

"But nothing's *new*?" She sounded crestfallen.

"No—what're you even talking about?"

"Ugh, it's nothing. Call me tomorrow, okay? Or tonight...if you feel like it."

"Okay?"

We hung up, and I shook my head, confused. "Something is up with my sister."

"Huh," Gabe said, but he didn't ask me anything further.

Huh.

He tipped his champagne flute against mine. "Cheers. To Wesley. That's amazing news."

"Cheers." My heart swelled with joy. "I can't believe he's awake and he's okay."

"I know. I didn't know what was going to happen. But he's a fighter, just like your sister."

We stopped and drank our champagne. Holding his hand, knowing that Hannah and Wesley were okay, I felt elated and calm for the first time in weeks. I squeezed Gabe's hand again, reveling in the newfound peace in my heart.

I turned and found Gabe watching me, another intense look on his face. "Have you ever been to a wedding before?" he asked.

"Sure—but nothing like this. I went to my cousin's wedding when I was twelve. It was a backyard-barbecue sort of thing."

"Which one do you like better?"

"I don't know. I was twelve, Gabe. The whole thing seemed very dramatic to me, even though we sat on folding chairs in my aunt's backyard. This is obviously much more sophisticated."

He smiled, but there was still something off about his face. "I mean do you prefer a smaller wedding? Or do you like all of this?" He motioned around the opulent reception.

"I don't...I don't know," I said, because I didn't. I'd never been a girl who'd dreamed of her wedding day. I'd dreamed of curing cancer and eliminating greenhouse gases. The only white garment I'd ever pictured myself wearing was a lab coat.

"Never mind." He shook his head as if he could read my thoughts. "Would you like to dance?"

I looked at the couples beginning to swirl on the dance floor. "Um..." I could barely walk in my dress.

"I'll lead," Gabe said, sensing my discomfort.

I finished my champagne, bracing myself for the worst. "Please don't let me trip."

He held out his hand to me. "Never."

Gabe held me close as we danced, so close that I didn't even have to pretend I knew how. My nerves melted away as I swayed against his chest, happy and content, oblivious to the crowd around us. He put his cheek against mine, not saying a word, just holding me in time to the music. At the end of the song, he kissed me deeply, right out on the middle of the dance floor.

Heat surged through me. I clung to him, oblivious to the dancers around us. I wanted more.

I always wanted more.

He kissed me again, gentler this time. Then he placed his forehead against mine. "I love you." His voice was husky.

I smiled at him, but he didn't smile back. "You know I love you too. But what's the *matter*? I feel like you're not telling me something."

"It's nothing." He reached over and stroked my cheek.

For the rest of the night, Gabe kept his hands firmly on me. We danced, we ate, we drank with his brothers, laughing and telling stories. He didn't let go of me once.

By the time the reception wrapped up, I wanted his hands everywhere. His touch burned my skin, and my body ached for him.

"My brothers want us to change and go to their suite for more drinks," Gabe said in the elevator ride back to our floor.

I smiled, trying to mask my disappointment. "Of course."

Gabe turned suddenly, pinning me against the wall of the elevator. He grinned wickedly. "I told them I had some important business to attend to first." He crushed his lips against mine, and I arched my back so I could mold my body to his. I could feel his erection pressing against me, hot and hard.

He broke free and looked at me, his brown eyes sparkling. "As long as that's okay with you, that is."

I grabbed him by the tuxedo lapels and greedily pulled him closer. "I thought you'd never ask."

***

Later, after we'd made love twice, Gabe sat propped up in bed, stroking my hair. He had that same thoughtful look on his face, as though something were eating at him.

"Are you upset about your mother getting married?"

He shook his head as if to clear it. "Not at all. Why do you ask?"

I ran my fingers along his jawline. "You just seem like something's on your mind."

He kept stroking my hair. "You are, as usual, correct."

I grinned, trying to lighten his mood. "That's because I'm brilliant."

"You *are* brilliant. Among other things."

"That doesn't sound good—what sort of other things?"

He tucked a lock of hair behind my ear. "Sometimes you're hard to read, babe."

"Really?"

"Really."

A warning alarm sounded inside my head, and I sat up. "Did I do something wrong?" We'd been social nonstop since we'd arrived in Boston. Introverted, uptight nerd that I was, I'd probably said or done the wrong thing. Maybe I'd embarrassed him.

"Of course not—boy, I am messing this up."

I sat there, my brow furrowed.

"My family loves you, Lauren. You can relax your forehead."

That made me feel better, but I continued to scowl, waiting for him to continue.

He sighed. Then he lay back, putting his hands behind his head, and stared at the ceiling for what felt like forever. I wasn't sure if he was going to say anything else.

All of a sudden, he laughed—a deep, guttural sound that seemed out of his control.

"What's so funny?"

He stopped laughing, but it took him a minute. "I'm *nervous.*" A funny look crossed his face, as if he smelled something repugnant or had a sour taste in his mouth. "This is a first for me. Obviously, I'm not handling it well."

"You're going to have to elaborate. I'm totally lost."

He propped himself up on one arm to gather his thoughts—at least I got to admire his sculpted bicep while I waited.

"You know how my mother was whispering to me earlier? That's what I'm nervous about."

I still had no idea what was going on. "Okay..."

"Although she wanted to talk about logistics, and I'm more nervous about the actual execution—and the outcome, of course."

"Of course. But can you tell me *what* the heck you're talking about?"

He laughed again. "This isn't going how I'd planned."

I said nothing, waiting for him to make sense.

Gabe sighed, raking his hand through his hair and getting up from the bed. He dithered around—at least I got to admire his ass and his muscled thighs for a moment, until he pulled his boxer briefs on. "Why are you getting dressed?"

He held out one of his old Harvard T-shirts for me. "Put this on. We can't do this naked."

That didn't sound promising. My scowl deepened. I wanted to stay in the warm bed, but I pulled the T-shirt on.

He patted the edge of the bed. "C'mere."

I suspiciously went and sat near him. He knelt on the ground in front of me, raking his hands through his hair, making it spike. I longed to smooth it, but I held back, waiting for him to speak.

"So—logistics. I need to get this out of the way first." He grabbed my hands and looked up at me. "I don't think this is the best timing, but in other ways, it's the absolute best timing—because it's now, and I don't want to wait anymore."

I nodded, swallowing over a sudden lump in my throat.

"But my mother said this was all she wanted for a wedding present, so I consider that her blessing."

I opened my mouth and then closed it.

"Babe. You know who I am, and you accept me. But *I* knew me before—and I know that I'm a better man because of you."

"Oh...thank you."

Gabe's eyes widened. "No—thank *you*. Because you've given me the life I always wanted. You've inspired me, and you inspire me every day. I consider it an honor to know you. I mean that. I love you so much, babe."

My eyes filled with tears, but I held them back. "I love you too."

"*Good.*" Gabe seemed to relax a fraction. "But back to logistics. My mother got married today."

"I know. I was there."

"Lauren, your genius is showing." He flashed a dimple. "Because this was her day, I didn't think this was the right time..."

I bit my lip. I wanted to ask: *The right time for what?* But I felt suspiciously like I might burst into tears.

"But she insisted it was. She said she was too old to have her thunder stolen."

"Babe?"

"Yes?"

"Can you *please* tell me what you're talking about?"

He laughed to himself, and I saw his dimple. I reached out to stroke his cheek.

He pulled the nightstand drawer open and brought out a small, square box, then looked up at me. "My father gave this to my mother—it isn't much. It was all he could afford."

I could see the muscles in his throat work as he swallowed, and I almost lost it.

He opened the box, and there was a ring inside—a simple gold band and a solitary, circular diamond.

"I wanted you to have this ring because it's special to me. I know how much my dad loved my mom—I love *you* that much. And I want to ask you: will you marry me? I want to spend the rest of my life with you."

I opened my mouth to respond and promptly burst into tears.

Gabe pulled me to him, cradling me in his arms. I thought he might be crying too, but I couldn't be sure. Once I finally calmed down, he pulled back. "Was there an answer in there somewhere?"

"Yes. The answer is yes."

A look of pure joy, the likes I'd never seen, broke out over his face. "I'm so glad."

He slid the ring onto my finger, and we both stared at it. "I can't believe it fits like it was made for you. I guess this really *was* meant to be." Gabe pulled me back into his arms, and then we both cried. This time, I was sure.

Once we calmed down, we sat on the bed and admired my left hand. "My mother would love this ring. I wish she could be here." Still, I felt her with me—breathing a huge sigh of relief.

"I wish I could've met your parents. They must've been amazing people."

"They were. They would have loved you."

He kissed the top of my head. "I need to call my mom. And you need to call your sister."

I sat up straight. "Did she know? Is that why she was acting so funny on the phone?"

Gabe nodded, looking guilty. "I asked her permission."

"That's *cute*—so why do you look like that—guilty?"

Gabe looked down, playing with the ring on my finger. "She got, er…a little excited."

"Of course she did. She loves you, and she's my sister. She's been dying for us to get engaged." But then suddenly it dawned on me. The thing that followed the engagement was *the wedding*. "Oh no. Oh boy. She's going to go crazy. We can't let her."

Gabe's jaw muscle tightened. "Well…she sort of already started. She's been texting me all weekend." He showed me his phone, which was filled with pictures of wedding venues, cakes, and links to different appetizer lists.

I dropped the phone onto the bed. "She's already planning a *menu*?"

"And she's been dress shopping. She made you a bunch of appointments at bridal salons when we get back." He held up his hands. "Don't shoot the messenger, babe. I'm just trying to prepare you."

"Oh…wow."

"The thing is, you can't say no to her."

"Of course not. We just got her back, and she's been planning both of our weddings since she was four." I might as well accept bridal defeat. If I had my way, Gabe and I would get married in a courthouse first thing Monday morning. But Hannah would have other plans—*lots* of other plans. I groaned. "She can do whatever she wants."

"I already told her that. I gave her the black American Express card."

I peered at him. "She's going to break it, you know."

"That's fine." He put his arms around me. "Let her have some fun. She deserves it."

I settled myself against his chest, putting my left hand up so I could still stare at it. "I can't believe we're getting married, I'm so excited!"

"So am I." Gabe wrapped his arms around me, a huge grin on his face. "And this is just the beginning."

"The beginning of what?"

"Of us, babe. The beginning of us."

***

Silicon Valley Billionaires, Book 3: HANNAH

Before She Can Put the Past Away... There's Hell to Pay

Hannah Taylor—the bright, bubbly publicity director of Silicon Valley's celebrated startup Paragon Laboratories—was kidnapped and beaten. Her bodyguard-boyfriend, Wesley Eden, was shot right in front of her. The responsible party? None other than Chinese mogul Li Na Zhao, who'll stop at nothing to steal Paragon's blockbuster biotechnology from Hannah's CEO sister, Lauren.

Now, Wesley and Hannah are back home and on the mend. Their relationship is tested as Wesley struggles to recover, and Hannah, fueled by the injustice of Li Na's actions, is out for retribution while refusing to acknowledge the PTSD she's grappling with from her kidnapping. Wes is convinced that Hannah is hiding the truth about her captivity, and he's determined to find out what really happened while Li Na had Hannah.

Out to protect her loved ones, Hannah is hell-bent on finally taking Li Na down, especially after she discovers that Paragon isn't the only Silicon Valley company in Li Na's cross hairs. Naturally, the ethically challenged Chinese CEO refuses to give up without a fight...

But she hasn't tangled with Hannah Taylor when she's bent on revenge.

HANNAH
SILICON VALLEY BILLIONAIRES, BOOK 3

CHAPTER 1

HANNAH

"Hey." I nudged Wes's shoulder and he groaned.

He pulled me, gently, against his chest. "Hey what?"

I nestled against his big body, warm underneath the blankets, while staying mindful of his bandages—and the wounds they protected. "I have to get going to work."

He kissed my forehead. "Stay for a while."

Feeling his arousal, I rolled my eyes. "Easy, stud. Dr. Kim said you need to take it slow."

"I know." He chuckled. "But you're awfully close, and you're awfully pretty."

"Aw, that's sweet—and it's a nice try, but I'm not going against doctor's orders." I slid off him and moved to the other side of the bed. I didn't want to tempt him, and the doctor said we should abstain for a few more weeks. We needed to be sure Wesley's heart was strong enough to withstand intense physical exertion.

His heart… I shivered, thinking about how I'd almost lost him. He'd been shot right in front of me, and I'd thought he was dead…

"Hey." Wes reached for me, pulling me closer. "I'm a little worried about you. You had another nightmare. Do you remember?"

"No." That wasn't entirely true—I had a vague memory of the dream, someone trying to grab me and hold me down in the dark. "Did I wake you up?"

"You did, but I don't mind. You said some stuff, though. You were crying."

"Oh. Huh. Sorry about that."

"You don't need to apologize."

I kissed his cheek. "You really are the sweetest, but I have to go. The nurse should be here soon, okay?"

"Okay." But he didn't sound okay. "Do you want to…talk about it? The dream?"

I got up, throwing on one of Wes's enormous T-shirts and a pair of my sweats. "Talk about something I don't even remember, that has no bearing on reality? Nope." I leaned down to kiss him again. "I'm going to grab us some coffee before I take a shower. Be right back."

Wes didn't say anything, because he didn't have to. The look on his face said plenty—he was worried about me.

He's being ridiculous, I thought as I headed to the kitchen. *He'd* been shot, suffered a head injury, and put into a medically induced coma. *He'd* had a minor heart attack while in said coma. I'd only been kidnapped by some assholes who held me captive in a dirty condominium—compared to what Wes had been through, I'd had it easy.

My sister, Lauren, and her fiancé, Gabe, were already in the kitchen. They were dressed and ready to go to their respective offices. Gabe was headed to Dynamica, the technology company he owned in San Jose. Lauren, of course, was heading to Paragon Laboratories, the biotechnology company she owned and where I worked as the publicity director.

Lauren's face lit up when she saw me. "Good morning." She wrapped me in a big hug and rocked me back and forth. She'd greeted me this same way every day since I'd come home, holding me like she'd never let go.

"Hi." The word came out muffled against her long, blonde hair.

"Is Wes up?" Gabe asked as Lauren released me.

"Yeah. I'm just getting us some coffee."

Gabe headed to our room. "I'll see if he needs help."

"Thanks." I turned back to Lauren. "Gabe's being so great about Wesley—seriously, I don't know what I'd do without him."

Gabe and Lauren had asked Wes and me to stay at their enormous estate in Palo Alto for a while. After everything that had happened, we all felt safer together at the compound. We were surrounded by Gabe's security-agent brothers, Levi and Asher Betts, a team of their top Betts Security agents, along with bodyguards from Paragon Laboratories. Levi and Ash were busy relocating their business from Boston to Silicon Valley, but they checked in often, keeping close tabs on the situation at home.

No one wanted to give Li Na Zhao—the Chinese CEO who'd been stalking Lauren's technology for over a year, and the woman responsible for Wesley's shooting and my kidnapping, among a multitude of other crimes—another chance to infiltrate our personal or professional lives. We'd tightened our inner circle, tripled our security and were closely watching one another's backs.

Since Wes had come home from the hospital two weeks ago, Gabe had taken it upon himself to get him up every morning and help him to the bathroom. At six-foot-two and two hundred twenty pounds of pure muscle, my boyfriend was a big guy. Even though he'd lost some muscle mass due to his injury and the ensuing atrophy, it would've been impossible for me to help him get around. If I'd tried, I think it would've embarrassed Wes—but he and Gabe joked about it; Gabe called it his morning workout.

"Gabe loves Wes—you know that. He's more than happy to help." Lauren poured two cups of coffee, one black for Wes and one with extra cream for me. She watched me as I took a sip. "You look like you didn't sleep that well."

"I slept great," I mumbled. "I'm going to make sure Wes is settled, and then I'll head to the office. Okay?"

"You don't have to come back to work yet," Lauren told me for the hundredth time.

"I know, but I want to. I need to feel like things are getting back to normal."

My big sister nodded, but she looked worried. "Fine, but make sure you have security with you at all times. Come and see me for lunch, okay?"

I grabbed the coffees and made a beeline for my room, before she could scrutinize me further. "Sure."

"Hannah?"

"Yes?"

"I love you."

That stopped me in my tracks, and my eyes filled with annoying tears—just like they did every time she told me she loved me, which was every five minutes these days. "I love you too. Now stop being such a sap, geez! Getting engaged has turned you into an emotional basket case."

"It's not because I'm engaged." Lauren sighed, picking imaginary lint off the fitted navy blazer I'd bought for her. "I'm emotional because I'm so happy you're back and that you're safe."

I put the mugs on the counter, pulling her in for another hug. At my lowest point back in that dirty condo, where they'd kept me in a dark room, I'd often wondered if I'd ever see her again. "Me too. Me too."

***

I paced back and forth at the foot of the bed. "Are you *sure* you're going to be okay?"

"Yes, honey, for the tenth time, I'm going to be fine." Wes gave me a very patient, and very irresistible, smile. He had one of those smiles that produced two vertical grooves on each of his cheeks; for some reason, I found them mesmerizing. I often traced and retraced those lines, wanting to memorize them with my fingertips.

But this morning, guilt overwhelmed me too much to be distracted by Wes's handsome face. My shoulders slumped. "But what will you do when you get hungry?"

"Get in the wheelchair, with the help of the nurse, and go get a sandwich. With the help of the nurse."

I grimaced, knowing he hated the wheelchair. He probably hated having a nurse too, but he never complained. "Speaking of sandwiches—I made you a turkey, bacon, and avocado one, on the ciabatta bread you like from the bakery downtown. It's in the fridge."

He beamed. "You're the best. C'mere." He patted the bed next to him and took my hand when I got close enough. "I know you're nervous about leaving me, but don't be. The nurse will be here, security's here, and I'm fine. I'm also thrilled that you're going back to work. I think it'll be good for you."

I brightened. "You do?"

"Yeah, I do. I know how much you love your job and your friends at Paragon. You've been rattling around the house for the past few weeks, totally focused on taking care of me—you need to get on with your life. I don't want to hold you back."

"Wes, don't be ridiculous! I've loved being home with you."

"It *has* been sort of awesome. But you know what's even better?"

"No."

"Now I get to see you in your sexy work clothes"—his eyes traveled appreciatively down my black dress to my leopard-print heels—"*and* watch the NFL draft nonstop without you constantly changing the station. Win-win."

"Ha." I reached out and stroked his cheek. "I hate to leave you, though." Suddenly, I found myself near tears for the second time this morning.

He captured my hand underneath his larger one, and I caught a flash of it again—his worry. "I'll be here when you get home, I promise. But I want *you* to promise you'll keep security with you today, even while you're at the lab."

I nodded. "I promise."

Careful to avoid smudging my makeup, Wes kissed the top of my head. "Go get 'em. And have a great day."

I looked up, my heart suddenly thudding in my chest. "I will. And Wes?"

"Yeah?"

We looked at each other for a beat, my courage faltering. "I—I love you."

His face split into a grin, showcasing those lines that I also loved. "I love you too. I'm pissed that you said it first, though. I had *plans.*"

"You did?"

He clasped my hands and squeezed. "Of course I did. I've been wanting to tell you for what feels like forever…I just wanted to be at the top of my game when I said it."

"So you could show off your big muscles while simultaneously declaring yourself?"

He laughed, but it sounded a little strained. "Something like that."

I leaned forward and kissed his cheek, then carefully wiped my lipstick off his face. "Well, I beat you to it. I'd say I'm sorry, but I'm totally not. Because…I love you."

"And I love you." He pulled me closer and deepened the kiss, lipstick be damned.

I felt dizzy by the time he released me. Wes was good at many things, and kissing was at the top of the list. I fanned myself and hopped up. "Woo. Okay. I better go before we violate doctor's orders."

Wes groaned. "That doctor's on my shit list."

I straightened my dress and winked at him as I headed for the door. "When you're better, we'll make up for lost time."

"I can't wait," he growled. "And honey? I love you."

I grinned at him. "I love you too."

Wes flashed the smile I loved. "I said it first this time!"

I laughed and blew him a kiss as I left, my heart feeling lighter than it had in weeks.

***

I texted the nurse on the way to Paragon, checking in on Wes. I texted her when I got to my desk. I texted her ten minutes later to remind her that Wes liked the special electrolyte-enriched bottled water in the fridge. Then I texted her again to make sure she'd received my text.

Finally, Wesley texted me to tell me to chill out and to please stop driving the nurse crazy. *Fine,* I texted back, *but make sure she gets you the right water, and don't forget your sandwich!*

PS, I love you.

Love you more, he wrote back right away. Hmm. I was going to have to prove him wrong about that.

I ached with missing him, but it felt good to be back in my sunny, cheerful office. When I'd been held captive, another thing I'd wondered about was if I'd ever sit at my desk again... I pushed the thought from my mind and plowed through our most recent sales data, which continued to surpass all projections, and started drafting a much-overdue press release. My office phone buzzed. "Hannah? It's Stephanie."

Stephanie was Lauren's assistant and a close friend of mine at work. She sounded frazzled.

"What's the matter?"

"I have ten messages already this morning from Fiona Pace. She won't stop calling—she said she needs an emergency meeting with your sister."

"What'd Lauren say?"

"She said she's too busy to take the call and that since her 'people person' is finally back, I should direct Ms. Pace to you."

Typical Lauren—she could solve any insane biotech problem you threw at her, but she couldn't handle talking to people. "When she calls again, put Fiona through to me. I'll take care of it."

"Thanks." Stephanie sounded relieved.

"I know how she can be—don't worry about it." I pulled up Fiona Pace's profile after I hung up the phone, wondering why she wanted to meet with Lauren.

She was the hard-charging CEO of BioTherapeutics, a hot new startup that had the industry buzzing with speculation about its enormous valuation. Reportedly, BioTherapeutics was developing an antibody therapy to help combat certain cancers. I scrolled through the company's pages, noticing that Fiona had assembled an all-female leadership team—no small feat in male-dominated Silicon Valley.

Previously, Fiona had been the CEO of several Silicon Valley companies. She'd also written a popular self-help book for professional women, which had made her a minor celebrity. BioTherapeutics was her most recent venture. I'd known her for years through SVWBA, the Silicon Valley Women's Business Association. She was past president of the association, where I'd also volunteered, and I considered her a friend. Still, I had to be on my game with Fiona. When she wanted something, she wanted it *now.*

But I knew how to handle her, and I was ready when Stephanie patched her through a minute later. "Hey, Fiona. It's been a long time. How are you?"

"Not good," she said immediately, sounding unusually rattled. "And I have a bad feeling you're going to understand why all too well."

My stomach dropped. "What…what do you mean?"

"I'd rather not talk about it over the phone. Can I come up? Can I meet with you and Lauren right now?"

"You're *here*?"

"I'm in the parking lot. I was hoping you could fit me in—it's important."

"Hold on—let me text Lauren and see if she's free."

I put her on hold and fired off a quick text to Lauren, wondering why in the hell Fiona Pace was sitting in Paragon's parking lot. Something had to be wrong, very wrong. Fiona's schedule was jam-packed. I'd tried to schedule a lunch with her two years ago, and we'd had to book it six months ahead of time.

I read the reply from Lauren and got back on the phone with Fiona. "We can see you, but it needs to be quick. Lauren's due back in the lab in a half hour."

"That's fine. I'm coming in now."

I hustled from my office to Lauren's. She hadn't been happy about the unscheduled interruption.

She jumped to her feet when I came in. "What does Fiona Pace want? I'm so busy today. There's so much catching up to do—"

"I don't know, but she sounded upset. And Fiona doesn't do upset."

"I don't like it." Lauren shook her head. "I have a bad feeling about this."

I nodded, my stomach churning with nerves. "But maybe she's working on another book and just wants to interview you."

"I think she would've scheduled that ahead of time, don't you?"

Stephanie buzzed in before I could answer. "Ms. Pace is here."

"Send her in."

Fiona Pace came through the doors, wearing a violet-colored sweater and a pencil skirt, her brown bob shining in the sun that streamed through the windows. She would've looked fabulous if her face hadn't been so drawn. "Lauren, thank you for seeing me on such short notice."

"It's a pleasure to meet you, Fiona. I enjoyed your book. It seems like BioTherapeutics is doing well—congratulations."

"Thank you, that means a lot." Fiona turned and pulled me in for a hug. "Hannah, it's so good to see you. I've been following your story—I was worried sick."

News of my kidnapping and the shooting at my house had been covered by the local press. Lauren and her attorney, Bethany O'Donnell, had done their best to keep the spotlight off Paragon and its violent entanglement with Jiàn Innovations, but people in the industry still talked.

"We've all been praying for you—me, Jim, and the girls—I'm so sorry about what you've been through. What a nightmare."

"Thank you. But I'm fine, and I'm thrilled to be back at work."

"How's your boyfriend?"

"Wesley's doing much better, thank you. He's home now, and he's going to start physical therapy soon. He's expected to make a full recovery."

Fiona squeezed my hand. "That's wonderful. I'm so glad."

We all sat down, and Fiona cleared her throat. "It's not often I find myself sitting in a parking lot, begging for a meeting."

"Why don't you tell us what's going on?" Lauren asked.

Fiona played with her rings. "Things are going well at BioTherapeutics—*very* well. We're getting close with the antibody therapy, and I think it's going to work. This could be big, a bigger innovation than we've seen in biotech in a long time. With the exception of your patch, of course."

Lauren smiled. "Of course."

"That's amazing news," I said. "So why do you seem upset?"

Fiona raised her gaze to meet mine, and I saw how hollowed-out she looked. "Because Li Na Zhao wants to steal the technology from me. And for the first time in my adult life, I'm scared. Scared, as in totally fucking petrified."

***

HANNAH, coming soon from Jack's House Publishing. Sign up at http://jacks-housepublishing.com/hannapreorder/ to be notified when HANNAH is available for preorder!

SPECIAL THANKS

Thank you to my readers! Every single one of you light up my days. I love hearing from you, and also that you think Mr. Betts is hot, too…it's so nice to know I'm not alone!

You can sign up for my mailing list at www.leighjamesbooks.com to be notified of new releases.

Thank you to Marie Force for being an amazing publisher, mentor, and person. Working with you has taught me so much—it's a privilege and an honor! Thanks to the wonderful editing and eagle eye of Linda Ingmanson. Also a huge shout-out to Holly, Julie, and the team at Jack's House for their work on this book and their continued support. I consider myself blessed to be able to work all of you!

I could not write without the love and support of my husband and my three children. You guys make every day worth it. And a special shout-out to my mom, who is always ready with a pep talk, and who told me to never give up.

About the Author

Leigh James is an author of contemporary romance and romantic suspense. She is a vocal lover of strapping alpha males in movies, books and real life, which makes her three kids roll their eyes and makes her husband feel appreciated.

When she's not writing, you can usually find her reading or watching Outlander, Game of Thrones, and Vikings (see penchant for alpha males, above). She has a degree in journalism from the University of New Hampshire, which is good for deadlines and word counts, and a law degree from Suffolk University with a Concentration in High Technology Law, which is helpful when writing about sexy tech billionaires with legal woes.

For more information about Leigh, please visit her website *www.leighjamesbooks.com*, "Like" Leigh on Facebook at *www.facebook.com/leighjames19author/* and follow her on Twitter @LeighJames19, Instagram at *www.instagram.com/leighjames_author/* and Goodreads at *www.goodreads.com/author/show/7231254.Leigh_James*. Join Leigh's newsletter at *www.leighjamesbooks.com/form* to be the first to hear about upcoming releases. She's loves hearing from her readers. Email her directly at *leighjames@leighjamesbooks.com*.

43232157R00157

Made in the USA
Middletown, DE
05 May 2017